SENDER UNKNOWN

Published by
LION STONE BOOKS
4921 Aurora Drive
Kensington, MD 20895
Telephone: 301-949-3204
Fax:301-949-3806

Cataloging-in-Publication Data
Lowenstein, Sallie
Sender Unknown/Sallie Lowenstein
p.cm.

Summary: Twenty-four-year-old Markham Perralt has just bought a house where ten to fifteen catalogs of children's toys are delivered in the mail daily. It isn't long before he decides to order from the catalogs, but he doesn't get what he expects.

ISBN 0-9658486-4-7
[1. Fiction -- new families 2. Speculative Fiction]

Library of Congress Control Number: 2002090957

First Edition
Manufactured in the United States

SENDER UNKNOWN
by
Sallie Lowenstein

Kensington, Maryland

FROM THE AUTHOR

The idea for *Sender Unknown* first came to mind when a friend related a strange tale to me. She and her family had just moved into a new home, previously owned by the county sheriff. Much to her and her husband's dismay, everyday, like clockwork, five to ten catalogs of very peculiar stuff, items they never would have imagined could be found in catalogs, were delivered through their mail slot. Naturally, these were not toy catalogs, but it wasn't long before my over active imagination had set to work and the beginnings of *Sender Unknown* were born. Of course, the story mutated and changed, as books do as they come to life. And, it was written and rewritten, as all books are, becoming more complex and polished as I went.

My books, whether they are novels or picture books, for the very young or for the very old, are illustrated. Although I have been writing for the last ten years, I have been a painter and a sculptor since I was fifteen, and so when I tell a story, I see the art work as I write it. The art is integral with the writing process for me, and every story demands a different kind of art, for each story is different from the last. As I wrote *Sender Unknown*, I saw the illustrations for the catalogs, but it wasn't until after the first draft that I knew the covers and pages of the catalogs I had envisioned would also act as the chapter headings. It was exactly the intergration and interweaving of art and idea that I had been looking for. Then began the arduous process of designing interesting and diverse catalogs in black and white, and of writing copy to go with them. To achieve the diversity of catalogs described in the story, I used different media, including clay heads of various characters which I scanned into my computer to look like photos and then combined with drawings or collage. It was fun, but also hard work, and I certainly have a greater respect for catalog designers and catalog copy writers than I did before I began.

The illustrations also required that I do a huge amount of research. I made extensive lists of different characters and material I could use for each catalog page or cover, and was disappointed when I couldn't use even a third of the total number of entries on the lists. In some cases, I made up the entries, but a large portion of the material on the illustration pages can be found in nursery rhymes, literature and myth, pulled from the collective imaginations of many generations. The characters of the children in the book were also a combination of my own imagination and that of world tradition.

I thoroughly enjoyed writing this book. It is the journey through the imagination that makes not only writing such a wonderful process for the writer, but also the reading of a book such a wondrous process for the reader.

You are welcome to write the author at lionstone@juno.com. She will write back.

CONTENTS

This book is dedicated to the young people in the writer's
group I work with, whose imaginations never cease
to amaze me:
Greg Benson, Paul Dean, Lori Green, Teresa Green
Victoria Lanaras, Erin McDonough, Sarah Rowley
Patty Sever, Jim Shirey and Sam Strongin

Special Thanks To:
Rachel Kenney, who once again provided me
with a wonderful title for my book;
John Kenney, who is always my first reader;
Frank L. Lowenstein, whose opinion I hold
in high regard; *Frank Lowenstein*, who found the
great mistake; and *Bob Kenney*,
my last reader, who keeps me afloat
and makes it all possible.

SOLD

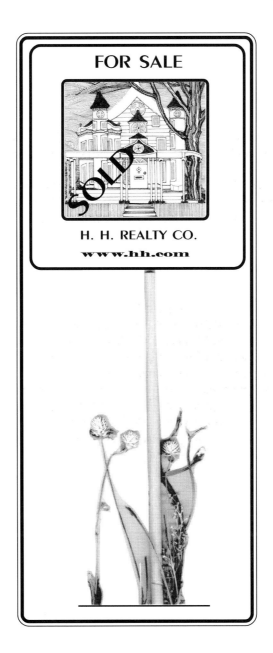

Mark leaned into the balmy wind that whipped at his tie and suit jacket, obliviously letting it play over him as he turned his ear towards the house he had just bought. He listened for the sound again. Maybe it had just been the old house moaning and fidgeting as the wind swept through it or maybe he had merely imagined it. The only thing he heard now was the silence of the still sleeping neighborhood around him.

He pulled uncomfortably at the tie, craned his neck and looked all the way to the top of the house. It stood among tall hickories, one of which actually grew through a hole in the floorboards of the wide front porch and then poked through another in its roof. The center of the house was flanked on either side by two round towers, crowned by coned roofs, perched like hats above old windows that wobbled with warped reflections. Between them, above the main entrance, a recent addition of a soaring crystal ceiling refracted sharp beams of sunlight.

Mark had rejected twenty houses before Herb Higgley, his frustrated realtor, had shown him this one. When he had liked it, Herb looked perturbed and asked, "Why this one, Mark?"

"Easy, Herb. It doesn't have red flocked wall paper on every wall or a big watchdog next door that leaps fences in a single bound and bites the neighbors. It doesn't even have toilets that groan like ghosts every time you flush them."

Despite his fervent desire to sell a home to Mark, Herb had asked, "You don't think it's too fanciful?"

"That's exactly what I like about it, Herb."

Herb bit his lip and said, "There's something you should know. This house has been unoccupied for more years than it's been occupied."

"What's wrong with it? Is the foundation cracked? Does it have termites?" Mark asked.

"No, no, it's really solid. Great craftsmanship on this old beauty." Herb actually pushed on the walls as if to prove it.

"Then why has it been empty so many years?"

"I don't know. That's what makes me nervous."

"Is it haunted?" Mark asked straight-faced, but dying to laugh.

"Of course not," Herb said quickly.

Mark ignored Herb's nervousness, and bought it on the spot for full price just to finally be done with it. Only maybe that had been a mistake. Maybe Herb had known more than he had told, but it was too late to worry about that now. He sighed, and forced himself to walk up the porch steps and turn the key in the lock. Beyond the marble-floored foyer was an enormous room, lined in tall windows and real wooden bookshelves that glowed with a warm patina. He wondered if anyone had ever filled those shelves. A few catalogs lay on them. He flipped through one absently and put it back on the shelf. He went into the kitchen with its twelve foot high ceilings and its walls delicately stenciled with deep green leaves and vines. Drinking orange juice here would be like eating in a jungle or perhaps in a forest, like the one of recently sprung saplings just outside the windows of the dining room.

He climbed the steps to the towers, his own footsteps thudding loudly in the empty house. He stopped to listen again. Nothing. It was abnormally silent, not a whisper from the wind, not a creak in the stairs. He shivered and for no real reason wanted to leave, but made himself keep going. There were six bedrooms altogether in the two, three-story towers, one bedroom on each floor, each with its own bathroom. Streaky light filtered through large windows, making the dust in the bedroom air wink. How long had it been since the last occupants lived here? Why had they really left? A sudden sense of foreboding overwhelmed him and he ran down the stairs and out the front door. He took a deep breath, relieved to be outside again. This was ridiculous, he reasoned with himself. It was his house now and in a week or so, it would no longer be empty. Maybe then he'd be able to shake the sense of strangeness he had just felt. It was probably only the idea of suddenly, at age twenty-four, being the owner of something akin to a mansion. He took another deep breath of fresh air. For better or worse, it was the new residence of Markham Perralt, but for now he needed to get to work.

He picked a violet out of the grass as he left, noting that in his yard the tiny flowers sprayed across the whole lawn. He was at the bus stop before he remembered he had left his new car at the house. Oh well, he could go back for it whenever he wanted. He hopped on the bus and felt himself relax as it curved through the back streets, letting him watch the landscape and the houses and the old people who still sat in their yards. People got on the bus, wended down the aisle and twisted their heads to look at him in his fancy suit and freshly buffed shoes. Two young women talked about their boyfriends and their children while they put a second coat of lip gloss on their wide mouths. This was nice. This was real, this was familiar.

His stop came up too fast. He didn't want to get off the bus, but like the good corporate boy he had recently become, he stepped off into the world of success. Mark sighed again. Another day at the office. He walked through the leaded glass front doors of Cannady & Company, greeted the doorman and the guards. His tenth high school reunion had done this to him. He had been perfectly happy wearing his yellow tennis shoes laced and held together with red dental floss, repairing and restoring old junk for wealthy people who wanted to own an odd item here or there. Perfectly happy, until the reunion. He shouldn't have gone. He shouldn't have given any of his high school classmates the chance to say, "Well, well, look who didn't amount to a hill of beans after all! Weren't you voted most likely to be the richest computer nerd in history?" Or, "Didn't you graduate when you were only fourteen?" And, "What happened to you? You just disappeared."

"Oh," Elsie Johnson giggled in his memory, "he became a fix-it-man! I went to him once with something my mother wanted restored and he did quite a good job." Her silly laugh tittered loudly around the room in the moment of silence that followed her statement.

That fateful reunion preoccupied his mind all day, and when work finally ended he had accomplished very little. He tried to stay late to finish up, but it was useless. All he could think about was that he didn't really belong in a big office, behind a shiny desk, dressed as if he was going to a birthday party every day. Nor did he belong living in a huge, fancy home, even an eccentric one, remodeled by someone who had apparently wanted to live in a castle. The truth was, that if it weren't for his job, he would keep right on renting the slightly rag-tag cottage at the edge of Old Willingham Park. If it had been up to him.

He straightened up his desk and went home to that cottage and shed the suit and the shoes and the socks and the tie and the shirt and dropped them on the floor. *That's where they belong,* he thought. *On the floor.* He pulled on his jeans and started to slip into his favorite tee

4

shirt and stopped. *Oh, To-Be-A-Kid-For-The-Rest-Of-My-Life* was printed across it. His sister had given him that tee shirt as a friendly insult the day she had gotten married. Kate had been right on target when she had given it to him. It had been his fondest wish to stay a kid, but since he had taken his job at Cannady & Company the letters burned into his chest whenever he put it on, as if he was telling a lie when he wore it. He folded it lovingly, neatly, stuck it in the back of a drawer and put on a plain blue one.

Whenever he saw Kate now, she beamed at him. "I am so proud of you!" she'd say. "A fancy car, new friends and now your own house. I am so proud!"

It had been easy to make Kate proud. He had simply gone to a company with a well executed, creative slant on his resume. *Previous position: Inventor.* (He had invented many hardware devices in order to repair old machinery.) *Education: Engineering.* (He had taken engineering in high school and he could build anything.) *Computers: Extensive experience.* (He had, after all, been a real computer geek, as his class had so aptly noted.) *Age: 24.* (He was young, but it meant they didn't have to offer him a big salary.)

He had been placed in an entry level position, but it hadn't taken him long to figure out how to devise innovative business programs, then complex game programs and novel marketing approaches. He got his first promotion in four weeks. Unheard of! In six months he had managed to become indispensable. It had been a struggle not to make it look too easy. It wasn't long until he was so valuable the company had offered him a special contract, wined him, dined him and given him someone to pick his clothes, and his cuff links, and to be sure his hair was cut so that he looked and acted as if he deserved the outrageous salary he was earning. He had appeared out of nowhere and no one had questioned it. The company stock had rocketed on his merit.

He pulled on his old yellow comfort socks and wiggled his toes, but he wasn't sure if it was enough to make him feel himself anymore. He wasn't even sure which person he was, Mark the money-man or Mark the fix-it-man. He had let his mind drift to a toy he wanted to restore when the phone buzzed him. It was Elliot, the personal manager the company had hired to help organize him.

"Hello? Markham, I heard you bought the house this morning."

"Uh huh."

"Congratulations! First thing tomorrow I'll make the arrangements for your move."

"No, no thanks, Elliot. I'll take care of it."

"Please, Markham, it's my job."

"Forget it. I don't have that much to move."

Mark disconnected and wiggled his toes again. At least he could move his own life from one point to another without help from his office. He would get some boxes for packing, hire a truck and try to sort through all the stuff he had. By the time a week was up, he'd be ready to move. He ran his fingers through his hair and went to the shower.

How had a guy like himself managed to end up with all these people involved in his life? He had always liked being solitary. He looked in the mirror and was surprised again at how neatly the haircut Elliot had advised stayed in perfect order, like the files in a file cabinet, each pale hair lined up against the next. He tried to mess it up, but it fell back into exactly the same place. The face wasn't his either. No more glasses to push up his nose under a shock of unruly hair. Elliot had insisted on replacing them with contacts. And no more smudges across his cheeks from his fix-it-up projects. He shook his head and stepped into the shower to try and wash off the perfection of success.

RHYMES

Dandy Humpty Dumpty, fancy fellow, sitting on wall.......30.00

Young King Cole, bowl, meerschaum pipe and 3 fiddles.......22.50

The Kid in the Moon, with moon and planet stickers......20.00

Little Girl with the Curl, sweet faced, push a button, has a tantrum.............35.00

Tom the Piper's Son and Pig, wigglily mechanical pig.....19.95

Peter Piper, Peter Pumpkin Eater, in pumpkin shaped box, orange clothes, and spoons for pumpkin scraping..........35.00

Mother Goose, flip over doll, one side is goose, one side is lady with large hat..................22.50

Little Nancy Etticoat, dressed in long white petticoat, carrying electric candle..............................15.95

The Boy of Tabago, comes with rice and gruel....:.........25.95

Young Miss Hubbard, accompanied by laughing wind-up dog, genuine bone, and cupboard..................40.00

The move had taken longer than he had thought it would. He didn't have any furniture of his own, but he couldn't bring himself to discard any of his projects or supplies. When he finally opened the door to the house, he sent the automated robot mover he had rented to pile boxes in two of the upstairs bedrooms. He was inspecting which of the other four to sleep in when he heard something fall onto the marble floor of the foyer. He peeked tentatively into the entrance hall. Mail lay just under a brass mail-slot that needed a good polish.

He scooped it up. All junk, addressed anonymously to "Present Occupant." Other than packages, junk-mail was the only real mail he had ever seen. He dumped it in a heap on the cold marble and went out for food, his hair still neat, but his shirt covered in stains from the exertion of moving. The grey-haired lady who lived next door stared hawkishly at him as he walked towards the bus stop and left his car standing in the driveway again. The bus was empty except for him and a ten-year-old boy. Mark sat down one seat ahead of the boy.

"What are you reading there?" Mark turned around and asked just to make a little conversation.

The boy slammed his book closed with an embarrassed look. "My mom makes me read."

"I kind of like reading books," Mark admitted.

"You must be crazy, mister! You ain't serious, are you?"the boy said as he slid out of his seat and popped into a seat three rows behind Mark.

Actually, Mark was serious. And he had all those book shelves to fill up.

"You got any kids?" the boy called forward.

"No," Mark said.

"Good, 'cause I bet you'd make them read."

"I might." It was his stop. He hopped off the bus and went into a café.

Mark's life seemed to be little staccato scenes: a moment on a bouncy bus, a moment in a café-stop, a moment walking down the street. It had a beat, like an old poem without rhyme, an out of tune nursery rhyme. His mother had owned a copy of such verses she had read to him and Kate at bedtimes. An image of it flashed across his mind. He speculated briefly on whether he could still get such a book, and then impulsively hailed a cab whose driver looked at him skeptically, held out his hand and said, "Thirty-five bucks up front."

Mark paid it and hopped in. The driver watched him nervously in the mirror.

"Where to, bud?"

"Book Stop at Third and River."

"Sure thing. So, you like books? Me too," the man said surprisingly. "Whatcha like to read?" He didn't wait for Mark to answer before he said, "Me, I like reading mysteries. Course nobody writes 'em anymore. Criminals don't stand a chance since high-tech got applied to crime scenes. Nowadays, cops got tiny cameras, communicators and computers embedded in their badges! Wasn't like that in my day."

The driver finally paused. Mark took it as a cue for his turn. The driver seemed awfully taken with the topic. Could he have been a criminal?

"Do you want the criminals to win?" Mark asked curiously.

"No, course not," the driver cut right back in.

"Isn't it good that there's less crime these days?"

"Course it is. Here you are at the Book Stop."

"But I don't understand. What did you mean?" Mark insisted.

"Aw, I just ramble a lot these days. Your meter is ticking."

"It's okay, I'll pay the meter."

The man cocked his head, appraising Mark. "You're too young."

"For what? To be a criminal?"

"Naw, not that." He paused and cleared his throat. "I don't wantcha to take this wrong, bud. I don't like crime no more than you do, but I remember when it meant something to solve a crime, what it felt like when you put the thing together with nothin' more than intuition and intelligence and imagination. Made a guy feel proud. Made me feel good. Now, get before you owe the machine a fortune. You ain't ever gonna understand anyways," the man said ending the conversation.

Mark slid his card through the credit-debit slot and ducked out of the cab, leaving the thirty-five dollars as a tip.

"Thanks," the man said through the open cab window.

Mark mulled over how old the cabby had been as he walked into the store. Sixty? Younger? Older? Had he been a cop or a criminal? He was still thinking about it when a clerk came up and eyed him critically.

"Can I help you? Would you like an interactive title or a book?"

"A book. A book of nursery rhymes, if you have it," Mark said.

"I don't believe we carry any. Do you have an exact title?"

"Nursery rhymes, uh, Mother Goose?"

The clerk was blank. Maybe Mark had the title wrong?

"You know, 'There was an old woman who lived in a shoe'," he quoted from his childhood. No response. "Or, 'Tom Tom the Piper's Son, stole a pig and away he run' or 'Peter Peter Pumpkin Eater'?"

"Pardon me?"

"It's for children," Mark said, finding himself feeling defensive.

A plump older woman came up and shooed the young clerk away. "I'm Wilma. Can I help you?" she asked Mark in a sweet, shaky voice.

"He wants a book called *Mother Goose*," the clerk called as he walked off.

"Oh my, I'm afraid I only have one used and rather dilapidated volume." She pulled a book off the shelf and laid it gingerly in Mark's hands. "You can look at it on the counter," she said, "and Charles will ring it up if you want it."

Mark flipped the pages carefully. The binding was cracked, and several frayed pages lay loose between the cover, but wonderful illustrations, whimsically drawn in black lines and creamy colors, prompted him to say, "Okay, Charles, I'll take it. How much?"

Charles frowned. "This must be a mistake. Who would pay one-hundred-and-fifty dollars for this?"

"Me," Mark said. "In fact, next time you get one of these books, call me." He laid his card on the counter.

"Don't hold your breath, young man," Wilma said from behind him. "They're rare and they aren't being published anymore, not even as interactives."

"Why not?" Mark asked.

Wilma raised her eyebrows and shrugged. "Take good care of this," she said as she wrapped the book in several layers of yellow tissue and slid it into a plastic bag.

Mark left, carefully cradling the package in his arms. The tissue paper peeped out of the bag with the innocence of a newborn's blanket. A feeling of protectiveness came over him as he looked down affectionately at the book and said to it, "Not to worry, I'll take good care of you. I'm a fix-it man. I'll fix you up and put you right."

RABBITS

Fat White Rabbit: repetitively says, I'm late, I'm late. Large, wind-up gold pocket watch included...........39.95

Brer Rabbit: trickster rabbit; briar patch ready for planting in garden....................25.95

Magician's Rabbits: 4 bunnies, magician's tricks and vial of magic, plus black hat 50.00

Weekend sun poured onto the floor where he was sleeping, splashed across his face and brought him to consciousness. The sounds of a lawn tender burping along and of trees being trimmed with an electric saw greeted his awakening.

He looked in the bathroom mirror and smiled. A hair had grown past the others and was popping up proudly. It was near noon. He brushed his teeth, pulled on his jeans, tied his tennis shoes and neglected his hair.

He heard the mail slot open and the now familiar slap of catalogs landing on the marble floor. Ten to fifteen catalogs arrived each day and were standing in a tottering tower in the foyer where he had taken to stacking them. He never opened them, never read them, just saved them for a project he had dreamed up. The only unusual thing happening in the house was their daily delivery. There were no particular squeaks or floorboard groanings. He hadn't found any secret doors or compartments. The windows didn't rattle when the wind blew. As far as he could tell, Herb had been absolutely right, the house was solid as a rock. So far, so good, except that Elliot would be arriving soon to "help" him think about furniture. Mark knew what that really meant. It meant that after six weeks of living in an empty house, Elliot was going to make him take the plunge and buy furniture. Today. Buy it today! Mark was just as happy thinking of the house as one, big, empty workshop, but Elliot kept pointing out that in six more weeks he was scheduled to host a formal office party. Elliot made it clear that no one else in the firm would think much of an empty house.

Mark slid his feet into his raggedy yellow tennis shoes and went into the kitchen: toast in the old toaster he had repaired, apple jelly from the fridge still labeled with the date he had made it, herbal tea and a serving of red Bing cherries.

He squatted at the table cloth he had spread on the floor in a square of sunshine, popped a cherry in his mouth and wondered how he could dissuade Elliot from the shopping trip. Elliot would say, "You can't live like this. You have money, you are rich, Markham, and the rich have furniture."

I don't care about being rich, Mark pretended to say to Elliot. *I don't care what anyone thinks.* But that wasn't true. He had cared. He had wanted to show all his ex-high-school-peers that he was a success, and that had brought him to shopping with Elliot.

The door bell rang. He jumped up, a cherry still in his mouth.

"Hi, Elliot," he said mushily.

"So I was right. No progress since my last visit," Elliot said, appraising the multi-storied foyer and the floor to ceiling windows in the large, bookcase-lined great room. "It has potential. Wait until we've been shopping, Markham. Let's see, curtains for the windows, knick-knacks for the shelves and rugs, and of course, furniture." He tapped the words into his notebook and slipped the little computer back in his shirt pocket.

"Here, sit," Mark said, stacking catalogs into a perch for his fussy manager. "I'm just gulping breakfast and then we can go." He popped the cherries into a bag and hurried through his tea. "Okay, I'm ready."

"Like that? You're going out like that?" Elliot spluttered, dashing his hand up through the air at Mark's attire.

"Yes, like this."

"But," said Elliot.

"Come on," Mark said, pushing Elliot out the door. He held the car door while Elliot crawled in over discarded candy wrappers, pop cans, magazines, and any number of rocks and pieces of wood that had caught Mark's eye.

"What have you done to your new car?" Elliot gasped as he sat on a rock.

"Nothing. It runs perfectly."

"Good grief!" Elliot said, peeling a candy wrapper from the bottom of his shoe.

Mark put the car into gear.

"Now then, let's go to Lathem's and Barrett's," Elliot instructed. "They have lovely accessories and items for the home."

"How about Lady Anderson's instead?" Mark said and headed in that direction before he got an answer.

"Where is that?"

"Not far. I saw a bed I liked there."

"Excellent! Then, it's off to this Lady Anderson's," Elliot said and relaxed into the cushion of his seat.

They bounced along over the pits and ruts in the street that led to the shop. The look on Elliot's face made Mark laugh.

"Markham, this is Junk Row!"

"So?" Mark said, feigning innocence.

"Markham, you can't buy anything here!"

"Why not?" The car turned sharply into Lady A's driveway. "Come on, Elliot. We're here."

"I will not get out here. For heaven's sake, Markham! You're rich, you don't need this stuff!"

"Have it your way," Mark said, sliding out as a black, mud-streaked dog padded up the dirt driveway. The dog stood on its hind legs and put its dirty paws on the shiny car. It sniffed at Elliot's window and let out a gruff bark.

"Wait for me," Elliot screeched, sliding out Mark's door to avoid the dog.

"Hey, Mark, how goes it?" Lady A asked as they entered the shop.

The only light in the dingy interior filtered in from the open door. Pieces of old wheels, rusty tools, chairs without bottoms hung on the walls; bins with marbles and screws and door knobs sat scattered about the room. Lady A fit right in. She wore a faded, blowsy shirt which covered two thirds of her long paisley skirt. She scratched under one of the many hats she always had pulled over her hair and down to just above her eyes. It was impossible to tell how old, how young, how slender or fat she really was, especially in the dim light.

"Do you still have that bed frame I liked?"

"Sure thing, but it needs some glue, you know?"

"I remember, Lady A."

"Who's the finicky, rich guy with you?" Lady A asked as Elliot tried very hard not to rub up against anything.

"Oh, him? He's Elliot."

"A friend?" Lady A asked.

Mark thought a moment. "Well, not an enemy. Elliot, this is Lady A. Lady A, this is Elliot."

"How-do-you-do," Elliot said properly.

"Pretty good," she said, then laughed an abbreviated chuckle.

"How does three hundred bucks sound for the bed?" Mark asked.

Her eyebrows lifted. "It isn't worth that much, Mark."

"No? Gee, I thought it was." He placed the bills on the arm of a broken-down rocking chair.

"I always bargain," she said. "Three-hundred-seventy-five."

"Done," Mark said.

"Aw, Mark, you took the fun from it."

He just added the seventy-five while Elliot sputtered.

"Could you deliver it?" he asked.

"Sure, in a couple of days." She smiled. "You got taken, you know."

"I wouldn't want to ruin the fun."

"Markham, the lady is quite right," Elliot said, running after him as they left. "You got taken and you left without even getting a receipt!"

Mark ignored him.

"Okay, it's your turn to pick a place, Elliot."

"Good, good. Letterfine's Furniture."

"Okay, Letterfine's."

The car sped along the highway, dropped off into the heart of town and pulled up to Letterfine's Valet Parking. The doorman frowned at Mark, but Elliot got a smile.

"They don't like my outfit?" Mark teased Elliot who just grimaced.

Inside, the walls gleamed with new paint and there wasn't a speck of dust to brush up against.

"Can we help you, sir?" a man with a fixed smirk asked Elliot.

"I hope so," Elliot said. "We need an entire household."

The salesman's eyes lit up and a little smile crept into the smirk on his face.

"No, no, Elliot," Mark said, stopping the man just as he opened his mouth to say something. "You get one pick, then it's my turn again."

Elliot grimaced. "This is not a game, Markham."

"No? Do you ever play games?"

"Of course, with my little Lisa, but she's three and you're an adult." Elliot practically choked as he spoke. "Could we just concentrate on furniture and do what we came for?"

"Sure, sure." Getting Elliot flustered was easy. Elliot was a one-two-three thinker, an all-in-a-line thinker. Mark had always jumped around like a madman: a one-five-two-seventy-back-to-fifteen thinker. Elliot just couldn't jump far enough or fast enough to avoid Mark's teasing, but it was fun to make him try. Mark would have to get Lisa a nice, old-fashioned toy.

A vaguely remembered, favorite stuffed animal came to his mind. It came into his memory like a snapshot, only so real it was as if he could reach out and touch it. There was the rabbit dressed in a little yellow sun suit and a red cap. There was his father with a matching hat and there he was, posed with his yellow boots. He could even hear himself muttering to the somewhat ragged rabbit, but couldn't make out real words.

"Markham?"

"What? Oh, sorry. Now, one item, your pick, Elliot."

"One item? Markham, please, get serious."

"I am. One item. What'll it be?"

Elliot stammered in frustration, but finally came out with, "A sofa."

"What kind of sofa are you looking for, sir?" the man who was waiting on them asked Elliot.

"Ask him," Elliot said testily.

"Him, sir?" the salesman asked.

"Yes, me," Mark said happily, spreading his arms so he couldn't be missed. "And I want that one," he added, pointing to a wooden frame that was turned and carved and buffed and piled high with silk-covered pillows.

"I see." The man ran his eyes up and down Mark's clothes.

Mark noticed he left the *sir* off that he used when he addressed Elliot. He smiled, took cash from his pocket and shelled out fifty, one-hundred-dollar-bills. The clerk's eyes popped. "See you," Mark said casually.

"Yes, sir, thank you, sir," the clerk called as he and Elliot left.

"Markham, why do you deliberately provoke people?" Elliot groaned.

"You must drive me to it."

Elliot winced.

"Come on, Elliot, relax, admit it, you enjoy it."

Mark hooked his elbow through Elliot's and dragged the man down the street whistling some silly tune he had known all his life. "Follow the yellow brick road, follow the yellow brick road. We're off to see the Wizard..." He was pretty sure his father had taught it to him.

ORPHANS FROM DISTANT PLANETS

CATALOG OF SPACE TOYS

<u>0R35</u> STICKY TONGUED TRIPIDIAN: tongue snaps out to catch flying insects; insect farm included (20th C.)...............................27.50

<u>OR 34</u> ORPHAN FROM CRESPICULAR XX: lost in space, with space capsule that spits sparks, shoots little rockets and flies on solar batteries (e. 21st C.) 45.00

By the end of the day Mark had picked: the bed, the sofa, a rag-tag but comfortable wing chair, a petit point foot stool, an antique rocker, a small love seat, a coffee table in wood and tile, and a large, second-hand Persian rug. Elliot had picked: two small lamp tables with glass tops, two cloisonné lamps, a large desk, two over-stuffed chairs, a kitchen table, as well as a banquet-sized diningroom table. But Mark hadn't let him order any chairs to go with it, which was driving him nuts.

"How is anyone going to sit down to dinner?" Elliot asked. "You have to buy chairs. Why not the ones that match?"

"Boring. That would be too boring. Don't worry about it."

"Please, Markham, let me order the chairs."

"NO, no no! What I do need you to do for me is this. Get me a list of all the children of Cannady employees."

"What? What does that have to do with chairs?"

"Nothing. I'm going to buy birthday presents for all the kids, so put their birth dates and ages down."

"Markham, can't you please stay on track? What about the chairs?" Elliot practically screamed.

"Oh, that. I'm making them. Now go home. You must be tired."

Elliot threw his hands into the air as he walked out, shook his head and threw his hands up again. Back and forth went his head and hands until he ducked into his car and drove off.

Mark laughed from the window, but Elliot was right about one thing. If he didn't get busy, he wouldn't have any chairs for the party.

He went into the kitchen and was about to bite into a peanut butter and jelly sandwich when there was a knock on the door. It was his grey-haired neighbor.

"Hi," he said, with grape jelly on his lip.

"This bundle was left on my doorstep today, Mr. Perralt. I don't want this act repeated. Please take care of it," she said, eyeing his lip.

He looked at the bundle she held out to him. It was more catalogs.

"Mrs. Williams, these aren't mine."

"They belong to your house. Everyone on the street knows that," she said unforgivingly and dropped the package at his feet. "No other house get these catalogs, except yours."

"I'm going to cancel them as soon as I can, okay?"

"Humph! I'll believe that when I see it," she said primly.

"Why?" he asked.

"Humph!" she said again. "All the owners have said that and not one of them did it."

She turned on her heel and Mark watched her strut off, her head thrown back, her nose stuck in the air. She was certainly overwrought about a few silly magazines, but still, it was curious that someone would pay to send them to the house long after the subscriber had moved out. And he had to admit there were an awful lot of them. Well, at least he could put them to a good purpose. He had the evening free. He would sort them by size and color. He licked the jelly. This was going to be a sticky job. His plans called for a lot of glue. He would gather the catalogs into tight bundles and configurations and then glue them into settees and chairs. After they dried, he would varnish them with a thick plastic coating and voila, Elliot would have chairs! He'd have pillows made in blues of every hue for his homemade seats. It would be surprising and Mark liked surprises. Kate said his delight in surprises had always made their mother edgy. The thought brought on one of his leaps of memory. A picture of his mother in her wonderful red high heels filled his mind. His mother had had a hard time getting shoes that fit, so she had worn those bright red, pointy shoes a lot, even around the house. Every time she had put them on, Mark had put on his candy-yellow galoshes that came up to his knees. For the whole year he was five, red and yellow had been his colors. Now memories of his mother always came to him in bursts of red and yellow thoughts.

He finished a glass of mango juice and took the top twenty catalogs off the pile, hugged them in his arms and carried them into what would be the sitting room as soon as his furniture arrived. He began laying the catalogs out on the floor. He had assumed they would come in standard sizes, but few of them proved to be of the same dimensions. He wondered at the number that were still being published in hand-held form and not merely being delivered through cyber space. No virtual catalogs these. They took up space, they got bent, they smelled of ink and paper. Color-splashed squares went in one pile, purple-hued rectangles in another. Textured and smooth covers, black and white, maroon and aqua began to form piles. A yellow and red one came to the top of a pile and on a whim he flipped it open. The first page declared:

THE MYSTERIOUS CONTENTS OF OUR BOXES WILL AMAZE
AND DELIGHT!
TAKE A CHANCE!

He opened another catalog that likened itself to *Knights of Old:*

NEED A HERO? NEED SOME HELP? ORDER NOW!

These catalogs needed better copy writers if they wanted anyone to buy what they sold. The next one promised a cleaner house:

WHEN YOU GO TO BED AT NIGHT,
IS YOUR HOUSE A SORRY SIGHT?
NEITHER FRET NOT FACE A FRIGHT,
THIS MONTH'S SPECIALS BRING DELIGHT.

Mark stood up and stretched. It had been a long day and he was tired. He picked one more catalog off the top of the leaning tower he had managed to stack and went to his bedroom.

He dropped onto his floor-bed and propped the catalog against his knees. The first page was a group photograph of dolls which appeared to be spin-offs of a movie, probably some old science fiction flick. One little boy doll stared at him.

"You don't just feel like an alien, you're supposed to be one, too! I know how you feel," Mark said to it.

The picture looked back at him from the page and Mark said in a little boy voice, "Please order me. I'm orphaned, just like you."

"Don't cry," Mark said to him. "I might just do that."

"You know, I'm from the first star system past Pluto. Please, please adopt me," Mark's boy voice said.

"Sure, kid," Mark said. "I'll get you for my niece Milly. She'd like you." He folded down the corner of the page.

A few pages more, and a little winged girl-doll caught his eye. Her arms were mottled with silvery patches that matched her silvered eyes. Her hair was intermittently spiky. Mark dog-eared the page, left the catalog on his pillow and went out to the foyer to gather a few more of the magazines.

Four were for fantastical children's clothing, some of which didn't look mechanically possible to get into. He set them aside. The fifth was filled with storybook toys. He passed by a shoe full of children that fit into different shaped holes. He ignored Red Riding Hood's wolf. He finally stopped at *The Shoemaker and the Elves*. He picked the smallest elf and marked it. Then he saw a boy doll dressed in silver and ignominiously stuck amongst the last few pages. *The Wizard-of-Lost-Land-As-A-Child Doll.* Further explanation said, *A doll of particularly vivid imagination.* He marked it, amused that someone thought the phrase "particularly vivid imagination" would make for a good sales pitch.

He stretched restlessly and decided on a walk. He saw people moving in their windows and a young couple necking in a sports car parked under a street lamp. Maybe tomorrow he'd call Kate and make sure he had all the family birthdays right. Then he would add them to his birthday-present-list and just order for everyone all at once. He liked the idea. It made sense. It made shopping easy. These catalogs were proving useful in more ways than one.

A man's voice greeted him out of the dark. "Hey, there! It's Mark, isn't it? I'm Larry Porter. I live at the corner, right there."

"Right. How are you, Larry?"

"Fine. Like the house?"

"I'm getting used to it."

"Uh huh, well, I sure hope so, because I've lived here eight years and the house has had four owners and been empty another four years. It's about time someone stayed."

"Why so many owners? Is it haunted?" Mark asked.

"Aw, come on, Mark, that's nonsense. Ghosts! What a joke." Larry laughed nervously and then asked as if just to make sure, "You haven't heard any strange noises have you?"

"Nope, nary a one," Mark said. *Except the sounds of catalogs falling through the mail slot every morning,* he thought to himself.

Larry paused before he went on. "You're still getting those catalogs, aren't you?"

Mark nodded.

Larry's face almost brightened with relief. "Now I think they're the most probable culprits in all this." He suddenly lowered his voice. "Nothing seems to stop them. Two owners ago, Allen Farnsworth tried everything to stop them. He e-mailed, he called, he complained, he even wrote snail-mail. Nothing stopped them. All that happened was that they sent him double copies. Have you gotten doubles yet?"

"I don't think so," Mark whispered back, playing along.

Larry scratched his head. "Allen even contacted the Postal Service as a last resort. But no luck. They said they were required by law to deliver anything that was still mailed."

"Through wind and rain and snow and hail, absolutely nothing stops the mail!"

"Hey, that's good. So, are they still coming?"

"Mailmen?"

"No, the catalogs."

"Of course. Actually, they're kind of interesting."

"Interesting? Do you have kids, Mark?"

"No, I don't. Why?"

"Because, those catalogs, they're all for kids, aren't they?"

"Mainly. Has anyone ever ordered from them?"

"You must be kidding, Mark! Who would order any of that junk? I mean, Allen said it was all fairy tales and storybook stuff! Kids don't like those kinds of toys anymore."

At least Allen had looked through them. "Do you have kids, Larry?"

"Sure."

"Would they like space creatures?" Mark asked.

"No. Nobody is ever going to find life out there. Old dreams. Dead dreams. More fairy tales," Larry snickered.

"Probably," Mark had to agree. "By the way, do you know how long the catalogs have been delivered?"

"Don't ask me. But you could ask old Bill Henley across the street. He grew up in the neighborhood."

"Thanks. Goodnight," Mark said.

Mark found himself back at the house sooner than he wanted. It felt good not to have anything on his calendar for the rest of the weekend. He sat on the front porch and took in the night. A still-warm fall wind tried to mess up his hair. When he did go in and look in the mirror, only the one lock of hair was tousled. A singleton, sticking out in lonely rebellion. He gently combed it down. It fitted in when put in place. If he could hide it there when he went to the office, he might be able to keep it.

The morning came and orange juice, scrambled eggs, tea and dirty dishes were done and over with. He eagerly returned to sorting the catalogs, but he didn't get very far. Instead, he spent the morning reading through them, picking gifts to buy for other people's kids that satisfied the kid in him. He hummed absently as he went until the phone interrupted him.

"Hey, Markie," Kate said. "I'm half-way to your house. I'm dropping by, okay?"

"Sure, I need a break."

"You aren't working today, are you?" she asked. "It's Sunday."

"No, no. Come on."

Ten minutes later she was knocking on his door.

"I haven't been back since the second day you moved in. How's the place coming?" She stopped. "Mark, what are you doing with all these magazines?"

"Making chairs," he said.

"Out of these?" She picked one up and dropped it back in the pile. "Catalogs? For toys? What goes on here? Where do these things come from?"

"They just come. They've been coming to this house for many years, apparently."

"Come on Mark, this is me, Kate, your sister. This is one of your pranks, isn't it?"

"It might be a prank, but I'm not the one playing it this time."

"Why don't you just call the companies and put a stop to it?" Kate said logically.

"Because I can use them." He didn't tell her there were no phone numbers or web sites on any of the catalogs, or that no one had ever succeeded in stopping them. It would have made her nervous, but Mark kind of liked it. It added to his view of the catalogs as a mystery and made the house more interesting.

"What can you use them for? They're trash!" Kate said, disapproval suffusing her voice.

"Well, I wouldn't go so far as to say trash," Mark said defensively. "They're sort of silly, but trash? Isn't that a bit strong? Anyway, I'm making them into chairs. Practical, purposeful, not silly at all."

"Chairs? Why don't you just buy some?"

"I want to make them, Kate."

"Mark, this passion for making things isn't going to affect your job, is it?"

He sighed. "I'm being good. Truly."

She thought a minute as she sipped at the tea he handed her in an old cup with a chip out of it. "Mark, are you happy?" she asked him, running her fingertip across the chip.

The question caught him off guard. He froze, unable to answer *yes*, unwilling to tell his sister *no* when she approved, was actually proud, of his new success.

"I'm okay. Who wouldn't be?" he said out loud, but silently answered himself. *Me? Happy? Not exactly.*

"Well, that is not a ringing endorsement, but as long as you're okay with it, then I'll stop worrying."

He nodded and sipped his own tea out of a cup with faded Victorian figures on it.

"How's my favorite niece?" he asked.

"She's fine. We just got her a new computer game-station. She loves that stuff. Spends hours on it. Her class is making computer generated imagery for their first grade video performance. It's amazing how much technology she has access to at her school. It's wonderful!"

"Great," Mark said despondently.

"That is also not a ringing endorsement. Come on, Markie. You're a techno whiz, why so negative?"

"Let's just avoid another argument and go on to another topic. I'd like to buy Milly a real toy. You know, one you hold and play with. A doll."

"Don't waste your money. Girls aren't interested in dolls anymore."

"I have plenty to waste," he said insistently. "I don't want Milly to miss out on anything."

"What could she miss out on? She knows more math than I ever did. She has access to more information than ever before and all of it is right at her fingertips. She can find out about anything she wants to know right on the Net. It's wonderful!"

"Uh huh. Look, Kate, I like computers, you know that, but there is more to life than what you do on a computer."

"Mark, you need to accept the times. Children are happier than they have ever been because of computers."

"Really? I see," he said.

"A third not-so-ringing endorsement! Okay, got to go, Mark. I'll see you next Wednesday. Don't forget, for dinner. I've ordered a superb meal from the Old-Time Meal Company. Come hungry."

"I'll remember." *And I'll bring Milly her doll,* he said to himself.

"Love you," she said, kissing his cheek. "And remember, do something about stopping those catalogs."

COWBOYS & ALIENS IN THE SKY

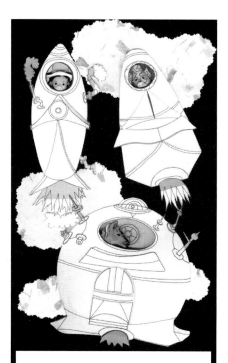

FIRE EATER OF YYSTER 12
(2004): Two-mouthed: eats fire
in one mouth, spits water from
other. Includes squirt gun.
FE12....................................55.00

BUFFALO BILL
(William Frederick Cody, 1883):
With complete set up for wild west
show in outer space, includes
mechanical buffalo.
BB.....................................125.00

MICROMEGAS, GIANT OF SATURN
(1997): Composed of snap together,
micro pieces. 10 feet across when
assembled.
MGS..................................125.00

He spent more time at work on Monday trying to peel the glue off his fingers so he could type up a project than he did typing it, and when he got home his fingers were still sticky. It made it hard to twist the key in the lock. A truck pulled up as he struggled with the door.

"We got your sofa, mister," the driver called out. "Where d'ya want it?"

"Okay, let me get this door open." The lock finally turned. He pushed through the door and tripped over an extra large pile of catalogs.

"Sorry," he said to the men who were waiting impatiently as he floundered to pick himself up off the floor.

"You oughta put a stop to all this here junk mail. It oughta be illegal," one of the men said, kicking at the catalogs.

"Just give me a minute," Mark said, scooping up as many of the magazines as he could and hurriedly setting them out of the way, wondering why everyone was so antagonized by a bunch of toy catalogs.

"Come on, mister, time is money."

"A minute more, okay?"

"We ain't got a minute." The man stomped in, knocking over more catalogs as two more movers pushed the sofa into the living room, scratching the floors as they went.

"How 'bout a tip, buddy?" one of the men said.

"A tip?" Mark glanced at the slurred piles of catalogs fanning across the floor and said, "No change, sorry."

"Cheapskate," the guy said. He kicked at the piles that were still standing, knocked as many down as he could and slammed the door as he left.

Mark sat down glumly in the mess. At least the catalogs he was ordering from were safely on the mantel.

"Knock, knock," a voice said. "Your keys were in the front door, young fellow."

"Oh, thanks. Can I help you?" Mark asked.

"You look like the one who could use help," the elderly gentleman pointed out.

"You might be right."

"Well now, just look at that sofa. With a sofa like that, why are you sitting on the floor in a pile of catalogs?" the man asked. He added almost as an afterthought, "I'm Bill Henley."

"I'm Mark Perralt. Oh, you're the man who has lived here your whole life."

"Since I was five, actually. Nice neighborhood. I'm fond of it. Larry Porter said you had some questions for me."

"Say, Mr. Henley," Mark said, standing up, "do you know how long these catalogs have been being delivered here?"

"Sure do! They started coming fifty-two years ago. Yes sir, they've been coming for a long, long time."

"Who ordered the first ones?"

"Well now, Charlie Rich lived here then," Mr. Henley said, pulling at his ear. "He was my friend. A little, short guy with big ears that looked even bigger because his face was small and he kept his hair trimmed close to his head. We used to play in a tree-house his Uncle Robin built him in one of the big trees. Me and Charlie and Petey. We were best buddies, pretending it was a fort and that we were fighting off rustlers or maybe monsters or sometimes aliens. We had overnights up there and pretended that we were star travelers as we stared up at the night sky. We dreamed dreams of great futures for all of us. Uh huh, those were happy days." Bill Henley had a far-off look in his eyes for a moment, and then something sharper took over. "Oh, don't listen to me. People say I'm getting senile. Anyway, when the catalogs started arriving, everyone in the family blamed Uncle Robin. He'd been staying with the Richs while he worked on a scientific project, but he disappeared right before the catalogs started coming, so they never really found out if he had ordered them."

"Did Charlie's family ever order anything from them?"

"Oh, no, no!" Mr. Henley said quickly. "It was bad enough the magazines kept coming. More and more of them."

"Why didn't anyone try to stop them from being delivered?"

"Oh, everyone who has lived in this house, including Charlie's family, tried that, but it's hopeless. For fifty-two years, catalogs have just kept on coming. Yep," he said, rising from the sofa where he had settled, "every owner tried and every owner failed."

"Then I won't waste my time trying."

"Good plan. Come by sometime. Bring a few catalogs. We can look them over like I used to with Charlie and Petey. Just like old times."

"Take a few with you. Help yourself, Bill."

"No thanks. I wouldn't want anyone to think I was too interested. Catalogs might start coming through my mail slot."

"You don't really believe that, do you?" Mark asked.

Bill Henley winked. "I'm not sure what I believe about those catalogs." He winked again and left.

Mark worked late into the night repairing the damage the delivery men had inflicted on his project, wondering intermittently about Bill Henley's reluctance to take even a few catalogs. He glanced quickly at the new mail the men had stamped on in their rush of impatience. Only one small catalog had escaped unmarked. It lay in the corner behind the door. It was the size and shape of a greeting card. *SPECIAL* screamed out in neon orange letters. *VALUE* followed in neon green. *Two for the Price of One.*

He stuffed it in his pocket and headed to bed. It was late and he had a big meeting with Mr. Cannady at eight-thirty in the morning. He yawned, closed his eyes and slept until the phone rang.

"Markham, where are you?" Elliot's panic-stricken voice sounded in the phone.

"Huh? Oh, I overslept!" Mark glanced at the clock. "I'll be there in half-an-hour."

"I'll try to postpone your presentation."

"Okay. Hey, Elliot, do you have that list of birthdays yet?"

"For heaven's sake, Markham! Concentrate! Get yourself here! Now!" He hung up with a bang.

For once Mark was glad his hair was so orderly. He shaved quickly and slipped into a freshly pressed shirt, clean socks and a dark suit. At the last minute, he grabbed a tie. He gulped juice and darted out the door, tie still in hand. He was knotting it as he came into the meeting. With a final yank on the knot, he went through the door.

"Markham, this is Mr. Randal Potter," Jerome Cannady said. "Sit, my boy." Mark noticed that Mr. Cannady's jaw fell as he dropped into a chair.

"Sorry I'm late. Let me get right to my presentation." Mark began. He gave the whole presentation and no one had a single question. "I'd be happy to address any issues," Mark offered.

Still no one spoke.

"Sir, Mr. Cannady, uh, is something wrong?"

"It's your tie, Markham," Carl Ellerby remarked.

"My tie?" Mark looked down. He had grabbed his eye ball tie. One big, bloodshot eyeball that pulsed little bursts of light every twenty-five seconds had been staring straight at everyone from the moment he had walked into the meeting.

Carl smirked nervously at Mark, or perhaps he was gloating. It was hard to tell with Carl.

He fumbled with the knot. "I am so sorry. Please forgive me. I was late and didn't realize which tie I had picked," Mark said as he rolled the tie and stuck it into his suit pocket.

"Quite! Well, perhaps now that the eye is off us . . ." Mr. Cannady said, letting the sentence hang in the air.

Mark hadn't meant to offend anyone, but it was funny: the tie, Mr. Cannady and best of all, Carl Ellerby who undoubtedly thought he had finally one-upped Mark over a necktie.

"Perhaps you could begin again," Mr. Potter said politely.

Mark worked hard to keep a smile in check. He cleared his throat to swallow a laugh, and began. It was one o'clock before they finished. Elliot was waiting in his office.

"Markham, where is your tie?" Elliot demanded immediately.

"In my pocket."

"You can't go around the office without a tie. Put it back on."

"Sure," Mark said, tying it quickly.

"No!" Elliot screeched. "Please, please tell me you didn't wear that horror into the meeting!"

Mark shrugged. "I'm going home to change my tie and maybe I'll come back, by and by, but Elliot, don't wait on me. I think I might take some leave. I'm sick if anyone asks. Come by the house later with that list I asked for."

SMALL **GIANTS**

Baby Cyclops: one eyed, giant ....65.

Baby Paul Bunyan: Giant woodsman with blue ox and ax ....55.

Goemagog: 2 snap together giants, leather and real hair. C.1590.................560.00

Giant Without a Heart: Removable heart from secret compartment........... 25.00

Thumbling: The doll telescopes from small to gigantic. C. 1816 .... 215.00

Golem: Red clay figure, white glazed face, hinged arms. 1560's 325.00

Goliath: Complete set with boulders, shoots rocks from spring hinged arm.
Biblical toy..75.00

Fee Fi Foe Fum Giant: With harp, goose who lays golden egg, and pot........ 20.00

King Kong: Baby great ape, push-button roar, turns head. 1930's.................. 65.00

Yeti: With real animal fur, makes large footprints (Tibetan)..........................35.00

Troll: Lumpy, ugly, plush toy, 1955..10.50

The Melting Giant: Ice giant, melts in heat, refreezes into original form....75.00

Giantof Dispair of Doubting Castle: Tears and moans roll from this giant...20.00

Atlas: Balances a huge replica of antique globe... 135.00

Cerne Abbas Giant: Carved from chalk (British)...10.00

ALL PRICES GOOD FOR THIRTY DAYS. ORDER NOW

Mr. Bill Henley was on his front porch when Mark got home at two-thirty.

"Hey, Mr. Henley, what can I do for you?"

"My, what a tie," the old gentleman remarked.

"Like it? It caused quite a stir today at work."

"I can imagine." Mr. Henley continued to stare at it as he said, "Listen, young fellow, my wife was making me clean out the basement. We're moving to something smaller, you see, and I found these old clippings. Thought you might like to have them."

Mark unfolded frail, yellowed papers. MAGIC REALM CLOSES AT WORLD FAMOUS AMUSEMENT PARK. LIFE ON MARS IS ONCE AGAIN REFUTED. GENETIC MAP MISUSED — CASE MADE AGAINST SCIENTISTS.

"Interesting," Mark said politely.

"That was the year," Mr. Henley said.

"What year?"

"The year the catalogs started coming and Uncle Robin left."

"You saved these because of the catalogs?" Mark asked.

"No, Uncle Robin left them in Charlie's basement. When Charlie moved he gave them to me as a memento. Of course, I didn't remember them until yesterday. Now I'm giving them to you, as a memento."

"Well, thanks very much," Mark said, not wanting to tell Mr. Henley that he would probably just discard the old paper.

"Okay," Mr. Henley said and walked away with a wave.

Mark shook his head, took the clippings inside and stuck them on the refrige under a big magnet. He gulped a drink and looked at them again as he kicked off his shoes, stripped off the now infamous tie and pulled his shirttails out of his pants.

All those things had happened in the same year the catalogs had begun to come. Pretty amazing. He took the clippings down and read them carefully as he nibbled on a peanut butter sandwich and gulped some milk. The story about the scientists had lines cut out of it in perfect rectangular gaps. He was about to go online to look at old newspaper files when he heard someone in the foyer.

"Knock, knock," Elliot's voice called. "Your front door is wide open. You'll have robbers in here if you aren't more careful."

"There isn't much to steal."

"Maybe they would take some of these catalogs," Elliot said wryly.

"Elliot, you made a joke!" Mark said.

"No, I didn't. I was serious. When are you going to throw some of them out?"

"When I don't need them anymore."

"Mark, you don't need them at all unless you're thinking of ordering via snail-mail," Elliot insisted stubbornly.

"Would that be too unsophisticated for a big shot like me?" Mark asked. "Elliot, why don't you ask for a reassignment?"

"I have, I have. They won't consider it. They think I'm really good for you."

"Yeah, but I'm driving you to distraction."

"True," Elliot agreed with him for once.

"I'm sorry, truly. I try to be good when I'm at the office, but by the time I get home, I just can't behave any longer."

"Sure, sure," Elliot said, pointing to the tie where Mark had tossed it. "And that is what you were doing today, being good?"

"The eyeball was an accident, I promise you." Mark paused before he impulsively said, "Ellliot, don't you ever want to inject a little excitement, a little imagination into the office?"

"No! Aren't you ever going to grow up, Markham?"

"Does everyone at Cannady's take inoculations against uncommon behavior?"

"Don't be silly," Elliot said.

"But if there was such a shot, you'd take it, wouldn't you? And Mr. Cannady would probably require proof of vaccination as a prerequisite for employment."

Elliot stood. "You're making fun of me again, Markham. Can't you ever restrain yourself?"

Mark grimaced. "Sorry. Did you get the list for me?"

"I wish you paid as much attention to how you are garbed and groomed as you do to this list," Elliot said, waving a computer printout right in front of Mark's nose.

Mark grabbed it and glanced down it. "Where's Lisa's name?"

"Lisa isn't on there. I'm only a consultant."

"Humor me. Put her name on the list," Mark said.

"Mark, you can't be serious about this. Why would you want to buy all these children birthday gifts?"

Mark paused as his mind jumped a space before he said out loud, "Because it's fun. I love toys." To himself he thought, *And I'll get to order from the catalogs!*

"Markham, stop this! You need to concentrate on work. I'm telling you, be careful at the office. It didn't go well today."

"Listen, Elliot, you worry too much. It went fine. I gave them a lot of stupendous ideas. I left them happy."

"You eyeballed them!"

"I did, didn't I?" Mark said, laughing happily. "Come on now, no more worries. Help me sort these catalogs by sizes so I can get on with my project."

"Why?" Elliot asked. "What are you up to now?"

"I'm planning a surprise for you. You'll be pleased."

Mark reached up and pulled the man down onto the floor with him. Elliot looked silly there in his shiny brown shoes and his starched shirt-collar.

Mark gave up and said, "You can sit on the sofa, Elliot. It suits you better."

Elliot stood and glared at Mark."I hardly came here to help you pile catalogs up into useless stacks. You left work before I could go over your schedule for the coming week. I would appreciate it if you would take the time to do it now, Markham."

"Just mark the calendar. I'll look at it later," Mark said.

Elliot went into the kitchen and marked the calendar. "Okay, done. Goodbye, Markham," he said curtly and left.

Mark put the finishing touches on the first chair that night. *Elliot's chair*, he thought. Tomorrow he would varnish the chair, but for now he was going to bed. He hoped the chair would make Elliot feel better.

As he took off his jeans to get ready for bed, he found the little catalog he had stuffed in his pocket. He gently straightened the roughed up edges and turned the pages. Giants was the theme. A picture of a child labeled Paul Bunyan; another called Irmaiian he had never heard of; the Cyclops, single-eyed and sweet-faced. A tiny catalog full of giants. He put it by his lamp. He would have Lady A deliver the bed tomorrow. He had ordered a feather mattress for the it, and the pillows for the chairs, custom-made by Mrs. Beatrice, Lady A's good friend.

The little catalog caught his eye again as he turned out the lights. "Good night, little giants," he said and went to sleep.

At breakfast he began ordering toys. He set the catalogs he had marked by his plate and sipped orange juice while he wrote down what he wanted. He had a total of seventy-one kids to buy for, but for the first order he only found twenty-three toys he wanted. Even though he was ordering from thirteen separate catalog companies, every catalog said the identical thing: *ALL Orders Final. NO Refunds, NO Returns. Use the address sticker on the last page when sending orders.*

He double checked his order to be sure he had what he wanted and decided to only order ten items. They weren't pricey, but it was hard to tell exactly what he was getting. The final list was:

1. Paul Bunyan, toddler with stuffed blue ox
2. Shoemaker's Elflet, complete with shoe repair kit
3. Nine-year-old Wizard of Lost Land in silver suit, shoes, tie and hat
4. Winged Wind doll from faraway star, glows in the dark
5. The last teen-boy from Ardromini Galaxy, complete with invisibility screen
6. NurseryRhyme Jack
7. Boy Cyborg, never before released toy
8. Orphaned, flying superhero, only eight-years-old, looking for a fine home
9. Mirabella, mind reader of Atlantis
10. Newborn from the fabulous lost cities of Mars

Delivery was promised within forty-eight hours of receipt of the order. He should have his purchases in time to take Milly her present on Wednesday.

He put the orders into envelopes, put the stickers on the fronts, noticing they weren't really addresses, just a series of numbers in three lines, and walked them to the snail-mail-box. It would be fun to see what he got. He bet Mrs. Williams and Larry Porter would be scandalized if they knew he was actually placing orders. Mr. Henley wouldn't approve either. But if he couldn't stop the delivery of the catalogs, why not enjoy them? He was late, so he rushed back to the house to finish dressing, but this time he checked which tie he was grabbing. Dark blue dots. Nice and conservative. Perfect for Elliot.

FATHERS

IN THIS EDITION

FAMOUS FATHERING TIPS
BY
PAPA BEAR
FATHER TIME
DADDY LONGLEGS
ZEUS
KING LEAR
KING MIDAS

The office had been bustling all week. Mark was about to take a candy-break when Mr. Cannady motioned him down the hall. "Come on, have a cup of coffee with me. Tasteful tie."

He had commented on Mark's tie every day since the eyeball incident. Mark doubted the famous-tie-mistake would ever be forgotten, but every day he just said, "Yes, sir. Thank you, sir." And then think, *Boring tie!*

"So how is the house coming, Markham?"

"Fine, sir. I've gotten some furniture, but it's a big house and it'll take me a while to fill it up."

"But you will be ready for the party? I'll be bringing some important clients."

"Elliot is being most helpful in that regard. I think he has already arranged the catering, sir." After a moment he added, "Do you think it might be more appropriate for someone established to host this party?"

"Markham, everyone takes their turn at Cannady's and yours is now."

"Yes, sir, but..."

Mr. Cannady frowned. "Mr. Perralt, I don't intend to discuss this. I'll excuse your hesitation because you are young and unattached. Do you need more help?"

"No, sir, Elliot is sufficient," he said.

It haunted him all morning that Mr. Cannady might give him another personal assistant. He would finish the house more quickly. Finish it. Go out at lunch and add to what he already had. A fancy music system, chests of drawers, fine china. His mind stopped. It wouldn't go anywhere. He couldn't think of anything else that would please Mr. Cannady and his clients. Oh, yes, he could fill the bookcases in the sitting room. That part would be fun. His mind stopped again. He sat down at his desk and made a list of each room and what it needed.

Foyer, no furniture there. Sitting room, six bedrooms, great room, dining room, small study off the sitting room, kitchen, six bathrooms, game room on the lower level, family room next to it.

He needed some new towels. His mind stopped again. What was he doing by himself in such a huge house? All he had ever wanted was a cozy place he could basically ignore and make things in.

Elliot walked in and looked over his shoulder. "Are you actually planning how to furnish the house? Bravo!"

Bravo? He stared at Elliot. *Bravo* was a dumb and affected word. He continued to stare until Elliot blinked.

"Elliot, I have no interest in this house. I'm a single man. What do I need with six bathrooms? The most interesting thing about this house is the catalogs, even though you and my sister and everyone in the neighborhood seem to despise them."

"We'll have to remedy that," Elliot said, failing completely to notice Mark's sense of desperation.

"Remedy what, Elliot? What are you talking about?"

"Being alone. A wife," Elliot started to say.

"No!" Mark said. His mind closed down. Stopped. Around him the office moved, the meetings loomed, but his mind had stopped.

"I'll be back," he managed to mumble as he stumbled off to the men's room. He had to get out. He leaned against the wall and felt the fire alarm under his shoulder.

Fleeing and fire alarm snapped together in his brain and without hesitation, he pulled it. People rushed out of meetings, copy rooms, bathrooms, and offices. They moved with funny little skittering steps, slides and downright running. Mark walked to the stairs and descended, whistling merrily, and left the building. It was only ten-thirty in the morning. He kept walking to the bus stop, got on a bus without looking where it went, got off in a strange neighborhood and waited. In fifteen minutes a kid with a knife came to him. Mark smiled, handed him six-hundred dollars, said good day, left the kid with surprise plastered across his face and walked home. It was after three by the time he got to his front door, but he couldn't go in. The door was blocked by three wooden crates. He scratched his head. What had Lady A sent him? A house warming present? No, she would never send him something he hadn't paid for. Maybe it was Elliot's idea. He slipped behind the boxes, opened the door, and stepped on the daily pile of catalogs heaped just inside it.

He scooped them into the corner and turned back to pull in the crates. Elliot's car came screeching to a halt as he was about to pull in the first one.

"Are you trying to get fired?" Elliot asked him angrily.

"What?" Mark asked.

"You heard me? You can't just leave for a day whenever you feel like it. What's wrong with you?"

"I'm eccentric."

"If you weren't so important to them, you would be dog meat right now, gone, finis, kaput. Don't you get it? You have responsibilities."

"What you really mean, Elliot, is if I didn't make them so much money I'd be gone, finis, kaput, dogmeat. I'm not important to them. It's the money I bring them they want. So, I won't get fired, will I, Elliot?"

"Probably not, but I might," Elliot said.

"If they fire you, I'll quit," Mark said calmly.

"No, you won't. Nobody would do that."

"Why not?" Mark asked, resting his elbows on top of the biggest of the crates.

"Money, this house, the car."

Mark laughed hysterically and then sobered up. "Yes, I would. I promise," he said seriously. "Maybe that is what I want. To quit."

"You're serious! You must be insane."

"Come on, Elliot, help me take these crates inside."

"What did you order?" he asked.

"Nothing. I thought you had sent them. The only thing I ordered were a few toys. Nothing to fill these." He gestured at the boxes blocking the porch and the door.

"Toys? You don't even have chairs and you ordered toys?"

"From the catalogs. I told you, they are the most interesting thing in the house."

"I don't understand you at all."

"I don't know what to say, Elliot," Mark said apologetically.

"Okay, forget it. Let's just get these crates off the front porch," Elliot said, bumping his elbow as they tugged the first crate through the door. "What on earth is in these boxes?"

"I have no idea. What I want to know is why they're all stamped *Open Immediately*. Do you think there's something in them that could spoil? Huge boxes of sausage? Or maybe a ten year supply of steaks?

Or eggs? I hope it's eggs. I'm not that fond of steak or sausage. What do you think?"

"How would I know?" Elliot said as they tugged and pulled until all three crates were in the foyer.

"Which one should we open first? Your choice, Elliot," Mark said, wiping at his face with his sleeve.

"Try the smallest one."

Mark went to get a crow bar to pry off the lid. When he came back, Elliot was examining the packing lists.

"Markham, apparently these are your toys. It says no returns! Please tell me some of it can be returned."

"Nope."

"Did the descriptions mention measurements?"

"Nope. No mention of size at all."

Elliot groaned. "Don't you know anything about children's toys? Always be sure you have room to store what you buy."

"Don't worry about that. The one thing I'm not short of is space. Come on! I thought you'd be proud I planned ahead."

This time Elliot moaned.

Mark placed the crow bar just under the lid. He was really thirsty from the walk. "Could you go in the kitchen and get me a drink of ice water while I pry off the top?" he asked.

Elliot vanished and Mark pried. The lid popped off without a sound.

Staring up at Mark was a small boy with large, pointy ears.

Mark slammed the lid back on the crate, cracked it and peeked in again.

"Can't I get out now?" a little voice asked.

"What are you doing in there?" Mark asked.

"You ordered me."

"I ordered a toy. Uh, which one are you supposed to be?" Mark stammered in confusion.

"Please let me out. I don't like it in here." He sounded as if he was going to cry.

"Don't cry. Just let me get my friend to go home and I'll help you out. Sssh, until he leaves, okay?"

Mark heard a sob.

"So what was in it?" Elliot asked handing him a glass.

"Shards. It's broken," Mark said. gulping down the water.

"See. You wasted your money," Elliot said with a satisfied, I-told-you-so smirk.

"Okay, okay, you were right. Now go home."

"I'll help you check the others," Elliot said.

"No, not now. Elliot, what do we still need for the party? Whatever it is, go buy it. Just do it. I'm not a party giver. Earn your keep."

"All of it? Even the furniture?"

"Do I still need furniture? Start with the kitchen stuff. I'll think about furniture."

"What kind of dishes?"

Mark held his palms up. "Your choice. Have fun, okay?"

"Now? I should do it now?"

"Sure, why not? Go!"

Elliot left shaking his head all the way down the drive to the street.

Mark grabbed the lid off the crate. The boy was sobbing softly. Mark reached in and gingerly lifted him out.

"Don't cry. Come on, I'll get you some milk."

"I don't like it here."

"I don't blame you. Where are your parents?"

The child looked at him blankly. "Didn't you adopt me?"

"No, I bought an . . ." Mark stopped and looked at the packing slip. "An Elflet."

"I'm Elflet."

"No, no, a toy Elflet. A doll, for a gift."

"I'm no doll. That's for girls."

"No doll. You're alive. That's correct," Mark said, feeling as if someone had dragged him into a bad dream.

"Yes, I'm alive," the little boy said. "Can you reach my shoes and also my blankie?"

"Huh? Oh, sure," Mark said, reaching back into the crate. "Anything else? What about this?"

"My shoe repair kit!" the little boy said and grabbed it from Mark.

"Okay, sit right there. I'm going to open these other crates and see what else I need to call the companies about, or maybe the police."

There were two more crates. He hoped there weren't any more mistakes or surprises.

"Don't you want me?" the boy asked, interrupting his thoughts.

"What? You don't understand, Elflet."

Elflet put his finger in his mouth and his blankie over his head. Mark put the crow bar down and picked the child up. He had no idea what to say, so he just patted his back. The boy hardly weighed anything, as if no one had fed him.

"When did you last eat?"

"I can't remember," Elflet said.

"Okay, let me pry off these two lids and we'll get a snack and then some dinner."

Elflet sucked his finger.

The second crate lid came off more easily. Mark took a deep breath and looked in. It came up to his chest and was full of straw. He couldn't see anything in it, so he dipped into the straw, swirling it around with his hand.

"Watch it!" a voice said. "Keep your hands to yourself."

Elflet pulled a pile of catalogs over to the crate and climbed up to look inside. "Nothin' there," he said around his finger. "Jus' a bunch of straw."

A snicker came from the crate. Mark rubbed his eyes. "Stay here a moment, Elflet. I need to get my list off the refrigerator," Mark said.

He dashed into the kitchen and grabbed for the list of what he had ordered, but it slipped from his fingers and glided under the refrigerator.

He was fishing it out when Elflet said loudly right by his ear, "Whatcha doing?"

Next to the little boy was a bigger boy.

Mark hooked the paper and pulled it out. He glanced at it quickly. "Uh, just out of curiosity, who are you?" he asked the bigger boy whose skin glowed lightly green.

"Traxon," the answer came in a kind of warbling trill.

"Traxon? You wouldn't happen to be from the Ardromini Galaxy?"

"Maybe," the voice warbled. "Where is this?"

"My house," Mark said.

43

"What galaxy?" Traxon asked impatiently.

"Milky Way," Mark said, wondering if he had finally lost his sanity.

Something thumped and Traxon vanished.

"Invisibility screen," Mark mumbled what was written next to the toy from Ardromini. "Come on, you two, follow me. Now sit, right there," he pointed to the sofa.

Elflet pulled up onto the couch and the cushion next to him sank, as apparently Traxon sat down.

Mark turned to the third crate. The top was split apart by a jagged gap. *Bang*, a sharp, shiny blade split the crate down the side. Out stepped an oversized toddler, ax and stuffed blue ox in hand. This kid was built like a truck, with cherubic cheeks and big blue eyes and a swatch of black curls.

"Give me that," Mark said, grabbing the ax. "Are you Paul?"

"Yes, me Paul," the child said.

"Good, that is good. Go sit next to them," Mark said, pointing to Elflet and the still invisble Traxon.

"And don't sit on me," Traxon said.

"Don't sit on anyone," Mark said. "Now, what are you guys doing here?"

They looked at him blankly.

"Read the instructions," Traxon said, fading out into a barely visible range.

"What instructions?"

Traxon waved his arm where a tag dangled, like the ones found on any toy.

"Genuine teen from Ardromini Galaxy. Needs high protein diet. Do not feed him processed sugar at all costs. At full growth, Traxon will be seven feet tall."

Mark turned the card over and read.

THE LEGEND OF TRAXON: In the year 10,265, the galaxy of Ardromini came under attack by the Yextil race. The beautiful cities made of round, rubber towers and glass platforms were reduced to glowing cinders and pools of black oil. The people of the galaxy hid in fear, waiting for the final Yextil curse. But from a distant rural mountain of Ardrominia Five came a young man with deep eyes and a strong jaw. He was only seven feet tall, small for his people, but he proved to be the salvation of his race. Traxon, invisible fighter of Ardromini Galaxy.

"That's a nice legend, but how do I send you back?"

"Can't, can you?" Traxon said.

"How did you get here?" Mark asked.

"You ordered me, didn't you?" Traxon said, cocking his head at Mark.

"Yes, but . . ." Mark began.

"Here is the receipt and it says right there, no refunds, no returns," the boy said, holding out a form to Mark.

"This must be wrong!" Mark said.

"You think? Did they deliver us to the wrong house?"

"No, I mean, yes, I mean they delivered the wrong items. There must be a way to return you."

"Did they? Deliver the wrong items? Doesn't the number on the receipt match the one on my tag?" Traxon warbled. "I don't want to go back into storage."

"I hungry," Paul said.

"Me, too," Elflet squeaked.

"Okay, okay, we'll go out to dinner," Mark said desperately. "Just let me get a jacket."

"I'm cold," Elflet said. "Do you have a coat for me?"

Mark wrapped him in a sweater that engulfed him. For good measure he pulled a skull cap down over the child's ears, which were rather pointy.

"Now, come on. Elflet, hold Traxon's hand, and Paul, you hold mine."

They went to the Drive-Through-Sup Shop. Traxon got a hamburger, Elflet a milkshake and chicken-bits, and Paul ordered a foot long hot dog with the works on it plus a milkshake and fries. Mark wasn't hungry.

The car was covered in crumbs and grease and Traxon looked a little greener than before after trying a gulp of milkshake. Maybe he really had a food allergy to processed sugar and the tag wasn't a joke. Kate might know what to do. They would go to Kate's.

They pulled up at her house and Mark hesitated. What was he going to say? "I ordered these kids from catalogs?" That wouldn't do. How about, "I'm babysitting for friends." But then, how would he explain later when their parents never came back for them? Maybe he would say he had taken in a few foster children. After all, the house was too big for just one person.

"Hey, Uncle Mark," Milly said at the door. "I didn't know you were coming."

"Uh, is your mommy home?"

"Uh huh. Who are they?" she asked, pointing at the boys.

"They're with me. Could you play with them for a little bit?"

"Sure, but that one looks green. Is he sick, because Mommy won't want me to play with him if he's sick."

"I think it's just an allergy. His name is Traxon and this is Elflet and Paul."

"Do you guys want to play on the computer?"

"I've never done that," Elflet said.

"You haven't? Weird. Well, come on and I'll show you how." Milly took Elflet's hand and led them towards her room.

UNEXPECTED VISITORS

BROWNIES

SANTA CLAUS

THE TOOTH FAIRY
Sprite, night-time visitor. Comes with supply of change.

A FAIRY GODMOTHER

LEPRECHAUN
Searching for gold, creates mischief in early morns.

ALIEN ABDUCTORS
Sneaky grey men stealing people off dark streets.

"**K**ate?" Mark called and followed her voice into the kitchen.

"You didn't get the days mixed up did you, Mark?"

"No, no, I just wanted to see my big sister."

"What's going on, Mark? You never just drop in, but I'm glad you did because I have a box full of stuff for you that's been stored in the basement forever."

"What kind of stuff, Sis?"

"Junk mostly, but Mom thought you would want it some day so I kept it until you got a place big enough to store it in. Some of it was left by Dad. I found it again when I was cleaning out. If you don't want it, I'm throwing it away."

"I'll take it when I leave. Sorry you got stuck with it all these years. Listen, Kate, I uh, well, I uh . . ." He stuttered into the truth. "I've, uh, I've become a foster parent."

"What? Mark, are you nuts? You can't even match your own socks. Elliot has to do it for you. What are you going to do with a kid?"

"Thanks for the vote of confidence, and it isn't one kid. It's three."

"Three!" She practically screamed. "Three? How could anyone give you three kids? You don't even own a bed!"

"I will tomorrow."

"Mark, this is a huge responsibility. Are you sure you can handle it? What will you do with the kids while you're at work?"

"I don't have the vaguest idea. Hire a baby sitter?"

"Mark, this is crazy!"

"Agreed, but what am I going to do now? It's too late."

"Where are they?"

"Upstairs with Milly. "

"I guess I should take some more cookies and milk to them," Kate said in a stunned sort of voice.

Cookies. Sugar. Traxon. Mark dashed out of the room and upstairs to Milly's room.

"Traxon, don't eat that. It has sugar in it."

Traxon dropped the cookie at his lips as if he had been burned.

"Are you trying to poison me, Earth child?"

"You're weird. I was just being polite, sharing my cookies. I thought everyone liked cookies."

"He's allergic to sugar, sweetie," Mark said quickly, patting her head gently.

"To sugar? No cookies?" Milly said in dismay.

Kate came into the room. "You know about allergies, honey. It's like Tommy and his allergy to nuts."

"Oh, yeah," the little girl said.

"Do you have some cheese? He likes cheese," Mark suggested.

"Cheese and crackers would make a nice snack, too," Kate said diplomatically. "Uncle Mark and I will get you all some."

She pushed Mark downstairs and into the kitchen.

"Mark, what's wrong with that boy?" she whispered urgently.

"He just has an allergy."

"His skin is green!" Kate observed. "That isn't normal."

"Allergic reaction, I think," he said quickly.

"That is some allergy. Is that why they gave him to you? Because no one else would keep him?"

"Sort of, I guess. And now I'm stuck," he mused out loud.

"Mommy," Milly called. "Paul pulled my hair."

"I think it's time for us to leave," Mark said. "Come on, boys, we're leaving!"

Kate pointed to a moldy carton, coated in grey strings of dust from long storage in the basement.

"Take that, too," she said. "And watch that child's diet."

They piled back into the car. Who was he going to get to baby sit three kids, especially three kids who had been sent to him through the mail in packing crates? No one was going to believe him. He didn't quite believe it himself. He kept glancing behind him just to be sure there were really three boys back there.

They pulled up to the house to find Lady Anderson banging on the front door. She turned as they got out of the car.

"Hey, Mark, I was about to give up. I got a truck and brought the bed on over. Who have you got with you?"

"Traxon, Paul, Elflet, meet Lady Anderson. Lady A, meet my three new charges."

"Charges? Where'd you get them?"

"Uh, it's a long story."

"I'll bet. I mean, I like you and everything, Mark, but who would let you take care of their kids?"

"I'm a foster parent. I, uh, guess if you have money you can arrange anything."

"Yeah? Well, I think you bought into more than you'll be able to chew. You already look pale and peaked. You don't have any energy since you took that new job. It's sucking the life right out of you."

"Could that be true?" he mulled as Elflet pulled on his leg.

"Can I go to sleep now?" the little boy begged.

"A kid who wants to go to bed? What did you do, put him under a spell, make a magic wish, or what?" Lady A said with a loud burst of laughter.

"Lady A," Mark said suddenly. "You don't think I've recently gone insane, do you?"

"Huh? Look at you. You live in a big house, drive a fancy car, make a lot of money. You've got what almost everyone wants. You aren't crazy, are you?" she asked.

"I just asked you that!"

"Well, answer your own question, then," she said.

"Okay. I live in a big house with almost no furniture in it because I don't really want any. All I truly want to do is make stuff and fix it, but I've managed to earn too much money to be able to do what I really want to do. Isn't there something nuts about that?"

"Well, now you have three kids to fill the house up. And, don't worry, they'll have it covered in junk and mess in no time, and every time they break something, you can fix it. How's that?"

"I wanna go to sleep," Elflet said loudly.

"Okay, go," Mark said.

The child began to cry softly.

"Mark, you have to put him to bed. You know, get him in his pajamas, get him to brush his teeth and all, and then kiss him goodnight."

Elflet looked up at Mark with big eyes. Okay, he could let the kid sleep in one of his tee shirts that he had shrunk in the dryer, he could fold up some blankets for a bed, and he would worry about the toothbrush in the morning.

50

"Come on, Elflet, let's go," Mark said and took a little hand in his.

"And a bedtime story and maybe a lullabye," Lady A called as they left together.

He stopped halfway up the stairs.

"Lady A, you seem to know a lot about kids. Could I hire you to baby sit tomorrow? I could bring them by your place before work."

"To me? Oh, no! But maybe I'd come here. How much, Mark?" she said from the bottom of the steps. He recognized her bartering voice.

"Fifty for three hours," he suggested.

"You're kidding? Fifty dollars per hour is more like it."

"Thirty," he said to please her.

"Forty-eight fifty," she answered quickly.

"Forty-five," he dickered.

"Forty-six, and that is my last and final offer," she said firmly.

"Done."

"Plus a tip if they're difficult or you're late."

He grinned all the way up the stairs. He'd known Lady A for years. He didn't know what she looked like under the hats and crumpled clothes or how old she was, but she was as reliable as the day was long, and she would be there in the morning.

"She dresses like Mother Goose," Elflet said.

"You know of Mother Goose?" Mark asked, really surprised.

Elflet nodded his head up and down, his eyes solemn. "But I never really met her."

SHOES

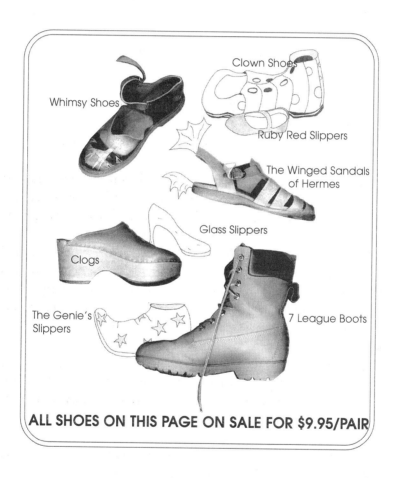

Clown Shoes

Whimsy Shoes

Ruby Red Slippers

The Winged Sandals
of Hermes

Glass Slippers

Clogs

The Genie's
Slippers

7 League Boots

ALL SHOES ON THIS PAGE ON SALE FOR $9.95/PAIR

He was glad Elflet had wanted an early bedtime. Paul had fallen asleep on the sofa, a lumpy wad hugging his blue ox. Mark had hefted him into his arms and laid him next to Elflet, covering them both with an old woolen blanket. That left Traxon, but when he went to look for him, the boy was nowhere to be seen.

"Traxon? Are you here?" Mark waited a minute. "Could you please visualize?"

No boy appeared, just his voice. "I'm going to sleep now."

"So?" Mark asked.

"So, I always protect myself when I sleep."

"You mean hide yourself?"

"Of course." Traxon's voice warbled.

"Okay, fine, but warn me if I'm about to step or sit on you?"

"You won't, I promise," the boy said.

Mark threw up his hands. "Okay, okay," he said and went into the kitchen. He was exhausted. Tea and cookies sounded wonderful, and maybe a warm soak in the tub, but he was too tired. Too tired to get the tea and cookies, and too tired to draw a bath.

"Goodnight, one and all," Mark said to the dark house. "Goodnight."

He thought he heard a noise in the middle of the night, but was too exhausted to get up and investigate, so he just turned over, pulled the covers over his head and went back to sleep. At five in the morning, he sat straight up in bed. Paul was crying. He knew it was Paul. It was a lusty bellow.

Mark fumbled about groggily looking for his worn, yellow tennis shoes he used as slippers. They weren't where he thought they had been. He padded barefooted into the hall and stumbled over something. He crashed to the floor, twisting his ankle sharply.

"What the . . .?" he growled angrily.

The light flicked on illuminating a bleary-eyed Traxon by the switch.

"What happened? Why did you yell?" the boy asked.

"Because someone left . . . " Mark paused, turning what he had tripped over in his hands, looking for a description for what he held. He rotated it between his fingers several times before he said, "I tripped on pieces of my yellow tennis shoes?"

Elflet peeped from behind a door. "I was trying to fix them up to look new for you."

"You took my shoes apart? Why?"

"Because elves repair shoes."

"But, you ruined. . ." Mark looked at Elflet's face and clamped his mouth shut.

"At least I didn't ruin your shiny black shoes," the little boy said, looking pleadingly at Mark.

"True," Mark said, trying not to look too sadly at his favorite pair of comfy shoes lying in pieces on the floor. He wished it had been his company shoes.

"Hungry," Paul said, chewing on the tail of his ox.

"Elflet, pick all this stuff up and throw it away. Then we'll all get a snack in the kitchen."

"Not me. I'm going back to bed." Traxon yawned as he spoke.

Graham crackers and milk seemed to soothe Elflet and Paul. Mark kept the lights dim and by the time they were finished, the two had sleepy faces and droopy eyes.

Getting up wasn't as hard as Mark had expected. He took an extra five minutes in the shower, checked his appointment calendar, breathed a sigh of relief that there was nothing pressing first thing at work, and waited nervously to see if Lady A showed up.

He stepped out onto the front porch, looking for the blowsy figure he hoped was coming, but the only person out was a young woman with a torrent of black hair curling down her back. He was nervous. It was close to when he should leave.

"So, are you ready?" the young woman called to him from the sidewalk.

"What?" he said, shading his eyes. "Is that actually you, Lady A?" he asked.

"Who did you think it was? Mother Goose?"

"No, no, it's just I've never seen you, uh, uncovered before."

She laughed, a deep sort of laugh. "I'm not exactly uncovered," she said, whirling about like a little kid, arms out, the skirt of her dress flying as she spun. "You like?"

He watched her, absorbed by the motion.

"Pull your eyes in, Mark. Where are the kids?"

"Asleep. Don't feed Traxon any processed sugar. He's allergic. They all have instructions on the tags hanging from their arms."

"What?"

"I'll explain later. I have to go," he said quickly and started to leave, but then stopped and asked, "By the way, what is your first name?"

"Won't Lady A do? I don't think I know you well enough to get that personal."

FEASTS, FÊTES & BÊTES

Feasts in Valhalla for Dead Heroes.................150.
Feast in Honor of Queen Esther.........................135.
The Boston Tea Party, on a ship.........................175.
The Feast of Sweets in The Nutcracker............125.
The Mad Hatter's Teaparty ....95.
The Beast's Magic Dinner for Beauty...............85.
Food from Cinderella's Ball, served out of glass
        slippers..200

Elliot was waiting in his office when he got there Wednesday morning. "Here is the menu for the party. Tell me what you think by the end of the day. And here is the guest list," Elliot said.

Mark glanced at it. "I've got a few people to add."

"Markham, this is the list Mr. Cannady provided. You can't add anyone. Now get ready. You've got a surprise meeting in ten minutes on the Peat and Peabody account."

"Elliot, I'm not going to the meeting unless you and Laura are added to this list."

"Markham, please! This is Mr. Cannady's list. I can't change it."

"Okay," Mark said, "but I can." He took up a pen, scribbled Elliot and his wife Laura onto the list and walked off to the meeting.

Peat and Peabody were looking for a new program that interacted with the arts. Mark adjusted the parameters of how they had been looking at the project, suggested some new interfaces, and got smiles and slaps on the back. Mr. Cannady got a signed contract.

Mark couldn't understand how no one else saw what he did. It was obvious to him. He just pulled one piece from over there, another from here, one from up there and it all snapped together. Building with thoughts and constructing something with wood and nails were not too different for him. Both were three-dimensional processes. The only difference was that when he built with thoughts he moved the pieces in his head instead of with his hands.

Mr. Cannady thanked him and Mark went out to lunch. He called Lady A from the café at which he usually ate.

"Mark, how could you tag them like they were stuffed animals or action figures? They're people."

"It seems pretty efficient," he said, at the same time he was thinking, *they were supposed to be action figures and dolls, not real live people.* And dolls and action figures came with tags sometimes. And it was efficient.

"And why don't you take away that invisibility toy from Traxon? Why would you give such a thing to a child? Children are supposed to be seen and not heard, but this one can be heard but not seen," she said angrily.

"I didn't know you could buy an invisibility screen," Mark said.

"Well, you must be able to or he wouldn't have one, would he?"

"Okay, anything else?"

"Yes, Elflet seems sad and two boxes were left at the front door."

"Oh, no!" he groaned. "Any strange noises coming from them?"

"What are you talking about, Mark? I opened them. One's a set of silver rimmed dishes and one is full of sheets and bath towels. Mr. Cannady, your boss, sent them as a house warming present. It was very nice of him."

"Thank goodness!"

"Yes, thank goodness! You needed towels. I couldn't find any for the kids. These kids need baths and Traxon needs to see an allergist for this green junk on his skin."

"Okay, okay."

"And I've got to leave by five. I've got a client meeting me at the shop to pick up some things."

"I'll be home. Promise."

He hung up. He had noticed that whenever Lady A was indignant, she became bossy. He went back to work, but couldn't concentrate. He looked over the party plans and glanced at a new project.

"Markham," Elliot said, startling him.

"Yes."

"Go home. It's four-thirty. You look exhausted and I'm supposed to remind you that you're having dinner at your sister's."

"What? Four-thirty!"

He grabbed his jacket and raced down the hall. He had to be home by five and if the traffic was bad, he was sunk.

Lady A was standing on the sidewalk with the three kids in tow when he pulled up to the house. He was late and she looked mad.

"You have to give me a ride, so I can make my meeting," she announced immediately. "Pile in, kids."

She shoved them into the car and climbed in next to him, drumming her fingers on the edge of the dashboard.

"Listen, Mark, you have to be more punctual if you want me to baby-sit for you again. I've got other responsibilities, you know. And you need to register Traxon for school. He's too old to stay at home. He can't even read."

"I can, just not in English," the boy sang out from the back seat.

"And," Lady A continued undeterred, "it wouldn't hurt Elflet to be in a preschool. He'll be ready for kindergarten next fall."

"Make a list," Mark sighed. "This is all too sudden."

"Oh, come on. The social service people must have prepared you," she said, unsympathetically.

"Oh right," he said thinking quickly, "but I'm a little disorganized. The absent-minded professor type."

She agreed with him.

"Will you come tomorrow?" Mark ventured timidly.

"I guess, but you'd better find someone more permanent," she said as she got out of the car.

He looked at his watch. Kate had asked him for seven o'clock. He'd have to bring the boys. If he hurried he could stop at a mall and get some other clothes for them and something to make Traxon's skin look less green. Makeup, maybe.

The mall was crowded with mothers and teenagers. The three boys stood at the entrance, staring, frozen by the activity. He tried to pull them into the foot traffic, but Elflet grabbed one leg and Paul the other, and clung to him. He couldn't move. He detached them and squatted down.

"It's only a mall. I won't leave you, okay?"

They didn't look convinced.

"I'll hold your hands. Traxon?" He swung around. The older boy was gone. "Traxon? Traxon? Where are you?"

Panic was crawling out of his stomach into his throat.

"This place is wild," a disembodied voice said.

"Come on, visualize, please. You can't shop if no one can see you."

"I don't want to shop."

"We won't be here long. Please cooperate, Traxon. This is hard enough as it is."

The boy reappeared right by his side and Mark quickly led them through the crowd towards the department store at the other end of the mall. Paul's grip grew tighter and tighter and tighter on Mark's fingers until they were numb. It felt like forever before they got there. The boys were nervous and Traxon faded in and out, but nobody in the store noticed them until they got to the children's department.

"Can I help you?" a woman asked uncomfortably.

"I need some outfits for these guys," Mark said.

The saleswoman was still staring at the boys. "What sizes?" she stuttered.

"Uh, I don't know exactly."

"Okay, uh, that one," she said pointing to Paul, "looks like a husky size five. This one, except for his feet, looks like a four slim, and the older boy is probably a size fourteen or sixteen?"

It turned out that two-year-old Paul took a six extra husky and refused to wear anything that wasn't blue. Elflet kept looking for green clothes and Traxon wanted nothing he saw, but settled for jeans and a black velvet pullover that made his skin look even greener.

The saleswoman had been right. Elflet had super big feet. Socks and dress shoes were a problem that went unsolved. The cosmetics counter was packed with women getting free makeovers. He circled it three times before approaching a middle-aged salesclerk who must have seen his hesitancy because she smiled pleasantly and said, "Can I help you, sir?"

"Uh, well, uh, I need to buy some makeup."

"What kind of complexion does your girl friend have?"

"Kind of green," he blurted out.

"Green?" the woman frowned.

Mark nodded rapidly. "It's for my kid brother, here. He got in some green paint and has his first date and he wants to cover it up."

"Oh my! It should be fairly dark for coverage, a little base, then blush. That should do it."

The bill came to fifty dollars. Mark dragged the boys into the men's bathroom. By the time he got them dressed and tried to cover up Traxon's complexion they had spent two hours in the mall and were late for the party.

"Sorry, Larry," Mark said when his brother-in-law opened the door. "No babysitter."

"Kate mentioned you had really lost it and taken in kids. Why am I not surprised they're with you?" Larry said irritably. "You should have known you weren't prepared to be a father."

"You're probably right, Larry, but here we are," Mark said, trying to keep from just leaving on the spot.

"Okay, okay, come in, all of you, I suppose."

The kids were quickly shooed upstairs to join Milly. Kate had invited friends and one of them happened to be a woman who happened to be single and happened to be interested in everything Mark did, at least until she saw the kids. Then her eyebrows went up and her interest in Mark went down. He was relieved and concentrated on the food. It was good. He enjoyed the tastes and felt a sense of calm come over him until a big fuss ensued in the kitchen where the kids were eating. Kate gave Mark a dirty look and ran in to see what was going on. Paul had eaten through the other kids' shares before they had even gotten to sit down. He had sneaked into the kitchen and gone from one plate to the next while everyone else washed their hands. Kate ended up giving all of them peanut butter sandwiches, being careful not to put jelly on Traxon's.

Everything seemed to be settling down, when an invisible Traxon whispered into Mark's ear, "Did Lady A remember to tell you about the two crates that came while you were at work?"

"Excuse me for a moment," Mark said and walked towards the bathroom. "Traxon?" he whispered, hoping the invisible boy was nearby.

"Yeah? What?" his voice said.

"Into the bathroom and appear, immediately, please. Okay, now, no more invisible spying or arrivals. And yes, I knew about the boxes of towels and dishes that Lady A unpacked."

"How about the other two crates that came? The two that said, *Please Open Immediately.*"

"What? Four boxes came today, not two? Open immediately? Get Elflet and Paul, right now. We have to go home."

Traxon and he left their bathroom conference. Mark made a botched set of excuses and apologized profusely, but knew he and the kids had ruined Kate's carefully planned party. She walked him to the door and closed it before he could say anything else.

"Is she mad at us?" Elflet asked.

"Yes," Paul answered.

By the time they got home, two large envelopes and four tightly sealed crates, not two, sat on the porch, blocking the front door.

ASSORTMENTS

ELFLET: Shoemaker's littlest elf

75.00

YOUNG MERLIN: Arthurian

95.00

LITTLE BABA YAGA: Walks on chicken legs

85.

WOLF BOY: Full-moon lover

100.00

WINKEN, BLINKEN & NOD 125.00

MIRABELLA: Young mind reader of Atlantis

120.00

THREE BOYS IN A TUB

150.00

METAL BOY: From Molten Volta 7

95.00

Mark tore open the envelopes. The first one said, "We are sorry, but we no longer stock the newborn from the lost city of Mars. We have credited your account and hope that you will order from us again. Thank you."

"Thank goodness and thank you," Mark said. "Thank you, thank you, thank you!"

He opened the second envelope. "The One-of-a-Kind Super Hero suffered a minor flying mishap and is not available for immediate delivery. Thank you for your patience."

Oh brother, I think this means they will still send him, Mark thought just as one of the crates rattled as though it contained a crowd rather than what he assumed was one child. What had they sent him?

"Here's the crow bar," Traxon said, making him jump. "You didn't order anything dangerous, did you?"

"Not that I know of, but then I didn't think I had ordered what I got when you came along."

"How come you ordered us when you didn't really want us?" Traxon asked, glaring at him.

Mark looked at the boy and Elflet and Paul. They were waiting, watching him, expecting an explanation.

"It's just that the descriptions in the catalogs were misleading."

"You don't really want us?" Elflet asked.

"I want you, I do! I just wasn't prepared for you," Mark said quickly.

The crate saved him. It thumped and banged madly at that moment, turning all their heads towards it.

"You better open it," Elflet suggested.

"I'm ready for it, whatever it is," Traxon said, taking a bold pose, feet forward, arms up.

"Look guys, whatever is in there, it's probably fed up with being closed in a box and that's why it's banging away like that," Mark said, trying to be reassuring.

He took the crow bar from Traxon, pried and pulled the lid up, and peeked into the crate warily.

"Well?" Traxon demanded.

"You can stand down," Mark said to him. "Come out," he said into the box.

A boy of twelve or so peeked over the top of the crate. He was devilishly handsome, blonde hair, brown eyes, lean and athletic. He immediately jumped straight up over the edge of the box and landed nimbly on his toes.

"You were making all that racket?" Traxon said.

"I needed a stretch."

"Who are you?" Traxon asked.

"Jack."

"Just Jack?" Mark asked. That didn't seem right to him.

"No, not quite. It's Jack-Sprat-Be-Nimble-Hill, at your service." The boy bowed.

"We'll continue introductions after I open the other three crates. Everyone has been in them way too long."

"You're telling me," Jack said.

Paul pointed at one of the boxes and in a little baby voice that seemed incongruous with his body, said, "Quiet! Sleepy?"

Mark sighed and tried to pry off the lid, but it resisted.

"Now what?" he wondered out loud.

"Say the magic words," a voice said.

"What?" Elflet asked.

"Wrong, wrong, wrong," the voice said.

"Please," Mark suggested.

"Not even close," the voice said gleefully.

"Oh, give it up. Stay in there if you want to," Traxon said.

"Silvery," Paul said, peeking through a hole in the crate.

"Aw, the baby guessed," the voice said.

They heard something creak and the lid slowly rose on a set of large, spring hinges. The child within was eight or nine, completely dressed in shiny silver including his top hat. His face was round and jolly and a pair of pince-nez glasses perched on his little snub nose.

"Who are you?" Elflet asked.

"It's not who I am now, it's who I will be someday. Tell them, mister," the boy said to Mark.

"The Wizard of Lost Land?" Mark read off the packing list.

"Bingo, my man, so says my tag. Is this Lost Land?" the boy asked pompously, waving his arm and with it, his tag, as he climbed out and jumped to the floor. His hair was close cut. Dimpled hands hung out of his sleeves and pudgy legs stuck out below his three-quarter length pants. Mark couldn't bring himself to tell the boy he didn't know where Lost Land was, or if it was.

Paul poked the wizard with a finger.

"Don't touch the goods, little boy."

"Wizard, huh? You do magic? That's how you kept us from opening the box?" Traxon asked.

The wizard looked at Mark and back to Traxon.

"Well, not precisely. I, uh, invent magic," he announced with what appeared to be a burst of inspiration.

"Invent magic? How's that? Is it real magic or not?" Jack insisted.

"Oh, my!" the wizard said.

"What's the matter?" Mark asked the little wizard.

"I don't quite have an answer," the boy said, suddenly deflated. "My memory seems to have a few holes."

He reached up to scratch his head, making his tag wiggle and dance as it dangled from his wrist.

"Here we go," Mark said, removing it. "It says, 'The Wizard of Lost Land, also known as Rollo Wiz, needs many things to tinker with. Delightful inventions shall come your way, as well as a bit of a mess. Workshop advised where supervision is available. At age nine, Rollo is committed to being a wizard.'"

"What's that mean?" Elflet asked.

"It means he's a tinkerer and an inventor," Mark said.

Mark wished he had come with a tag when he was born, so his parents would have known what to do with him. It was helpful, especially if you weren't like everyone else.

"Hungry," Paul declared loudly, breaking into his reverie.

"Me, too," the chubby Rollo said.

"I think Paul can show you where to get some food, can't you Paul?"

"Uh huh," the toddler said happily. It was hard to keep him out of the kitchen.

"Traxon, could you make some popcorn for everyone?" Mark asked.

"No," Traxon said. "Let's open the next crate."

A loud crash came from the kitchen. Mark dashed in to see what had happened. Two chubby boys were flat on their backs surrounded by broken glass and cookies from the shattered cookie jar.

"Anyone hurt?" Mark asked, picking each child up and shaking the glass off of him. Rollo clutched three cookies in his plump hands and Paul was already stuffing as many as he could into his mouth. "I'd say you're fine. Clean up, and don't you dare eat all those cookies," Mark said, starting for the broom.

From the foyer he heard, "Wow! You'd better come down from there."

"No!" a voice cried out. "Oh, no, I dare not."

Mark dashed back towards the porch, but didn't make it past the foyer. The older boys had pulled the last two crates inside and pried one of them open. Everything was blowing about. The air was full of straw. Catalog pages were flapping, shredded paper was flying in mini-whirlwinds and Styrofoam packing peanuts floated like big white beans in the wind.

Mark looked up and shaded his eyes as he tried to focus on what was moving above them. Traxon and Jack were on the landing above the foyer looking up as well. Mark craned his neck and saw something fluttering against the ceiling.

"Come down," Traxon begged.

"Calm down," Jack said, balancing on a railing for a leap.

"Jack," Mark shouted, "get off that railing."

Okay, Mark thought. *What am I going to do?* "What's your name?" he called to whoever was hanging in the air up there.

"Ailithe," came back in a feathery voice.

"Ailithe, please come down."

"No," the whispery voice said.

"Uh, are you the Wind Child I sent for?"

She didn't answer this time, but everything flying about in the air moved faster and more wildly.

"I sent for a Wind Child, but I had no idea you would cause such a mess. Could you please turn down the breeze?"

67

"No." The word blew about between all the confetti-ed scraps and dust that filled the air.

"Why not?" Mark asked, not watching Jack, who leaped at that moment, grabbing out towards Ailithe.

"Got her," he cried as the wind subsided. He grinned just before he realized he was hanging by a girl's ankles high above a cold marble floor. "Oh, no!" he cried.

"Hang on," Mark called, completely bamboozled as to what to do. It was as if all of them were frozen, suspended in the moment: Traxon with a perplexed look, Elflet in mid-screech, Paul squeezing his ox to his chest, Jack a scream about to exit his open mouth and Mark motionless with his brain at absolute stop.

Only the girl seemed to move. Her gossamer wings beat softly. Her arms and legs were etched in halos of silver, her eyes were large black holes in a gleaming face. Surreally, as if in animated slow-motion, she lowered herself and the boy hanging onto her ankles to the floor below them. As soon as his feet touched down, he let go and she shot back up into the heights.

Traxon moved. A sigh instead of a scream escaped Jack. Paul released his strangle hold on the poor ox. Elflet giggled. Mark sat down on the floor and waited for his brain to jump-start, but it didn't, as if it was numbed into permanent shock or shutdown.

"How do we get her down?" Elflet squeaked.

Mark shook his head, trying to clear it so he could come up with a solution. The best he could do was to plead. "Ailithe, please, can we talk? Tell me what's wrong. I'm sure I can help."

"What are you?" she asked.

"What?" he said, perplexed.

"What are you?"

"Uh, humans, well, most of us anyway," Mark said, hoping that it was true.

"Why am I here?" she asked.

"He ordered you out of a catalog," Traxon called.

"Why?" she asked. "Why did you do that?"

"It was a mistake. I'm sorry," Mark said. "The catalogs didn't mention any of you were real."

"Cause if they did," Jack said, "nobody would order us."

"People want children, but they wouldn't order them from a catalog," Mark said.

"Where would they get them from?"

"Well, an orphanage or a social service organization."

"Then why did you adopt us from a catalog?" Jack asked, hands on his hips as he awaited an answer.

"I didn't know I was adopting anyone. I told you, I thought you were just toys."

"Oh," Elflet said. His little face wrinkled up as if about to cry and Mark didn't know what to say.

"Look out," Traxon said. "She's about to make a big breeze again."

Everyone looked up to the top of the ceiling. "Ailithe, please, couldn't you just be nice, sweet like a little fairy, and come down from there?" Mark asked hopefully.

"What's a little fairy?" she asked.

Mark dredged up another distant memory from his childhood. "It's a magical little person with wings."

"I am certainly not a fairy," the winged Wind Child said most emphatically.

"No, I suppose not," Mark said.

"Are you ever coming down?" Elflet asked.

"I don't know yet."

"Ailithe, could you just drop that tag on your wrist down to me, then?" Mark asked.

She looked at it querulously and dropped it saying, "Take this strange gibberish."

It twisted slowly, twirling in the breeze made by its owner. Mark grabbed it.

"Introducing Ailithe, winged Wind-Child of a distant world. Distrustful of everyone, she cannot resist piano music. Concentrate on understanding and be gentle with this delicate being."

Mark ran to his stereo, picked a Beethoven sonata and turned up the volume. The girl swung around in mid-air and glided into the great room on a gentle breeze.

"Where's the piano?" she asked.

"It's a recording," Mark said, staring at her.

Her face was flat, her lips a thin, rouged line. Between short spiky sections, the hair on her head was fine and silky. Her ears lay flat against her head. Thread-fine, mesh-covered wings grew from her protruding shoulder blades and imbedded into the skin on her arms and legs were sparkling half-round spots.

"I like music," Paul declared.

"Do you?" Ailithe asked. She seemed to hang midway between horizontal and upright positions.

"Mark!" Traxon yelled. "Did you forget the last crate? It's been here a real long time now."

"Come watch the other kids," Mark said, "while I open it."

Although Mark knew it was impossible, this crate appeared to be seamless. The sides, the top, and the bottom were all one piece. He tapped on the box, listened, his ear to its side, but heard nothing.

"If anyone is in there, tell me if you're okay," he called, his mouth close to the side.

Nothing. He lifted his head and listened. He had heard something, but it was gone now. He tapped at his ear, and then clearly, someone said directly into his mind, *Look on the bottom of the box.*

"What am I looking for?"

Push the button.

He tipped the box up and there in a recessed niche was a button. He pushed it and the sides of the box popped apart.

There was only one of his orders that this box could contain. "Are you Mirabella?" he asked the petite girl perched on the pieces of the box which had opened like a clam shell.

She nodded.

"The mind reader of Atlantis?"

Another nod.

"Okay, can you come with me, please?"

She shook her head.

"Come on, please. I'm really tired. I've had a bad day. I need help here. If you can read my mind, you know I need you to cooperate." He crossed his fingers behind his back.

She nodded and stepped daintily after him. He guided her into the great room and sat her with the others. There they were, sitting on his sofa, seven children he had no idea what to do with.

"Bedtime," he announced. It was the best he could do. "Come on, I'll get you blankets and towels."

They all seemed to be engaged in getting ready for bed, so he went downstairs. He pushed the crates back onto the porch to the sides of the door and began sweeping up the trash in the foyer from the Ailithe whirlwind, when someone yelled through the still open front door.

"Hey!" a man's voice shouted. "I got your mail. Where do you want it, mister? I had to come back this late 'cause you had your door blocked before. How am I supposed to deliver your mail if I can't get to the front door?"

Mark turned quickly. The mail man. Maybe he could stop the catalogs. He moved to the door and looked out just as a bundled package of catalogs came flying through the air and hit him full in the face.

TO THE RESCUE

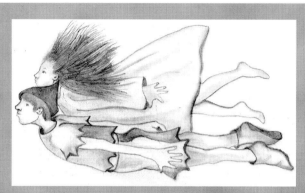

PETER PAN- and it's off to Never Never Land -- 55.

Also available:
Captain Hook and the Lost Boys
The Merry Men and Lady Marion
The Kingdom of Monkeys

ROBIN HOOD- steals from the rich and gives to the poor -- 55.

RAMA - virtuous rescuer from Indian myth and poem -- 50.

He woke to the phone ringing. Blood was dripping out of a cut on his cheek and his right eye was swollen shut. He scrabbled around, following the shrill sound of the phone until he found it, grabbed it and heard Elliot ask, "Is that you, Markham?"

"Yes," he mumbled.

"What's the matter with you? You sound awful."

"Accident," he managed.

"Are you okay? I'm coming over, Markham."

Mark sat on the cold hall floor, the phone in his lap, trying to concentrate. It was awfully quiet. Why was that bad? His head was pounding, and his cheek was bleeding, and why was it bad that it was so quiet? He couldn't focus.

They are all asleep, a little voice that wasn't his own said into his head.

What? he thought.

Jack and Traxon, Rollo and Elflet, Paul and even Ailithe. All asleep. It's okay. Don't worry.

That was it. That was why the quiet was bad. Seven children in the house.

But, they're asleep, Mirabella thought to him again.

Thanks, he thought back, grateful not to have to speak.

I told them you weren't dead. Your brain still buzzed human thoughts.

Good, go to sleep now. I'll be okay.

Who's Elliot? she asked.

Friend, he thought groggily. *Goodnight, Mirabella.*

A sound in his mind cut off and he assumed she had gone to sleep.

He dozed off to awake to, "Why did you leave those crates on the porch? It looks so dreadful! Oh, my word, Markham, what hit you?"

Mark pointed to the bundled magazines coated with spattered blood.

"Oh, my! I don't quite understand, but I'll get some ice," Elliot said, flipping on the light. Mark heard a squish, squish noise as Elliot stepped on a few mislaid cookies. Then he heard, "Good grief! I'm going to get you a maid service." Finally he came back with ice wrapped in a towel.

"I think you need sutures," Elliot said as Mark held the ice to his eye. "I venture to say, you won't make it to work tommorow. I'll have to cancel all your appointments."

"Not going to a hospital."

"Why not? You need to see a doctor."

"Got kids upstairs."

"What? Markham, I think you may be delirious."

"Foster kids."

"You took in foster kids? When? Why? What on Earth for?"

"You forgot to ask how," Mark said woozily.

"You're right, how did you get these kids?" Elliot added.

"Tell you when I'm feeling better."

"We'll call a baby sitter. Who do you use?" Elliot asked.

"Call Kate. Maybe she'll come," Mark said. "Her number is on the refrigerator."

Thirty minutes later, a sullen Kate appeared at the door, squeezing between the crates. When she saw Mark, her anger faded.

"Good grief!" she cried.

"Can you stay with these kids he's taken in, so I can take him to the hospital?" Elliot asked her.

"They're asleep," Mark said.

"Good. I'll stay, but they'd better stay asleep."

"Thanks, Kate," he said, trying to smile, but his face was too swollen and stiff. She walked him to the car and as she closed his door for him, he said, "There are seven of them now."

He heard her yelling angrily after him as they pulled away.

"Seven kids?" Elliot said. "You took in seven kids? Seven!"

Mark lied a little. "It's a big house. It felt empty."

"Someone let you take in seven kids without checking on whether you had help or not?"

"They didn't care. I'm rich enough. I'll hire someone." Mark didn't want to talk. His tongue was heavy, his words came out like mush, his face hurt.

"You're single, young, know nothing about kids!" Elliot yelped.

"Better than their being crated up somewhere." His words were slurred. He wished Elliot would notice and stop quizzing him.

"Children aren't locked up, Markham. They are humanely cared for until they can be placed with responsible parents. "

"You know what I mean," Mark said.

"Markham, who hit you with that bundle of magazines?"

"Mailman. Threw it at the wrong moment."

"What do you mean?"

"Crates were there. Swung the catalogs over and *pow*!" Mark motioned to his face.

"Did you order more toys for those kids? Is that where the crates came from? You just can't stay out of trouble, can you?"

"Can I explain later?" Mark said. "My face really hurts. It's hard to talk."

"Sure. Sorry," Elliot said sincerely.

Mark wished he had been able to tell Elliot the truth, but he never would have believed him, and it was better not to convince him that Mark was completely crazy. He sighed and sank into pain and tried not to worry.

SECRET IDENTITIES

FROM SECRET ADMIRERS

RUMPELSTILTSKIN: Say his name, get your way for the day --2.50
THE MAN IN THE IRON MASK: Smuggled missive from a prisoner-- 2.00
SCARLET PIMPERNEL: Roses are red, the Pimpernel said , violets are blue,
I love you -- 3.50
ALIENS IN HIDING: Sending out love notes from exile--5.00

It was five in the morning before Elliot brought him home. The stitches hadn't been painful, but he was woozy and diagnosed with a concussion. Kate was asleep on the sofa, but sat up with a start when she heard them come in. She felt under the couch, searching about for her shoes. She leaned over and peered under the sofa and stuck her hand under it again. Alas, it came back empty except for the dust that covered it.

"Okay, I give up, Mark. When you find them, call me. The kitchen is cleaned up, by the way. Feel better," she said, gingerly kissing him before padding out the door in her bare feet.

"I'll move those crates so you can get in and out more easily. Later, I'll send someone over to break them up and cart them away," Elliot promised.

"Elliot, could you just have the crates put in the back yard with the first three?" Mark said, vaguely imagining them as playhouses for the kids.

Mark practically fell into bed. He closed his eyes and dreamed about flying cookies and pieces of shoes floating through the air and children hanging out of tree houses in the backyard.

His eyes popped open at seven, as something bumped the mattress from underneath. He forgot about his head and leaned over to see what it was. A pair of green eyes stared out of the dimness that always lay beneath a bed. Mark raised his head carefully back up, as his bruised eye throbbed.

"Elflet, come out," he said.

"Hi, Mark," the little boy chimed.

"What are you doing under there?"

"Fixing Kate's shoes."

"Fixing? You mean you took them apart?"

"Uh huh."

"Elflet! You have to stop trying to fix shoes."

"But it's what elves do!"

"But you aren't too good at it," Mark explained wearily.

"Then send me to school so I can learn."

Mark groaned. "I don't think they teach elves to repair shoes at schools these days."

Mark swung his legs over the edge of the bed and stood unsteadily. "You don't look so good," Elflet said.

"I look better than those," Mark replied, as he glanced miserably at the pieces of leather that had been his sister's shoes. He splashed water on his face and looked in the mirror. He looked like a war zone. Ailithe appeared by the edge of the door.

"I'm hungry," she said.

Mark stared at her. Her wings were gone. "Where are they?"

"What?" she asked.

"Your wings."

"I retracted them. Traxon told me I might scare someone."

"Oh!"

Mark wondered how to hide her face. It was pretty alien itself.

"Okay, I'll try to come fix breakfast, but give me a few minutes."

"We called Lady A," Traxon said as he came into the room. "Get back in bed. She's on the way."

"Why did you do that?"

"You're sick, we're hungry, and there is nothing in the cupboards."

"I feel like the old lady who lived in a shoe," Mark stammered.

"You can't be a lady, you're a man," Elflet pointed out seriously.

"Okay, okay, get everybody up here."

They must have all been out in the hall because they flooded into the room instantly.

"Everybody on the bed. Jack, in the bookshelves is a Mother Goose book. Go get it and I'll read to you all until Lady A gets here. No bouncing and no bumping my head, okay?"

Paul crawled into his lap. Elflet pressed up against his shoulder. Ailithe fluttered down and perched behind him. Mirabella sat lady-like on the edge of the bed. Traxon squeezed in next to Ailithe. Rollo sank the edge of the mattress with his little round body and Jack took the last place at the foot of the bed.

Mark paged through the book gently until Traxon yelled, "There's Jack! Read what it says."

"'Jack be nimble, Jack be quick, Jack jump over the candle stick,'" Mark intoned.

"Why would I do that?" Jack asked. "That's not me."

"You must be a very good jumper," Ailithe said solemnly, "or you would get burned."

"If I jumped a candlestick, I would never get burned," Jack said indignantly. "Wanna see how high I can jump?" he asked, climbing off the bed.

"Sure!" everybody yelled.

"No," Mark said. "Not in the house. Later, outside."

Jack crawled back onto the bed and that was how Lady A found them. She stood in the doorway, open-mouthed. "You look awful, Mark. And where did all these children come from?"

He smiled as best he could.

"Did you bring groceries?" Jack asked.

"Food," Rollo and Paul said like twins and rushed out of the room.

"Better hurry, all of you. I do believe those two could finish off all the bagels and fruit before you others even get to the table. Three, four, five, six and seven," Lady A counted as they ran out.

"Mark, how could you take in more kids? You couldn't handle the first three," she pointed out, standing there in a bright yellow, flowery dress that hung from her in her usual untailored way, her hair tucked once again under one of her more voluminous hats.

"It wasn't planned. I promise," he winced as he moved his head.

"But you signed the papers for them, didn't you?" she insisted.

"Uh, I suppose I did, didn't I?" he said, thinking of the order forms, knowing that wasn't what she meant.

She stepped on a piece of shoe. "What is this?" She examined it carefully, shook her head and threw it in the trash. "I'll call this week to register them for school. Have they had their physicals and are their shots up to date?"

"Stop," he moaned. He hadn't even considered documentation for the kids until Lady A had just mentioned it. He searched quickly for a way to divert her.

"They haven't sent me the records yet, so wait on school. Give me a little time here. I can't deal with it right now."

"Sorry," she sighed. "I'll go check on the kids."

He gave his own sigh of relief as she vanished in a bright flash of color, but she was right. The authorities would be after him if he didn't have official documentation for the kids. But how was he going to get such papers for two apparently alien children, one child from a mythical lost continent, two storybook boys, a nursery rhyme Jack and an elf who was a terrible cobbler?

It made him laugh, which hurt his face. They weren't really who the tags said. They couldn't be. It was probably someone's idea of a bad joke. Then again, the catalogs had been coming for fifty-two years. Who would keep a joke running for that long?

Mirabella came to the door, licking her fingers. "I brought you a sugar-glazed doughnut," she said. "They're your favorite."

"You read my mind?"

"Only what you thought out loud," she said.

"Listen, Mirabella, don't tell anyone anything you hear. Someone could think that, well. . ."

"I was crazy?" she finished his sentence for him. "Don't they have any imaginations?"

"There you go again," he said, "repeating what I was thinking."

"Okay, I'll try to be careful," she said.

"If you go to school and do that, it could be dangerous."

"When am I going?"

"Of that I'm unsure. I have to find a way to get everyone papers."

"Get them any way you can?" she asked, this time repeating his own silent question to himself out loud.

"Go on, now," he said. "I need to think private thoughts."

His private thoughts were a muddle. Even for him, there were too many pieces to try and fit together. Finally he decided to concentrate on something practical. He needed documentation for them. He could hardly admit he had ordered them from a catalog, that he had actually bought children.

Elflet tiptoed by his door clutching someone's shoes.

"Elflet, come in here."

"Yes, Mark?" the little boy said as he tried to hide his own pair of huge, green elf-shoes behind his little back. "I was just going to show them to Rollo," he whispered.

"Why?" Mark asked suspiciously.

"He thought he could add retractable roller skates to them."

Mark beckoned to the child, put his face right in Elflet's and said slowly and seriously, "Absolutely not."

"Okay," Elflet said, hanging his head down.

Mark managed to get out of bed and get dressed.

"Lady A, can you drive a car?" he asked leaning on the door frame.

"No," she said.

"Then call me a cab, okay? I have an errand to run."

"To where, to do what? You should be in bed."

"These kids need toys to play with," he said.

"What? You're hurt. They can wait on toys, Mark. Go back to bed!"

"No. They're already thinking up all kinds of things to do that I wish they wouldn't. If they have toys, they may be distracted. Call a cab and, oh yes, don't take off your shoes if you want to walk out of here with them on your feet."

"Are you delirious?" she asked, feeling his forehead.

"No, I am not. Call that cab before the kids do something drastic."

"Mark, this is ridiculous. What could they do?"

"I don't want to find out. Call the cab."

Forty minutes later the cab honked and Mark made his way gingerly out the door, down the walk and into the back seat, where he gasped as he lay his head against the cool glass of the cab window.

"Where to, bud?" the cab driver asked.

"Toyland," Mark said, sinking further into the cushions and closing his eyes.

"Gonna buy some new kiddy gimmicks, huh?"

"I was thinking of board games or tool kits or maybe building toys."

"Uh huh! When were you last in Toyland? When you were five? All Toyland carries these days is videos and TV tie-ins. There isn't a toy store left in the city that carries building toys or board games."

Mark sat up and peered at the driver. "It's you," he said.

"Hey, hey, I remember you now, too. You're the let-the-meter-run man," the cabby said. "So where to?"

"Where do you suggest I go for some real toys?"

"I don't got no suggestions."

"Then how about the Book Stop again?" Mark asked.

"Sure, if that's whatcha want. Just let me turn around and we'll be on our way."

Mark relaxed. A thought crossed his mind. "Hey, last time I rode with you, you said no one could commit a crime because of all our technology. Do you think that would apply to, say, getting fake papers for people, too?"

"Of course. People don't vanish and turn up as someone else no more. Everybody is on some data base. All their fingerprints, voice prints, gene prints even. You know that. I know that. Why're you asking me?"

"Yes, I know all that. But what if you weren't trying to change your identity? What if someone didn't have an identity to begin with?"

"Sure, whatever you say, mister."

"Humor me. What then?"

"Bud, they give everybody on earth a universal ID the moment they come out kicking and screaming. There ain't no 'extra' people in the world. If you think you found somebody extra, take a tissue sample, find a hair or finger nail clipping and run a check on it. I promise you, it'll come back with an ID."

"Some way I knew you would know a lot about all this," Mark said.

"Yeah, well, that's 'cause I was a cop until they took all the satisfaction out of it. I mean I wasn't helping anybody no more. They didn't need us. They had computers," the cab driver said bitterly.

"So, how would you like to help me beat the computers?"

"Aw, come on, bud. How're ya gonna do that?" the man said, laughing and shaking his head. Abruptly he quit laughing. "Hey now, I don't want no trouble. You're talking dangerous stuff here. You ain't serious, are ya?"

"What if I know someone who doesn't officially exist, who isn't in the data banks? Does that interest you?" Mark asked.

"You're nuts. It ain't possible."

"Suppose it was possible. Would you help me? Could you?"

"Nope, not me. You need the right computer codes to enter an identity into the data bank and the codes are unbreakable."

"Just suppose that I could break the code, would you know how to fill in and enter the forms to add a new ID to the data bank?"

"Make up a new ID for someone?"

Mark waited as the cab driver thought it over.

"I might know how to get it forged and filed in the computer, but you can't do it 'cause nobody can break the code!"

"But if someone could, you could do the rest?"

"Probably, yeah."

"You're hired, if you want the job," Mark said softly but clearly.

"What'dya say?" the cabby said, watching Mark in the mirror.

"Nothing, sorry. I'm a little out of it. Look, can I request you when I need a cab?"

"Sure, just ask for Pete. I'll come for ya, but, bud, don't go talking like this to nobody else."

"Thanks," Mark said.

"For what?"

"The advice and humoring me."

They pulled up to the Book Stop. Mark handed Pete a big tip.

"Wait for me," he said. "I'll pay the meter."

When Mark came out with a box full of books, Pete was still there mulling over a crossword puzzle on the vid-screen in the cab. Mark slid the box onto the seat and crawled in.

"Home, please. I don't feel so well."

"Good idea. You don't look so good," Pete said.

"I got hit in the face by accident last night," Mark explained.

"Were you even supposed to be out and about?"

"No," Mark admitted.

Pete carried the books inside and set them down in the foyer.

"Nice house, mister," Pete said. He glanced at the stacks of catalogs and then listened for a minute or two with his head cocked. "You got kids, huh? Nice sound, the laughter of kids. How many up there?"

Mark sighed. "Seven of them right now."

"Well, the way you look, I think you should send home the ones what don't live here, and tell 'em to come back and play another day. Give your own kids them books you got and go to bed."

"Right. I think I'll do that. Thanks, Pete," Mark said and sank onto a stack of catalogs as the door closed.

"You're home," Rollo said. "What'd you get?"

"Books. Mainly puzzles and mazes and stuff like that. Activity books. Crossword puzzles. Can you read yet, Rollo?"

"Of course, sir," Rollo said with a little pout.

"Good, here. Take these books with you and explain the instructions to everyone. I'm going back to bed. Hey, Rollo," he added as an afterthought, "see if you can teach Traxon to read English."

Lost Lands

Lady A was shaking him. "Wake up, Mark. You've got a problem with Rollo. He's crying and crying. I can't get him to stop!"

"What? Why? Okay, give me a minute," Mark groaned. He splashed water on his face. He felt better. His face was still purple and tender, but he wasn't as shaky as he had been. As he went into the great room, he could hear Rollo. The boy wasn't just crying, he was wailing loudly. Elflet had his hands over his ears, but the other kids were nowhere to be seen.

Mark took Rollo by the shoulders and said, "What's the matter? Tell me, Rollo."

Tears rolled down the boy's cheeks. Rollo pulled a dog-eared copy of *The Wizard of Lost Land* out from behind the sofa pillow and dropped it on the floor with a plunk.

"Where did you get this?" Mark asked.

"I found it in the box in the basement."

"What box?"

"The dusty one. The one that says *Markham* on it," the boy sobbed.

"What does it matter where he got it?" Lady A asked.

"It doesn't," Mark said. "That's the box Kate just gave me. I didn't know there was a book in there."

"Did the book make you sad?" Lady A asked Rollo, ignoring Mark altogether.

"I am not growing up to be a fake! I am not!" Rollo wailed again. "I'm going to be a real wizard and not just invent stuff to make me look like I'm one. You'll see. I'm going to be a real wizard!"

"Rollo," Mark said. "It's only a book. It's a story is all. You're a real person. You can be whatever you want."

"My tag said I was the Wizard of Lost Land, only he wasn't a wizard at all. He was just a fat guy who went off into the desert for a vacation trip and got lost. The warriors of Lost Land found him wandering, delirious, shouting out meaningless words that sounded like they were spells. They took him back to their city, and asked him to use his magic to bring rain to their land. He told them that before he could make it rain, he would have to perform fifty-six other spells. Then he tricked the warriors of Lost Land by inventing things that made it appear he had performed a spell: optical illusions that made people disappear; great balls of smoke that hid him from their view; glasses that made everything look tiny. Soon the people believed he was a true wizard. The years went by, but because the people couldn't count, they never knew how many spells he had performed. They trusted him, but he was a fake, a liar! Nothing more! And they never got their rain!"

"I read that book once, Rollo, and if I recall correctly, the wizard's tricks made the people of Lost Land happy, even if he couldn't make it rain."

"It doesn't matter! He wasn't a wizard," Rollo insisted. "He was a fake! A fake!"

"Rollo, I'll talk to you in a minute. Let me pay Lady A so she can go home," Mark said as quickly as he could before things got out of hand. He rushed Lady A to the door. "Thanks, really. I don't know what I would have done without your help today."

"Oh, no you don't. You can't just brush me out the door! How could you give a child a provocative book like that?"

"I didn't give it to him. He found it in the basement."

"Well, you should be more careful of what you leave lying around."

"Yes, I should," he agreed.

"Those books offer awful role models for children. How could you be so careless?"

"But, you and I, we're realistic, down-to-earth role models, aren't we, Lady A?"

She stared at him a moment and suddenly laughed, brightly. She kissed him on the good cheek, patted his shoulder, and left at last.

Mark took a deep breath, composed himself and returned to Rollo. He picked the book up and flipped through it. "Okay, now then. I think you should ignore this old thing," Mark suggested. "It's just a silly book."

"It's about me, Mark, when I'm grown up," Rollo said sadly.

"Rollo, don't you see, that can't be true. You are still a boy, how could anyone know what you'll be like in the future?"

"But you said you ordered the young Wizard of Lost Land, and then you got me. And that old guy in the book is the Wizard of Lost Land. So, he has to be me."

"Look, Rollo, the wizard in the book isn't real. You are. You'll grow up to be whoever you want to." Mark poked the boy and said, "Real. You are real, right now and forever more, Rollo."

Rollo pouted. "Are you certain, sir?"

"Yes. Now, how about some pizza from Pizza Pizzazz?"

"Sure." Rollo smiled a little. "Sure, pizza."

Mark went to place the order. Rollo followed him, still frowning. "Now what, Rollo?"

"Mark, if that guy in the book is me as an old guy, then what?"

Mark shook his head. This wasn't a good sign. Maybe food would distract him. "Rollo, go wash your hands."

"But, Mark," the boy began again.

"We'll talk about it another time," Mark insisted.

He turned to find Elflet pressed against a wall, clutching another book. "These elves know how to repair shoes!" he said accusatorily, holding out a flimsy paper back. "Why don't I?"

"Where did you get that?" Mark asked.

"I found it," Elflet said.

"In a dusty box? In the basement?"

"Yes. Why can't I fix shoes, too?"

Mark flipped through the book. "These elves are older than you," he pointed out.

"Not that little one, right there," Elflet said, putting his finger on an illustration.

"You'll learn. Don't worry!"

"Promise?" the little boy insisted.

Mark looked at the boy. "I'm pretty sure of it," he said.

Elflet wandered off.

"Do you really believe he'll learn to be a cobbler?" Mirabella asked from where she stood on the staircase.

"Have you found a book about yourself, too?" Mark asked, ignoring her question.

"No, not me. Atlantis is lost, you know?"

"Do you remember anything about it?"

"Not a thing, really. I try, but I can't seem to recall anything, except that wherever I was, it was really cold. I don't like the cold too much," she said and shivered. "Atlantis was one of the words in a crossword puzzle book. In the back it had a glossary, but it said almost nothing about it. Do you know anything about Atlantis, Mark?"

"Not really, except what your tag said. That it was a beautiful city that sank into the ocean."

"That's what the glossary said, too. Don't they know anything else?"

"I'm sorry," Mark said, thinking that somewhere he had read Atlantis was warm.

Maybe she was lucky. So far, the information the kids were finding about themselves was only upsetting them. Maybe books weren't such a good idea after all, not that he had given Elflet and Rollo the books they had found. He wondered if books upset most kids so much.

"Hey," Jack said, joining them. "I looked through that whole Mother Goose book and I'm not any of the Jacks in there. I am especially not related to that Jack-and-Jill guy. What a goof-up, falling down the hill and breaking the only good thing he had to wear: his crown. Think what that girl Jill must have thought of him. Doofus, doofus, doofus! I'd never embarrass myself like that! What other Jacks are there? There must be someone better."

"I have no idea," Mark said.

"Could you find out? Because I don't wanna go on not knowing who I'm gonna be," the boy said.

"Enough, enough, I've had enough!" Mark said loudly. "There is the doorbell. The pizza is here. Let's just go eat, okay?"

They divided up the slices. Everyone munched very quietly. Finally Mark said, "Listen guys, nobody knows who they will be, not exactly, until they grow up. Books are just stories. They aren't about complete people. There is a lot that isn't filled in about book characters. Where did you all get the idea that you could find yourselves in storybooks?"

"From our tags," Traxon pointed out.

DETECTIVES

Ailithe fingered her face in the mirror Mark had just finished hanging in the room she shared with Mirabella. "Could you get me some paints and brushes?" she asked.

"Do you like art?"

"I'd like to paint my face," she said as she floated off absently. She rarely walked anywhere and a little trail of dust seem to swirl at her feet wherever she hung.

He heard the catalogs fall through the mailbox. He heard the scurry of feet. The kids had taken to looking through all the new catalogs that came. Rollo and Elflet had started cutting them up and putting them together into picture books.

The doorbell rang and he heard little feet skittering to get away from the front door. Mark opened it, noticing there wasn't one child left about. It was Pete.

"That job offer, is it still available?" the man asked. "I quit my job."

"Sure, yes, I still need the help."

"Good, but I can't start for a coupla weeks. I gotta find a place to live first."

Two weeks? Mark couldn't wait two weeks.

"If you want, it includes room and board, if you can stand living here," Mark said before he could stop himself.

"Stand living here? Can I stand living in this here fancy house? Sure, sure, that'd be fine," Pete said, shaking his head. "That is, I mean, well, what is it exactly ya want me to do? I don't wanna do nothing illegal. Too embarrassing to end up in jail with a buncha senior citizens I put there while they were still young. Probably dangerous, too."

"I don't know if what I want to do is legal or not," Mark answered honestly. "Is there a law against getting papers for people who don't have any?"

"That again? I don't know about no such law. Maybe there ain't one 'cause whatcha wanna do can't be done, so nobody's gotta worry about it," Pete said.

"I'll pay you to try to make it happen," Mark said, "but it has to be done carefully."

"You wanna be sneaky, huh? Well, first you'd better run a DNA check on these people without no identities. Make sure it's true."

"Can you do that?" Mark asked. "Arrange the tests clandestinely?"

Pete didn't answer. He looked past Mark into the foyer. "Can I come in?" he asked.

"Sure, of course, come in," Mark offered.

Pete walked past Mark and glanced into the rooms. "Big house, huh?" He whirled around and said in a whisper, "How'dya do it?"

"What?" Mark asked mystified.

"Manage to get the money for this place. Didya do something illegal?"

"Illegal?" Mark said loudly. "I didn't do anything illegal! Whatever gave you such an idea?"

"'Cause you keep asking about beating the cops at their own games! I figure you already done it."

Mark laughed, a short bark of a laugh. "I thought you might have been a thief because of what you said, but it turns out you're an ex-cop! No, no, I work for a big corporation, and I make lots of money legitimately."

"Oh? You don't look like the rich type."

"Wait until the morning when I go to work. Then I'll look just like the rich type."

"Okay, I need a job. How much you willing to pay?"

"What do you think is fair?" Mark asked. "This is important to me, so I'm willing to be generous."

Pete scratched a tonsure spot on the top of his head.

Mirabella whispered in Mark's head, *Who is that man?*

"Pete," Mark answered out loud accidentally.

"Yeah, yeah. Don't rush me, I'm thinking about it."

"Well?" Mark said.

"I don't got much choice about this. I need a job. Okay, ten grand plus expenses, just for this one job, and I ain't gonna bargain. I gotta think about what'd happen if I get caught."

"If it's illegal," Mark said.

"Yeah, if! Let's hope it ain't."

"Fine, ten thousand. Wait here and I'll get you your samples. There will be seven of them."

"Seven?" he heard Pete say.

He found all the kids huddled in the kitchen and snipped a single hair from each one, putting each into its own bag. He labeled them by letter and gave all the kids little bowls of raisins.

"First step," Mark said, handing the bags to Pete. "DNA checks. Get the results and if I'm right and you still want the job, you can move in whenever you want to."

"Okay," Pete said holding the bags up to the ceiling light. "But even if they turn out to belong to someone already on the data base, you owe me at least five thousand. If you need any more of my services after this, it's gonna cost you more."

"Deal."

Pete left scratching his head, looking first at the bags and then back at Mark where he stood on the front porch.

LITTLE TERRORS

Goldilocks - 20.00

Red Chief - 15.00

Anansi- 25.00

Georgie
Porgie
10.00

Dan, Dan
Dirty Old Man
17.00

Pecks Bad
Boy
15.00

Tom
The Piper's
Son- 15.00

The Little Girl
with the
Curl - 35.00

Little Johnny Green -
20.00

Trickster Coyote- 35.00

Charly, Charly
Stole the Barley - 12.00

Pete was back in three days. It was seven on a Saturday morning, and for once the kids weren't storming down the stairs and into the kitchen, drumming spoons on tables and spilling juice and water onto the floor and counters. Mark was peacefully sipping tea when he heard the knock. He padded barefooted to the front door. Pete was rubbing the top of his head again, shifting from foot to foot.

"Okay, I got some news for you." Pete paused and waited for Mark to say something. When he didn't, Pete continued. "I got the DNA profiles."

"And?" Mark asked calmly.

"And none of these samples match with nobody. But you knew that, didn't you? The really big *but* is, there's a couple of profiles that ain't possible at all. No way. My lab guy wouldn't go beyond saying they might be some sort of synthetic DNA, which he pointed out was illegal. I told him it was probably a mix-up. Was it?"

"Wait a moment," Mark said out loud. *Mirabella*, he thought as loudly as he could, *bring the kids down, now.*

We were giving you a rest, she thought back.

Thanks, but I need you, now. Get dressed. Come down.

"Come on, Pete. Would you like some coffee or a cup of tea?"

"Not really. What I wanna know is where you got those seven samples? The black market? Overseas? Are they doing experiments over there without anybody knowing about it?"

"Patience, Pete," Mark said. He heard the patter of small feet coming their way. The children peeped into the great room. "Come on in, guys. This is Pete. He's going to help us," Mark announced to six little faces. Paul toddled in and crawled into Mark's lap.

"I hungry, Mark," he said. He stuck the tail of his ox in his mouth and chewed it.

"We don't want Pete to think you're rude. Introduce yourselves nicely," Mark said.

The older children lined up and said, "Traxon, Elflet, Mirabella, Jack, Rollo."

"And me Paul," the little boy said, snuggled up against Mark.

"And where is Ailithe?" Mark asked.

"She didn't think Pete was ready for her," Mirabella said sweetly.

Mark thought at her, *Did you invade Pete's private thoughts?*

No, she thought back. *I can only listen to the thoughts a person airs publicly.*

Mark gave her a dirty look. *Humans think all their silent thoughts are private.*

Pshaw, she thought at him, picking up one of his own phrases.

Pete counted the kids, pointing a finger at each one as he said, "One, two, three, four, five, six? These are the samples you gave me to send to the lab? Where is number seven?"

"Hey," Traxon said. "Don't talk about us like we're numbers!"

"Sorry, kid," Pete said. "Which are the ones that ain't real?"

Jack was in his face so fast he was a flash. "We're all real. All of us. Got it?"

"Back off, son," Pete said to Jack sternly. "Where'd you get these kids, Mark?"

Traxon practically snarled, but Mark pulled him away.

"Don't tell him," Elflet squealed. "He won't believe you anyway."

"Calm down, now," Mark said.

"What's wrong with him?" Pete asked, pointing at Traxon.

"Food allergy," Mark said. "Okay, guys, breakfast time."

The kids headed to the kitchen.

"Pete, I really, really need papers for them."

"Yeah, but you know, papers ain't gonna make those kids normal," Pete said. "Where'd you get them?"

"Foster children."

"Uh huh. Well, you think, maybe, just maybe, you made a mistake taking 'em in, 'specially so many of them?"

"You might be right, but here they are, flesh and bone. The only things they lack are identities."

"Yeah, the only thing," Pete sighed. "Okay, I'm in, but you gotta tell me where these kids really came from."

"I can't yet," Mark said, expecting Pete to lose it, but he didn't.

"Why not?"

Mark sighed this time. "Because I don't know. I guess this gives you a chance to prove how good a detective you are, Pete."

"You ain't kidding about that! Listen, you want me to solve this, you gotta give me a few details to work with."

Okay, Mark thought, *I must have lost it here. I can't tell an ex-cop a story that makes me think I'm nuts. What can I expect from him? But what choice do I have?* He paused after a deep breath and said, "I can't tell you everything yet. You'd think I was more than crazy, but I promise, as soon as you find out a few things, I'll tell you all I know."

Pete stared at him.

"Sit down, sip some coffee."

Pete stared again and finally sat. Mark handed him a cup of steaming café au lait. The man frowned and said, "Did we agree on ten thousand? Not enough, not for this."

"Twenty thousand, then? Is that enough?"

"Twenty? You're scaring me, how much you want this. I gotta think it through."

"Please, Pete! I need you to trace the origins of some catalogs that come to this house every day. I need to know who publishes them, how long they've really been coming to this address, who has lived here in the last fifty-five years and whether or not anyone else gets these catalogs. Can you do that?"

"Maybe, but why're you so hung up on these catalogs? And about those kids? How do they fit in with the catalogs?"

"I wish I could tell you, but I don't actually know. The answers are in the questions I just asked, I hope," Mark said. "Pete, move in. Get to know the kids. They're really nice kids, maybe a little unusual, but lovable all the same. And see if you can find out the answers to what I asked you, okay?"

"You're being pretty mysterious, but I like you and you pay awful good. You know I checked you out and the kids aren't the only ones who are a little strange. You were brilliant in high school. Graduated when you was only fourteen, then you wandered around kinda aimlessly for a few years. Finally settled in to make your living for five years fixing up stuff, a fix-it man living on the edge of financial security. Then one day you go to this Cannady & Company, a sorta middling successful company, and apply for a job. In nothing flat, you climb the ladder and sorta coincidentally, Cannady & Company starts climbing up the money chain at the same time. Soon it's in the top ten companies in the country and you're filthy rich and respectable. Coincidence? I got this premonition it's more than that!"

"Well, at least I know I hired somebody good."

Pete sighed and scratched his bald spot. "Okay, I'm in, I guess, but I got a dependent. You got room for her, too?"

"This dependent is a woman?" Mark asked warily.

"She's female, if that's what you mean. My granddaughter. Her ma and pa can't take care of her no more. They've tried, but she's got all kinds of problems and they can't handle it. She'll be here on Monday. Whatcha say?"

Mark needed Pete, needed him badly. So there wasn't much else for it. After all, what was one more child in a house full of children?

"Okay, that gives me time to let Lady A know."

"That the same Lady A that runs Lady Anderson's on Junk Row?"

"You know her?" Mark asked. "She's my babysitter."

"I was a cab driver, remember? I know everybody. Okay, gimme some catalogs so I can get started. I'll check back with you on Monday after I pick up my granddaughter."

Mark took Pete to the storage room where he and the kids had stacked the catalogs. The kids had sorted them by title. There were one-hundred-seventy-seven different titles so far. He picked one up and tossed it over to Pete.

"See if you can find the publisher for that one. And if you need an expense account, let me know," Mark said.

"Hard copy, still," Pete commented. He flipped through it. "But the rules have changed. You used to hafta put who published catalogs on the cover. Addresses, phone numbers, disclaimers and all that stuff. I guess that would be too easy. Nothing like that here. Is it on any of them?"

Mark shook his head *no*. "They come through the mail every day," he said, "except Sunday."

"The old mail schedule!" Pete exclaimed. "Okay, give me a handful. I got a friend I'll go see. Kinda a fly-by-night guy, but smart, and he keeps in touch with what's going on in what's left of the underground. I'll see what I can dig up."

"Good. I'll see you Monday when I get home from work. Thanks, Pete," Mark said.

Pete left with a package of catalogs in his arms and Mark sighed with relief. That had gone better than he had expected.

The children spent the rest of the day nervously fidgeting over Pete's visit, clinging like mice to the edges of the walls for security. They slid into bed early and Mark found them with the covers pulled over all seven of their heads, but by Sunday afternoon they were happily screaming in the backyard when someone unexpectedly knocked on the door. Mark opened it to find Elliot with his head cocked in the direction of the noise.

"Elliot, what are you doing here?"

"Mr. Cannady called and told me to swing by and get you. It's an emergency."

"I don't work on Sundays," Mark said.

Elliot almost hissed. "Markham, we work when Mr. Cannady says!"

"I can't go. The kids are in the backyard. I can't just leave them there alone."

"Mark, how did you get suckered into taking in seven kids? Send them back."

"Listen, Elliot, I'll call Mr. Cannady myself. Maybe I can solve this problem over the phone."

Elliot threw up his hands. "You can try, I guess."

"Mr. Cannady?" Mark began when his boss picked up the phone.

He didn't get far before Mr. Cannady said, "Markham, we need you here now. We have investors in from overseas. We have a major proposal on the table that needs your input, or I'm afraid we could lose their support."

Elliot grabbed the phone, "He'll be there, sir. Yes, fine, within the half hour."

"Elliot, I can't go."

"Yes, you can. I'll watch the kids. Go. Get ready and just go."

Mark gulped. "I don't know about this, Elliot."

Elliot pushed him towards his room. "Get dressed. Go, it'll be fine. I can handle it."

As Mark shrugged into business clothes, he heard Traxon come into the room.

"What's going on, Mark? Why is that Elliot here?"

"Traxon, listen, please, try to be seen as well as heard. I have to go in to work. Elliot is going to baby-sit you guys. And, tell Ailithe not to fly or brew up another wind storm."

"Isn't this Elliot guy pretty uptight?" Traxon asked.

"Yes, yes, he is! Please, ask everyone to be good. You don't want to give Elliot a stroke, do you?"

"Okay, I'll tell everyone, but Paul is hungry."

"Order Chinese. Tell Elliot I'll pay him back, okay?"

Traxon nodded, faded slightly and sauntered out of the room.

"Oh, brother," Mark muttered, crossing his fingers, and went out to his car.

WIND-UPS

TEDDY TIME :
Little bear who loves to ride. If he hits a barrier, he turns and goes around. Not recommended for under 2, due to small parts.

4572A 15.00

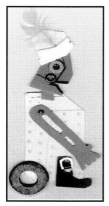

CHATTER BOX :
Wind her up and let her roll. See this little toy entertain your child for hours at a time, with many a story, rhyme and talking-time.

1X32BB......................13.00

DRAGON ROLLER :
Look out! Here comes a fire-breathing, fearsome dragon, but he can be easily tamed by feeding him animal crackers.

5Q66DD..........................15.00

COOKIES :
Variety packs with 50 species of animals. 10 lbs.

2Q66DC...............................4.99

101

He couldn't keep his mind on the meeting. He kept imagining Elliot in the face of impossible but absolutely real children. Would he become hysterical? Would he call the police?

He tuned in to the meeting. Mr. Cannady was speaking to him. "Cannady & Company is expanding. We want to develop a new class of toy that we manufacture and distribute ourselves. Only we're stumped. All of our trial tests show indifference on the part of children to anything we've come up with. What we need is a new approach, a new idea that kids can't resist. If we can do that, these ladies and gentlemen are prepared to infuse our company with a lot of money."

"Uh huh," Mark said, thinking about Elliot, imagining him caught in a maelstrom of fall leaves, tripping over an invisible foot or plugging his ears with his fingers to keep out a mind invader.

"Mr. Cannady says you're the right man for the job," someone said, "that a new computer game concept will be a snap for you."

"Really? I'm flattered, but he may have misjudged me. My taste tends to be pretty old-fashioned. Real toys, manipulatives, books, dolls, trucks."

"He's kidding. Great sense of humor, a bit of a prankster," Mr. Cannady reassured the investors. "He's an absolute genius with computers. You'll be amazed."

Mark sighed. "Sorry. Give me all the research you've done and a few months and I promise you some ideas at the very least."

"As I told you, his demeanor is disarming, but I promise you'll be pleased, ladies and gentlemen."

The investors left.

"Markham, do you realize what an opportunity this could be? You'll have a completely free hand! Fun! New toys for a new age! Right up your alley!" Mr. Cannady exclaimed as soon as he and Mark were alone in his office.

"Sure," Mark said unenthusiastically. "How long do I have?"

"We want a five-year plan. You have a six-month timeline here."

"Okay, but right now I'm going home."

To rescue Elliot, he thought in his mind, imagining the man shoeless with an ax through his bare foot. Thank goodness he had locked up the ax.

SIBLINGS

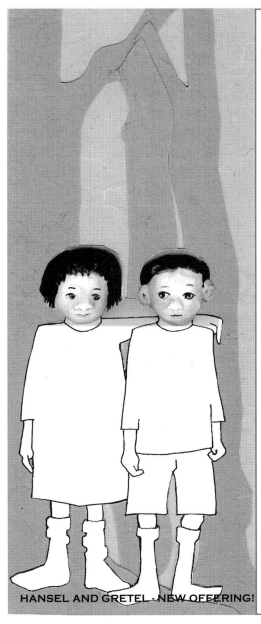

HANSEL AND GRETEL - NEW OFFERING!

JESSE & FRANK JAMES:
FAMOUS BAD BROTHERS,
AVAILABLE IN THREE SIZES
JJ.......................25.00

CINDERELLA'S SISTERS:
THREE UGLY GIRLS, WITH
EXTRA BIG FEET AND
FANCY DRESSES.
CS.......................33.00

ELIZA & THE 11 SWANS:
BEAUTIFUL ELIZA, 11 LIVE
SWANS. NEED PENS.
E11.......................45.00

3 LITTLE PIGS:
1 PINK PIGLET, 1 SPOTTED
PIGLET, 1 BROWN PIGLET.
RUBBER OINKERS ON
REAR ENDS.
3P 45.00

3 LITTLE KITTENS:
TINY LITTLE NEWBORNS,
COME TUCKED INTO
MITTENS.
3K.......................20.00

7 CHINESE BROTHERS:
STRONG BOY, BIG WIND,
HUGE FEET, FEARLESS
HEART, LONG LEGS, IRON
MAN & BIG MOUTH. MAY
BE PURCHASED INDIVID-
UALLY OR AS A SET.
7CB..............(SET)50.00
(EACH) 10.00

HANSEL & GRETEL:
BROTHER & SISTER, COME
WITH BREAD CRUMBS FOR
TRAILS.
HG.......................20.00

Mr. Cannady called him into his private office first thing Monday morning and closed the door.

"Listen here, Markham, I want you working on that toy idea at least seventy-five percent of your time. And I want to see one fantastic proposal. There's a lot at stake here."

"I'll do my best, sir," Mark said.

A frown creased Mr. Cannady's forehead. "No, Markham, no. You *will* do it! That is the only answer I want to hear."

"Yes, sir," Mark acknowledged unhappily.

"Good. Now, go. Work!"

The problem was, Mark couldn't come up with a single idea. His mind had always closed down when people told him what to do. When he was younger, whatever he was told to do had just slid away, conveniently half-heard and quickly forgotten. It was one reason why fixing things had fit him so well. He could jump from a part of one project to another project altogether, interchange mechanisms between two projects or start something completely new, and it didn't matter in what order he did it, or if he did it at three in the morning or ten in the morning or five in the afternoon.

Mr. Cannady's ultimatum had slid off him and pushed him into a black hole where no light could pierce the gloom surrounding his mind. He sat at his desk and doodled, first one small familiar face and then another until there were seven.

Elliot stuck his head in at noon. "I need to speak to you about the dinner party. Is now a good time?"

"Sure, sure, come in."

"Good," Elliot said. "All thirty couples who received invitations have said they are coming."

"Does that include you and Laura?"

"Yes, if that's what we must do to get you to give this affair, Mr. Cannady said we could come."

"Gee, how nice of him."

"Yes, it was. Now about the chairs?"

"I guess we won't be able to have a sit-down dinner, after all."

"Markham! Please!"

"But, I will open the observatory dome so the starlight can shine in," Mark said magnanimously.

"I didn't know there was a dome," Elliot said, distracted for at least the moment.

"Someone had plastered the ceiling over it. I found it above the top of the left tower when I stuck stuff up there in the attic the first week. I opened the ceiling up, but the mechanism that controlled the eye of the dome was broken. So I fooled with it and now it works nine times out of ten. A little more oil, a little jiggle here and there, and it'll work every time."

"That would be a lovely touch," Elliot conceded, then added a little pensively, "but what about chairs?"

"Forget about chairs. Let me tell you about the beautiful telescope I restored and mounted beneath the dome. I installed a circular, fold-down iron-worked staircase to reach it. Who needs chairs when they can climb such a staircase and magnify the stars? Come on, Elliot, if you bring candles and flowers, it'll be presentable, don't you think, without chairs?"

"I give up, I give up!" Elliot threw his hands into the air in his trademark gesture of total frustration with Mark.

"At least I've been thinking about this. Doesn't that please you?"

"Chairs would have pleased me," Elliot muttered. "Okay, okay, what color flowers and candles do you want, Markham?"

"Red and yellow," Mark said quickly.

"Red and yellow, red and yellow? No chairs and yellow and red flowers!" Elliot moaned loudly.

"Now, Elliot, it is really quite a lovely color combination."

"Markham, I'm worried about you. Don't you understand the importance of this?"

"If you weren't worried about me, I'd be worried about you. You like to worry, Elliot. Just choose the food and I'll take care of the flowers. Now go, go have your lunch. I have a call to make."

Mark picked up the phone and dialed home. "Lady A? Hi, how are things? Uh huh. Listen, a man named Pete and his granddaughter may arrive this afternoon. They're going to be living with us." He paused to let Lady A yell a minute. When she stopped for a breath, he said, "Put the girl in with Mirabella and Ailithe and give Pete the empty tower room."

She moaned on her end of the connection and asked how many more people he was going to take into the house. It was getting full. Would he just happen to have a few more beds stashed somewhere? Did he ever check to see if he had enough sheets? When was he going to stop?

Mark laughed. "Why, I'm going to buy more beds from you. What did you think? Do you have any?"

She hung up. Something between tenderness and amusement passed through his mind as he imagined her sitting dejectedly on the stairs, muttering to herself over his eccentricities.

The afternoon didn't go any better than the morning had. Finally it was time to go home. He tidied up, which wasn't hard, and hurried out the door before Mr. Cannady could find him.

"Those people didn't come yet," Lady A told him as soon as he walked in the door, "but your sister is here with her husband. I'm leaving. Goodnight!"

"Why so fast?" he asked.

"A date," she answered curtly. "See you." She stopped and turned around. "Do you ever go out on dates, Mark?"

"Seven children don't leave me with much personal time," he said.

"But you won't have them forever. They're only foster kids."

Yes, I will, he thought. "I'm hoping to adopt them," he said out loud. "Well, bye."

She frowned at him disapprovingly and left. Mark considered who would date Lady A. She wasn't exactly his image of a romantic partner in her slouchy clothes and floppy hats. He should have been happy for her, should have been, but instead he felt a twinge of regret. She did have a certain appeal, especially when she dressed as she had the first day she had babysat. With a pang of loss, he wondered again who her date might be. Was he jealous? Feeling vaguely left out, he turned to face Kate and Larry where they waited in the small study behind the left tower.

Larry was pacing impatiently and tapping his thumbs against each other. He looked up and did something with his mouth between a grimace and a smile.

"Mark!" He began quickly. "Kate and I felt obligated, well, obligated to give you some advice."

"About what?" Mark asked.

"Those kids you seem to have, uh, adopted," Kate said.

"Oh," Mark said.

"Oh! That's it? Oh!" Larry pounced with what was obvious glee. Mark had never liked him. "As an attorney, I think you should know, unless you register them for school, you will be held legally responsible."

"Oh," Mark commented again.

"Markie," Kate pleaded, "please, please, send them away before you ruin everything for yourself."

"I can't," he said simply.

"Why not?" she demanded.

"There is nowhere to return them to. Non-returnable." He smiled.

"You are impossible, Mark," Larry said and stomped towards the front door. "Come on, Kate. I told you it was useless."

She turned back at the last moment and said, "By the way, where are those shoes I had on the night you got hurt?"

"Gone?" he asked.

"Gone! Look for them, and when you find them, call me," she said angrily and left, hurriedly following her husband.

As soon as the car was out of sight, Mark laughed loudly.

"What's going on?" Jack asked.

Mark just laughed louder and harder.

"What's the matter with you?"

"Nothing. Nothing. It's just so much fun having you guys around," Mark said, affectionately messing up the boy's blonde hair.

109

SCARY FOLK

WERE WOLF: Clawed gloves, furry mask, full moon mobile ....35.
GOBLIN: Short, rubbery skin, bad complexion, wrinkly face ..40.
BIG BAD WOLF: Hairy guy, interested in filling his tummy .....50.

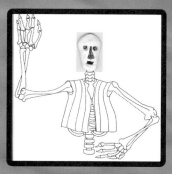

SKELETON: Rattles when he walks, assembly directions........50.
ZOMBIE: Activated when the lights go out, walks alone ....45.
CANNIBAL: Carries shrunken head and large cooking pot.....30.
SEA SERPENT: Water immersible, sinks ships, eats sailors ...40.
VAMPIRE: Attachable bat wings, sips bottled blood, kisses necks
  and hates garlic. Sleeps in the day, roams at night ....50.

Pete arrived after all the kids were in bed and Mark had just immersed himself in a good e-reference on the history of games. The man looked haggard.

"Where's your granddaughter?" Mark asked.

"I got her out in the truck. It was a long drive to get her."

"You drove? Why didn't you fly, Pete? I would have given you an advance."

"Couldn't. Didn't wanna expose her to a lotta staring. I shoulda told you. She's kinda different."

"So? You think that matters in this house?" Mark asked.

"She's white," he said wearily.

"White? What does that mean? As opposed to what?"

"No, I mean she's fifteen and all white. Hair, skin, eyes, everything white."

"An albino?"

"Yeah. Her name is Fiona, and she's kinda frail. The syndrome makes her vulnerable, you know, to light and stuff. Her parents gotta work and just couldn't afford to take care of her no more."

"Well, go get Fiona and bring her inside. I'd like to meet her."

"You don't care?"

"She's why you took the job, isn't she?"

Pete nodded and rubbed his bald spot. "You sure about this?"

"Pete, she'll fit right into this nut house."

"Thanks. That's what I thought, too."

He reached behind him and pulled in two fat suitcases and a stuffed bear and dumped them through the front door.

"You can have the last tower room and Fiona can share with Mirabella and Ailithe."

"Okay," Pete said.

He went back to the truck he had parked on the street. Mark saw him and half-heard him pleading with someone. Finally a shadowy whiteness moved towards the house, while Pete gave the truck door a loud thump.

The whiteness drifted towards the porch, standing just outside the light cast from the open door.

"I want to go home, Grandpa," it said.

"No, darling, we can't. Go on now. This is gonna be home."

Mark saw the girl put on a pair of dark glasses as she entered the flood of light from the house.

"Hi, I'm Mark," he said, extending his hand to her.

She took it hesitantly. Her grip was light and papery.

"I guess it's okay," she said, looking around her. "I'm awfully tired, Grandpa."

Pete nodded. "Come on, sweetheart, you can take the bed in my room for tonight."

They vanished up the stairs, Fiona hugging the bear to her chest.

Pete came back and said. "I'm surprised. She's ready for bed. Usually she prefers to be up at night and sleeps through the daylight hours. I guess she's really, really tired."

Mark nodded. "How about some hot chocolate?"

"Naw, but I could use a cup of coffee. Listen, Mark, those catalogs of yours, they stopped officially publishing them years ago."

"Really? Then why are they still coming? How is it even possible?"

"That's what you're paying me to find out, but you gotta be patient. You didn't think it was gonna be a snap or you wouldn't of hired me, wouldya? Have you ever tried ordering anything from the catalogs?"

"Yes."

"And did they deliver? Or was it a hoax? See, it could be a scam."

"They delivered," Mark said.

"You got the merchandise you ordered, huh?"

"Well, it wasn't exactly what I had expected, but I got it."

"So, it was bait and switch. That's an old gag. Did you return it?"

"I couldn't. No returns, no refunds. It says so in big letters on every catalog!"

"If they send you what they promised. Otherwise you should be able to return it."

"Not in this case," Mark said. "Look, see if you can find out more. There must be records of who published them originally. What about starting there?"

"Okay, but I gotta warn you, this stuff was called junk mail in my day, and I don't think nobody kept very good records of it. This could be real hard to track down."

"I understand. I'm going to bed, Pete. See you in the morning."

"Hey, Mark, mind if I ask why this is so important to you?"

He thought about it for a moment. "I'm not sure how to answer that yet, Pete. I'll see you tomorrow."

Mark turned off his light and crawled into bed. It was a good question. At first it had been because he had wanted to return the kids to whomever had sent them. Now he wasn't so sure they belonged anywhere or there was anyone to return them to. To Ardromini, to Lost Land, to Atlantis? Was it all just a huge hoax? It had to be, didn't it? He closed his eyes and tried to sleep, but couldn't. He tossed and turned, rolled over and finally got up. The problem with the hoax idea was that the kids would have to cooperate to pull it off. Who could have trained and drilled them into playing roles as realistically as they did, especially the little ones? And what about Mirabella? Nobody could fake being able to read minds, could they? How did you fake flying? Or being able to become invisible? He took a deep breath to clear his head. He was trying hard to make sense out of the situation, but logic and realism didn't seem to fit into the puzzle no matter how he turned them, tried them, or wedged them into the picture.

Something rustled on the stairs, breaking his thoughts. He stopped to listen, but the sound was gone, if it had ever been there.

Even though none of the kids fit all the details of who they were supposed to be, the discrepancies worked both ways. They might indicate it was all a huge gag, but they were also what made it all seem plausible.

Another wispy rustle froze Mark in mid-thought. This time he didn't move, just listened until he heard a little giggle.

"Okay, get in here," he called softly, wondering which of the kids it was.

Two heads peeked through the door frame.

"Elflet, Fiona! What are you two doing out there?"

"He's trying to fix shoes and I'm reading," Fiona answered for them.

"Elflet, whose shoes do you have this time?"

"I can't say," he answered.

"Why not?"

"It's a surprise. Please don't make me tell."

"Elflet, you can't keep doing this. Those shoes don't belong to you."

"Then you'll buy me some of my own?" he said, brightening.

"So you can take them apart?"

The boy's ears wiggled when he nodded yes.

"Elflet, I am not going to buy shoes so you can take them apart. You are not a cobbler. I don't think anyone is, anymore."

"And that's a shame," Fiona said quickly. "A real shame, because most shoes hurt my feet and a cobbler could solve that."

Mark looked at her. "I guess you're right, but Elflet doesn't seem to be the answer. What are you reading?"

"*Dracula*," she said, hugging a book close to her.

"I've never read it," Mark said. "Is it good?"

"It's really scary, not like the wimpy movie versions."

"What's scary about it?" Elflet asked.

"It's about vampires, the living dead. They crawl out at night and suck your blood!"

Elflet hid behind Mark's leg. "I'm out at night. Will they get me if I stay up and watch for them?"

"You could wear garlic to ward them off," Fiona said, and patted his head.

"Okay, bedtime, both of you," Mark said.

Elflet scampered off, but Fiona turned and asked, "There aren't any real vampires, are there?"

"No, there aren't. You're too old to believe such a thing."

"But, Mark, there aren't supposed to be any cobbler's elves either, are there?" she said hesitantly.

"Elflet is not much of a cobbler and there are no vampires," Mark promised. At least not in the catalogs he had looked through so far.

He closed the door to his room and went to sleep thinking about garlic.

PUMPKINS 'N COSTUMES

Devil:bright red, with trident, tail, torch
smoke pellets ------12.95

Pilgrim:authentic coat,pants,fancy belt &
buckle -------------9.95

Clown: big shoes and makeup----6.95

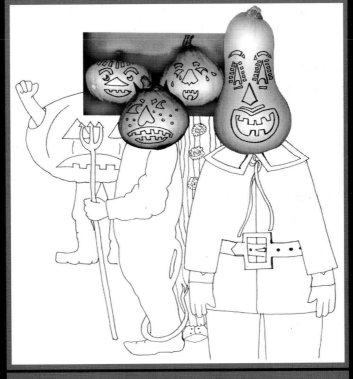

Jack-O'Lantern: Big, fat and orange, made
of crepe paper and plastic bags ----5.00

The phone rang early. He grabbed for it, tangled himself in the cord. Only half awake, he mumbled into the receiver.

"Hey, Mark, it's me." It took him a minute to recognize Lady A's voice. She was going to be late, she said nasally. She had a little cold.

"Take the day off. Pete will be here," he said.

She promised to be back the next day.

"Uh huh," he said and plunked the phone back in the cradle, groaned and rolled out of bed.

Breakfast was quick and dirty, and Mark was just out the door when Mrs. Williams stopped him. She never addressed him by name. She always began in mid-thought. "You have children staying with you who should be in school."

"Yes, ma'am," he said politely.

"Well, why aren't they? They are quite noisy. Quite a nuisance. Why aren't they in school?" she repeated.

"I hope to have the situation resolved soon," Mark said, trying to skirt the issue.

"Humpf!" she said, and went back inside with a bang of her front door.

Mark spent the day trying to forget the old lady's interest in the kids. The office was abuzz with activity that added to his distraction. Finally he shut the door to the hall and closed his eyes to see if he could get the privacy to dream up the new game, only to have the buzzer go off.

"Meeting in five minutes," the computer secretary hummed. "Four minutes, fifty-five seconds." It went on with the countdown.

Mark hated those countdowns. He turned off the voice to the computer, closed his eyes again, but the connection he had been making was gone, broken, lost. He ignored the meeting altogether. Why bother? He had nothing to report.

As he went home that afternoon, he noticed the small houses that lined many streets had plastic pumpkins merrily set in their windows. By the time Mark had been in first grade, schools had banished All Hallows Eve. Costumes vanished from stores. Candy corn disappeared from grocery shelves. All that was left of the holiday were these little plastic pumpkins. When he was ten he had found a snapshot of a two-year-old Kate smiling broadly from under the brim of a witch's hat, but when he had asked his mother if he could get dressed-up for Halloween, she shook her head and said, "Not any more, Markie."

The traffic was sparse for once, so he got home early. He wandered absently into the kitchen, grabbed a handful of raisins and popped them in his mouth, just as Jack rolled a huge, orange pumpkin through the kitchen door.

"What is that for?" Mark exclaimed.

"It's a pumpkin. A real pumpkin!" The boy looked up with delight written across his face.

"But for what?"

"For Halloween. I'm carving it out to make a play house."

"Why? For whom?"

"For all us kids. You know that's where Jack-Sprat kept his wife, in a pumpkin shell," Jack said and began rolling the pumpkin again.

"No," Mark corrected him. "That was Peter the Pumpkin Eater."

Jack pouted. "I wanted it to be a Jack."

Mark shook his head.

"Hey, hey!" Pete said interrupting them. "Now that's a big pumpkin! I ain't seen a real pumpkin for Halloween in years. Where'dya get it, Mark?"

"Ask Jack," Mark said.

"Where'dya you get it?" Pete asked.

"We ordered it out of a catalog. Cool, huh?" Jack said.

"What?" Mark shouted. "Jack, do not order anything else, do you hear?"

"But it was free to anyone who had a receipt for a previous order!" The boy protested loudly.

"I don't care!" Mark shouted back.

Pete intervened. "Come on now, calm down, it's only a pumpkin. In fact, look at that pumpkin! It's something! My pop used to carve one with us when I was little. I remember. He'd cut off the top and scoop out seeds and a ton of goopy stuff. Then he'd scrape at the inside of the shell until it was clean. If you're gonna cut and scoop you'd better roll it back outside where it won't make such a mess. Get going, boy. I'll get the knife and be out in a second."

Pete was good with kids. Mark sighed as boy and pumpkin exited the kitchen.

"Hey, where'd this come from?" Pete asked, holding up Paul's ax. "Ain't it a little dangerous to have around?"

"How did that get out of the closet? I thought it was locked up."

"Whatcha you doing with it at all? You ain't secretly an ax murderer, are you?"

Mark grimaced. "It's Paul's. It came with him."

"You gotta be kidding. Who'd give a toddler an ax?" Pete asked. He went out to the kids, muttering about the idiots who would give a baby a dangerous toy. "Lock it back up somewheres safer," he called back to Mark.

Pete would have been even more surprised to know that Paul knew how to use that ax. He went to the door and watched Jack and Pete, saw Jack put his hands to his mouth and watched as the kids appeared, floating in from all corners of the yard, between blowing leaves and old trees.

"Okay," Pete said in a booming voice as he distributed spoons. "As soon as I get the top off, dig in and scoop out the seeds and the goop. Save as many of the seeds as you can and toss the rest to the birds. But try not to get the goop in the grass."

Seven hands armed with spoons stabbed into the pumpkin. Scoops of goop began flying through the air and landing in a big bowl. Laughs and giggles filtered over to Mark.

"They are having such fun," Fiona said, standing beside him.

"They are. Why don't you go out, too?"

"Oh, I can't. I'm quite allergic to the sun. I get a horrible reaction to it. No pigment in my skin, you see."

"Then would you like to bake cookies with me? And maybe we could spice some cider, as well."

"Sure," she said. "I like the kids, you know. I've never had friends before. They're nice and they're funny, too."

"Yes? And maybe a little strange, don't you think?"

"Sure," she said, as he pulled sugar and butter and raisins out of the refrigerator.

"I guess they can't help it, though, being odd," Mark added.

"Grandpa said you took them in when no one else would."

"Sort of," Mark agreed.

They worked quietly, the spices simmering in the cider. The sounds of high, young laughter came to them from outside, punctuated by a few deeper guffaws from Pete. The afternoon sun took on a softer light, touching the golden, ruddy leaves as the limbs they hung from swayed in the wind.

"This is perfect," Fiona said.

Mark felt the warmth of the oven as the cookies swelled inside into delectable lumps of sweetness. The two of them washed the dishes together, and cleaned the counters. He pulled out the eclectic collection of old tea cups with which he had filled a whole cabinet, and set them in neat rows to await the cider. He looked out the window and the autumn light turned a sprinkling of leaves to yellowy-green and brushed the tips to true gold. Mark smiled happily, Fiona hummed an odd melody, and the moment was held in the air until seven famished children and one exhausted man rushed through the doorway.

"Cookies!" they screeched in delight.

Only Jack and Traxon stood aside as the rest practically jumped on the table grabbing for the treats.

"Mark, could we carve the illustrations to a story into the pumpkin?" Jack asked.

"Why would you want to do that?" Mark questioned the boy.

"We'd put it on the front porch with a light inside it and when people knocked on our door, we'd tell them the story. It'd be great! Please," he begged.

"But why would you want to do that?"

"I don't know why, we just want to. Please!"

Mark noticed that all the kids were suddenly silent as they waited for his answer.

"What story do you want to carve?" Mark asked.

"I don't know. I don't know many stories," Jack said.

"Let me see," Pete said, scratching the top of his head again. "Let's see, we've got a little boy named Paul with a stuffed ox and an ax, how about the story of Paul Bunyan?"

"That's me," Paul chimed.

"You know his story?" Traxon asked.

"Wait, I thought you were making a house, like Peter Peter Pumpkin Eater," Mark said. "How did we end up with Paul Bunyan?"

"Mark, nobody lives in a pumpkin. It's all slimy inside. After a few days ants and fruit flies start to eat it," Pete told him.

"Yuck!" the kids all yelled with gusto.

"Come on, Mark, let them do it," Pete said.

"Okay, okay, but do any of you know how to carve a pumpkin?" Mark asked.

Their faces fell.

"We thought you could do it, Mark," Mirabella said. "You can make anything."

"Me? I've never carved a pumpkin in my life."

"Oh, come on, Mark, you can do it. The kids are right, you're great with your hands," Pete said.

"Then you'd better tell me this story," Mark said to Pete, "so I know what to do."

It was Paul Bunyan and the Blue Ox who proved to be named Babe. Mark stabbed and carved and cut until he had blisters. The story ended up encircling the whole pumpkin. The ox looked okay, but Paul Bunyan was a little lopsided.

"Is that what Paul is gonna look like when he gets bigger?" Jack asked curiously.

Mark shrugged.

"I think he'll be handsomer than that," Fiona said. She had joined them as the sun had begun to set. She made a hazy sort of figure in the dimming light, her white hair flying in the breeze.

They half carried, half rolled, half pushed the pumpkin to the front porch and lit a candle inside just as the sun set, turning the day to dusk.

"There," Jack said proudly. "Will you look at that?"

"Let's roast the pumpkin seeds," Rollo said.

Mrs. Williams strolled by out on the sidewalk. "What is that?" she screeched indignantly, pointing straight at the pumpkin. "You can't mean to leave *that* on your front porch!"

"Why not?" Traxon said.

"Listen here, young man, jack-o'-lanterns are forbidden. Everyone knows that."

"Why?" Mark asked.

"You know why!" she exclaimed. "Everybody knows why."

"I don't. Tell me why, lady," Jack said, thumping the pumpkin.

"For heaven's sake!" Mrs. Williams said with ever greater indignation. "You are a very rude child."

"Oh, come on, Mrs. Williams," Mark said. "What harm can it do?"

She was insistent. "It's a jack-o'-lantern."

"Not really, lady," Pete said. "You don't see a Jack's face on it nowhere, do you. This is a story pumpkin. It's about Paul Bunyan."

"That's me," Paul said delightedly.

"That's disgusting. The child thinks he's an imaginary person," Mrs. Williams cried. "You should all be reported."

"I'm real," Paul said, a tear coursing down his fat cheek.

The woman stared at the toddler before she said, "I am calling the authorities."

"We'll move the pumpkin," Mark said quickly. "The children didn't mean to offend you."

"Do it immediately! I declare, I can't imagine what goes on in that house of yours." She turned and walked past, muttering under her breath.

"That old lady is a bully. She'll be back with more demands until she does call the cops," Pete growled.

"Are we in big trouble?" Traxon asked.

"No, I'm sure we aren't. Okay, let's move the pumpkin, and then everybody, inside. Go eat your cookies. Fiona will serve the cider." Mark shooed the kids inside.

The kids straggled quietly in to the cider and cookies while Pete and Mark rolled the pumpkin into the back yard again. Mark leaned against the big, round, orange squash and sighed.

Pete leaned against a tree and watched him. Finally he said, "Mark, it's time for you to tell me what's really going on around here."

"I guess so."

"Past time, really," Pete said.

Mark sighed again. "You know the catalogs? Well, I placed ten orders from them."

"Yeah, so you said. But you didn't get what you ordered, right?"

"Not exactly."

"What's that mean. Exactly what didya get?" Pete persisted.

"I ordered ten action figures and dolls. They looked so cute and I have to admit, it appealed to me that they were unusual and imaginative. I ordered baby Paul Bunyan, one boy Wizard of Lost Land, one boy from Ardromini with invisibility screen, one generic nursery rhyme Jack, one Elflet from the Shoemaker and the Elves, one mind reader from the Lost City of Atlantis and one Wind Child from another world."

"Hold on! Are you saying you were dumb enough to place ten orders at once from mail order catalogs? And they weren't toys?"

Mark nodded. "My other three orders weren't available. One is permanently out of stock, one is back-ordered and one is recuperating, whatever that means."

Pete nudged Mark over and took a seat on the pumpkin. "Okay, I've got Paul and Elflet and probably the Wind Child, and oh yeah, Jack. What about the others?"

"Rollo Wiz, the Wizard of Lost Land. Traxon of Ardromini. Mirabella, beware of your thoughts," Mark finished up the list.

"Do you really believe this, Mark?"

Mark closed his eyes for a moment before he answered. "All I know is the kids don't have official identities, they can do some pretty unusual stuff, and I have no idea who sent them or why."

"Geez! I'm surprised you didn't go straight to the authorities when it all started," Pete said.

"What would the authorities have done with a bunch of imaginary kids who just happen to be inhabiting flesh and bone bodies?" Mark asked, voicing the question he had given up asking himself weeks ago.

"I dunno. But it woulda been their problem, not yours. Guess it's too late now."

"Pete, I need to locate who publishes those catalogs before my neighbors decide I'm an unfit parent and get the authorities to take the kids away. Who knows what would happen to them!"

Pete scratched his head and then shook it hard as if trying to clear it. "Why ten?" he asked. "Couldn't you have been more practical?"

Mark threw his hands up in the air in an imitation of Elliot. "How was I supposed to know they weren't just toys? Come on, let's get some cider before it's all gone."

They went inside. Paul was happily munching, Fiona was reading and the others were playing marbles on the great-room's Persian rug.

"Where is Traxon?" Mark asked.

"I don't know," Jack said immediately.

Mirabella corrected him. "Yes, you do!"

Mark looked at Jack. "Out with it, young man."

"Can't you leave me alone?" Jack snarled at Mirabella.

"You shouldn't have been whispering about Mrs. Williams," Mirabella said. "I can hear words as clearly as thoughts, you know."

Mark took Jack's arm and demanded, "What's going on? Tell me right now!"

"Okay, okay, let go. He's gone to haunt Mrs. Williams a little bit. You know, moan a little and make things creak and stuff. Just to teach her a lesson, that's all. She deserves to be taught a big lesson."

"Oh, no!" Mark groaned. He spun around. "Mirabella, call him back. Tell him he'll be in major trouble if he doesn't get back right now. Do it, please."

"I'll try," the girl said, "but I can't promise anything. He was awfully mad. He might not hear me through his anger."

Pete rolled his eyes. "I don't believe this mess."

Mark ignored the remark and watched Mirabella. She stared straight ahead, squinched her face together and abruptly fell backwards into Mark.

"I got through," she said, smiling broadly.

"Sure thing, see, she got through," Pete said, waving his hand at the empty air.

Traxon walked through the door looking dejected. "Why'd you stop me? I could have taught her a lesson."

"Traxon!" Mark growled at the boy. "Don't disappear. You stay and face me."

Traxon had an unabashed smile plastered across his face. "You can't tell me you didn't want me to haunt her, just a little bit?"

Mark looked at the boy sternly. "Into your room, and don't even think about sneaking out! What you just did was rash and dangerous and cruel."

"Okay, but it was worth it. Oh, yeah, it was," he said and clicked his fingers all the way up the stairs.

Mark whirled about, his patience finally snapping. "Everybody, go get in your pajamas, right now. Go!" he yelled.

Pete was staring at him. "It's true, isn't it? All seven kids and three more on order?"

"Yes, I'm afraid so."

"You ordered ten children? Boy oh boy, we are in big trouble!"

Mark nodded again. "Trouble. Are you ever right about that!"

Pete sat down in a chair. "Couldn't you have started with a less grandiose order?"

"Be grateful. I almost placed twenty-three orders," Mark admitted.

Pete stared open-mouthed. Finally he said, "Okay, okay, what have we got? The catalogs come from nowhere for more than fifty years and the kids don't got ID's and you don't got papers for them. We've got a mess is what we've got!"

Mark shrugged and nodded his head *yes*.

"I'm gonna get real busy on this, but I gotta tell you, this may stump even an old pro like me."

"Be careful, okay?" Mark said. "It has to be done subtly so nobody else finds out."

"You don't need to tell me that," Pete said and went up to his room.

Mark, Mirabella whispered in her voiceless way. *What is Pete's secret?*

What? What do you mean?

I hear him telling himself not to think about it.

Do you know what it is?

No, only that he thinks about it often.

He thought back to her. *Pete's older than I am. I'm sure there are lots of things in his life that he might not want to think about. Be polite, don't listen in, okay?*

Okay, Mark.

FOR NOW IT'S EIGHT O'CLOCK

ROCK-A-BYE BABY:
Summer nighties and panties with matching blankies. In soft pastel colors of your choice. Cotton and fleece.
Newborn - 18 months 25.00

THREE JOLLY HUNTSMEN:
Horse covered pajamas, with free gift of three old fashioned hobby horses.
Sizes 2 & 4 ....15.95

TWINKLE TWINKLE LITTLE STAR:
Available in nightgown, sleepshirt or pajamas. Glow-in-the-dark stars on black or navy background. Recording of lullabye included.
Sizes 2, 4, 6 & 8............................30.00

SUMMERTIME:
Mama, Papa and baby pillows accompany matching towels and bathrobes. Monogramming available. Comes in fish or sunshine prints. All soft, natural cotton.
To 24 months; adult sizes.............45.95

ON THE GOOD SHIP LOLLIPOP:
Matching quilts, pillows and bean bag chairs, covered with lollipops. Matching nightshirts for boys and girls. Order all the matching items and get a year's supply of lollipops.
Sizes 4, 5, 6 & 8...................43.00

LITTLE BOY BLUE:
Multi-shaded blue tights and nightshirts. Comes with blue alarm clock with horn-like buzzer.
Sizes 2,4, 6............................32.00

WEE WILLIE WINKIE:
Nightshirts and nightcaps, special nightlights in candle shapes and a cookoo clock that sounds at 8:00.
Sizes 12 & 24 months.............37.95

ORDER NOW!!!!

Lady A arrived hatless, her eyes red, and her hair in a wilder tangle than usual. Plus, she was twenty minutes late.

"Are you okay?" Mark asked her.

"I will be," she said, turning her head aside so he couldn't quite see her face, but he thought she was crying.

"Listen, if you aren't up to this, I could stay home."

"Go, Mark. Go on to work. I can handle it."

"What happened?" he asked, not budging.

"Nosy, aren't you? Okay, I'll tell you." She swung around and faced him. He couldn't tell if her nose was rosy from crying or from the cold she had. "My date was a jerk. I should have known better, since my father set it up. He can never leave me alone!"

Mark knew he should say something, but the best he could mumble was, "Sorry." He was immediately surprised to discover he wasn't sorry and in fact felt relieved.

"Yeah, thanks. Now go, get, go on to your job," she said fussily.

"First, let me introduce you to someone," Mark said, wishing he hadn't asked about her date, wishing he hadn't even known about it. He called into the kitchen and Fiona came out shyly, looking as if she wanted to flee.

"Lady A, this is Fiona, Pete's granddaughter. Fiona, this is Lady Anderson who looks after everybody when Pete and I are gone."

"Hey," Lady A said, "I'm glad to meet you."

"Likewise," Fiona said and darted back to the safety of the kitchen.

"She's like a bird," Lady A commented. "Now, you'd better go."

He was about to leave when the phone buzzed. It was Elliot, of course.

"I'm glad I caught you, Markham. Mr. Cannady wants you to go to a breakfast meeting at the Purple Parrot Restaurant down at Fourteenth and Peacock."

"Now?"

"Now, for breakfast," Elliot said again. "Have you thought up any ideas for that game?"

"No, not a one, but I have a while yet."

"What have you been doing all week? Mr. Cannady's not going to be at all pleased."

"Is he checking up on me?" Mark asked.

"Yes, of course he is. There's a lot at stake."

"I'll think up something on the way over," Mark said and slammed the phone down. Mr. Cannady was reneging on his promise. Mark didn't have six months and he didn't have a free hand.

His mind went a mile a minute on the way over, but the car got caught in traffic and only went a mile every fifteen minutes. He tried to concentrate on the game, but he couldn't. He was becoming more and more absorbed by the kids and less and less by his job. He hoped Mrs. Williams was all right. If she couldn't tolerate a jack-o'-lantern, how would the old lady handle a ghost? With denial, he hoped. But what if it was hysteria, what if she panicked, what if she called the police? Then what?

He pulled up to the restaurant and put a token into the auto-valet-parker. He straightened his suit and tie, ran his nails through his hair and decided to grow it back out.

"Good morning, Mr. Cannady. Sorry if I'm late. The traffic was abominable."

"I ordered for you already," his boss said. "Thank you for coming. Now what ideas do you have for our toy?"

"I have six months, sir."

"It turns out we need it sooner. What have you come up with?"

"How long do I have?" Mark asked.

"Two months or a little less. Now, what have you come up with?" Mr. Canady asked insistently.

"I'm still working on it. I'm not ready to present anything yet."

"Uh huh. Markham, Elliot says you seem to be baby-sitting quite a number of children."

"Actually, I am foster-parenting them," Mark corrected Mr. Cannady. The man frowned just as Mark made a quick mental recovery and blurted out with a gulp, "I'm using them for inspiration."

"Really! You mean you are foster-parenting kids as a test group?"

Mark was afraid to speak, so he just nodded, waiting to see if Mr. Cannady would swallow the explanation.

There was a moment of silence before his boss said delightedly, "Brilliant, truly brilliant."

"The only thing is, I didn't quite count on how busy I would be." That was the truth. "But I have come up with one idea for an interesting computer game," Mark began, hoping he could fudge his way through the rest of the meeting as neatly as he had just twisted the truth about the kids.

Mr. Cannady interrupted. "Okay, I'm ready to be surprised again. Spit it out."

Mark smiled, although he really wanted to excuse himself to the facilities and crawl out the window that was a requisite for all bathroom escapes. He swallowed and launched into an idea he had only vaguely examined. "This is very rough." That was an understatement. "The premise involves an invisibility belt that the player must acquire. Once the player acquires it, he or she can slip into any number of situations unnoticed, and can, for instance, stop a war, spy on enemies and competitors, or even pretend to be a ghost." *Or escape unnoticed from a bad situation*, he thought to himself.

"No, no ghosts. You should know better. Industrial espionage, wars, spies, but nothing too extreme here. I like the belt. Nice touch of technological projection, but only develop realistic uses for it."

"Oh," Mark said. "Well, it's just a first model. I'll keep working."

Mr. Cannady wiped his lips, stood, briefly shook Mark's hand unenthusiastically and walked away. Mark's food came five minutes later. He didn't bother to eat it. He paid the whole check and left, fuming mad.

He got back into his car, got back into the wall-to-wall traffic, and let his thoughts run free. It hadn't been such a terrible proposal. Then again, it hadn't been so great either. Look how inventive Traxon could be with his invisibility screen! Look at all the trouble the boy had gotten into already. Maybe even suggesting such a piece of technology wasn't wise.

By the time he left work at the end of the day, he had decided to try something altogether different, he just didn't know what. He left with a huge headache just as Elliot was walking out as well.

"You don't look so great," Elliot said.

"Bad headache again," Mark said. "Is there anything demanding on my schedule for the next few days?"

"I don't think so," Elliot said.

"Good, just in case I need a few days off. Sick leave," Mark added quickly.

"Call in, okay. I hope you feel better, Markham."

What would make Mark feel better was a vacation. The traffic was light and he got home early again, but this time the street was alive with people milling around Mrs. William's house.

"What's going on?" he asked a woman standing next to him.

"Oh, poor Mrs. Williams has lost her mind! She came screaming out of her house saying she had seen a ghost! She banged on all our doors, ranting and raving. They had to take her away." The lady *tssked*.

Mark swung around, pushed open his own front door and slammed it behind him.

"Traxon!" he bellowed. "Get down here this instant!"

"It wasn't me, honest, Mark," the boy warbled as he faded in and out of view.

"Don't lie to me!" Mark raged.

"He isn't," Lady A interjected. "Calm down, Mark. Traxon, quit fooling with that toy of yours and stay where we can see you."

"It was me," Fiona said from where she was huddled under the staircase. Tears streamed down her face as she trembled from the crying. "I just took her some cookies. I thought of it as an apology, but she thought I was a ghost." She wiped at her tears. "I tried to explain I was an albino, but she went wild. She scattered the cookies everywhere and smashed your pretty plate to smithereens and then she started pounding on me with her fists all rolled up into little balls."

"Are you all right?" Mark asked, taking her hands and pulling her into his arms for a hug.

"Why do people think I'm a monster?" she cried, pushing away from him and running upstairs to her room with Lady A hurrying after her.

"Me and Ailithe heard screaming and ran over. The door was wide open," Traxon said. "Mrs. Williams had a shard of pottery in her hand. She was trying to cut Fiona, so Ailithe batted up a storm and I knocked the shard out of her hand. Mrs. Williams took one look at

Ailithe and went screaming into the street, going from one house to the next, rapping on doors, screeching hysterically about ghosts and hauntings and how it was all because of you and us."

"Okay, I owe you an apology," Mark said, feeling knots tying themselves in his stomach, but trying to stay calm. "Thank you for helping Fiona, but I hope you learned a lesson here. You cannot haunt anyone! Go read or something for a while."

Mark sat down. If anyone believed Mrs. Williams, he and the kids were in big, big trouble. Maybe they'd be lucky. Maybe people would be too unimaginative to believe a hysterical old lady. He rubbed his eyes. He hoped Pete had had a better day than he had. Maybe he had been able to trace some of the catalogs.

"Mark," Fiona whispered from behind him. "Can I talk to you?"

"Sure, of course you can."

"I'm sorry I made things worse."

"Oh, I don't know about that," he said. "This street probably hasn't seen an exciting event in a long, long time."

"I feel so bad for Mrs. Williams. She was so scared!"

"I guess so," Mark said.

"She really thought I was a ghost. She was terrified of me."

"That's sad," Mark said.

"Everyone denies what they see. Even Lady A makes herself think the kids are normal!" Fiona said softly.

"You don't think they are?" Mark asked.

She laughed with a rusty sound, as if she hadn't laughed in a long, long, time.

"Oh, Mark, we both know they aren't. Where did they come from?"

"I wish I knew," Mark said.

"Me, too," Fiona said. "I just watched Rollo invent a projection machine that blows things up into gigantic 3-D images. Elflet spends hours staring at how shoes are made and Mirabella reads minds, which isn't possible, is it?"

"It's all very strange," Mark agreed.

"That's all you're going to say? Mark, I'm truly ordinary compared to them."

"Absolutely, but we know you are real, Fiona, with real parents, and neither you nor I are sure about where the rest of the children came from. Now, want to help me and Lady A put together dinner?"

"Sure," she said, sniffling a little, but her eyes were dry.

Pete got home while they were setting the table. It was an ordeal to cook for eleven. Fiona was a big help, and Mirabella knew what needed to be done, without being told. Mark could barely remember what his life had been like a month ago. It scared him. Sometimes he tried to imagine re-crating the kids and sending them back to somewhere, anywhere. He could never do it. Besides, the crates had become an elaborate play structure in the backyard and probably couldn't be extricated anyway.

"So, any news?" Mark asked Pete.

"Yeah, those catalogs are almost untraceable. I did find out where a few of them were mailed from, but the cities I traced them to are dead ends. It's eerie. Here we are, living when you can find out anything about anyone, and a buncha catalogs are outta our reach, have slipped right on through the cracks."

Mark was wondering what else was lost that no one knew about, when Pete called out, "Hey, Mirabella, where were you before Mark uncrated you?"

"I don't know. All I remember is, I was always cold before I woke up in the crate. I was scared."

"I bet," Pete said. "Any of you remember anything? "

The answer was the same all the way around. *Nope. Nothing.*

Pete shook his head, chagrin written across his face. "I heard something happened next door," he said. "It was all over the news."

"I'll tell you about it later," Mark said, gesturing for Pete not to pursue it right then. "Okay, guys, clean up while Pete and I talk."

They stepped onto the porch. The trees stood iron grey under the high street lights and the first truly cold fall air turned their breath to smoky wisps.

"Cold suddenly," Pete remarked.

"Yes. Pete, we have to go to work on those papers. Mrs. Williams was so spooked by Traxon's visit that when Fiona took her some cookies, she freaked out. She thought Fiona was the ghost that had been haunting her. The cops came and the whole neighborhood gawked as they took her away! Fiona was in tears."

"Is Fiona okay? Why can't people leave her alone? She's just a kid," Pete fumed. "Just a sweet kid."

"I think she's okay now. We have to move on this, before things really get out of hand," Mark said again.

"Mark, it don't seem likely we're gonna find those publishers or whoever shipped the kids to you. Maybe we better take other steps. Can you really break computer codes? 'Cause like I said before, if you can break the computer code, I know a guy who can forge papers for the kids, 'specially since we already got the DNA samples to register.

"What about Ailithe and Traxon? Their DNA isn't going to pass inspection."

"Cross your fingers no one notices a little abnormality. People are pretty complacent. Might give us an edge. Don't got much choice," Pete said. "I'm gonna go check on Fiona."

Mark stayed on the porch. He sat in an old wicker rocker Lady A had sold him recently. As he rocked, the chair scraped a loose floor board tapping out a slow, creaky rhythm. Mark began to relax. Paul and Elflet found him there, and crawled into his lap, the book of nursery rhymes in hand.

"Read, please," Paul said and put his thumb into his mouth.
"Yes, please," Elflet added.

Peter, Peter, pumpkin eater,
Had a wife and couldn't keep her,
He put her in a pumpkin shell and there he kept her very well.

Peter, Peter pumpkin eater,
Had another, and didn't love her;
Peter learned to read and spell,
And then he loved her very well.

The boys giggled.

"Another," Paul said sleepily.

Wee Willie Winkie runs through the town,
Upstairs and downstairs, in his nightgown;
Rapping at the window, crying through the lock,
Are the children in their beds?
For now it's eight o'clock.

Hey, Willie Winkie, are you coming now,
The cat's singing grey calls to the sleeping cow,
The dog's sprawled on the floor and doesn't give a cheep,
But here's a waking laddie, that will not fall asleep.

"I like books," Elflet said. "We don't have a Peter or a Willie."

"No, we don't."

"Come on, Paul," Elflet said suddenly jumping down.

"Where are you going?" Mark asked.

"To look through the catalogs for a Peter and a Willie."

"Just look. No ordering, and put the catalogs back when you're done," Mark called after them. Through the doorway, he could just see their little legs pumping up the stairs. He rose and went inside, leaving the chair rocking emptily, squeaking gently.

He took a pad of paper and a pen and sat cross legged on the floor of the great room. The house slowly quieted. He could hear Pete's grainy voice singing some familiar melody as he put the kids to bed.

Mark started scribbling ideas for a series of computer games based on impossible technology. It was ironic. As long as it was technology, it was okay for it to be impossible. Technology was concrete. It made things concrete, but also put them out of the reach of real physical contact. In some way it disconnected the mind, distanced it from feeling. Abruptly, his mind jumped, closed down for a second, and he found himself making a list of toys that would be fun to build from old parts and bits and pieces of discarded stuff. They wouldn't do much except whir and turn, and be used to pretend with. He hadn't been particularly interested in toys before, but this was really fun.

He tossed the pen down, crumpled the plans, and put his head in his hands. The headache was back. He stretched out on the floor and closed his eyes. Quiet enveloped him and he slept heavily through the night.

BRAINIACS AND INVENTORS

Professor Challenger

Henry David Thoreau: 1862, with copies of "Walden", maps of the natural sites of the 1800's.

Guttenberg   Galileo   Dante

Beethoven   **Virginia Woolf**

Isaac Asimov   **Wright Brothers**

Thomas Edison

Odd John   Dr. Charles R. Drew

Plato: modernized version of toy from 347 B.C., voice activated, this toy responds via computer chip in Socratic dialog.

Frank Lloyd Wright: 1959, American, comes with drafting pens, drawing pencils and large rolls of paper.

SIR ISAAC NEWTON

Carlos Glidden   Tom Swift

Michaelangelo: comes with paste-up Sistine Chapel stickers

Aristotle   **Madame Curie**

Thomas Jefferson   Bach

George Eastman: 1932, with original Kodak box camera and celluloid film.

George Elliot   Rube Goldberg

Jules Verne: 1905, French toy with, full-sized hot air balloon.

Leonardo Da Vinci

He called in sick in the morning. His head was still pounding. He brewed his favorite peppermint tea, took a cup into the study and sipped at it. Warm sunlight poured in through the window panes and cast shadows and squares of light onto his desk, warming him to almost-sleepiness. He listened to the kids bickering in the kitchen over who got the last bowl of the fruit-popped cereal. Slowly his headache receded. He pulled out his private lap-top. It weighed only six ounces and was no bigger than an envelope for a greeting card. He had built it from cannibalized parts and had never registered a code name for it on the Net. He had preferred to remain anonymous and disconnected. Now he was glad. It would make him less traceable. Not impossible, but it would definitely take more effort.

Lady A was late for the second time. When she finally arrived, she looked harried and glanced over her shoulder a lot.

"Someone is following me around," she said.

Mark went to the window. "I don't see anyone out there." He stepped onto the porch and looked up and down the street. No one.

"He dropped out of sight about two blocks back. My father sure knows how to pick them."

"What do you mean?"

"It's the guy my father set me up with. He won't leave me alone."

"He followed you here?"

"Yes!"

"Okay, I'll take care of it."

The idea of someone following Lady A to the house made him nervous. He didn't want any extra scrutiny right now. He put on his coat and went for a walk, and kept his eyes roving. No one. He walked a little further and turned back. Still no one.

"Well?" Lady A asked.

"Nothing. No one. Relax, he's gone."

"Yeah, maybe," she agreed. "Thanks."

He settled in front of his little computer and hit a few keys.

"Wow, that's the smallest computer I've ever seen. Look at the quality of that screen and it's so tiny," Lady A said, looking over his shoulder. "Where'd you get it?"

"I made it. I use it when I want privacy. Have you fed those terrors in there yet?"

"No."

"I just brewed some mint tea. Help yourself."

She went back in the kitchen. He hit a few more crucial codes and waited. It was slow, because it worked differently than other computers, but for his purposes, it was safer than the usual paths. Pete came in with a cup of coffee, a bagel and a doughnut just as the screen popped up.

"Good, your timing is impeccable, Pete. We're going to break a code this morning. What data bank do I want?"

"On that?" Pete asked and pointed at the little screen.

"Why not?"

Pete shrugged and pulled up a chair. "You're just planning to sit down, right now, and crack the code?"

"Yes," Mark said. "Close the door."

"Okay." Pete pulled up a stool made of glued catalogs and perched next to Mark. "My contact said to try idt_cd.per/abiz/file/org."

Mark hit the keys. *Not Accessible* came up on the screen. He calmly touched *delete*, and then entered an access code he had discovered while he was still a kid. And it worked. It always worked. He had sent the subtle decoding virus out years ago almost as a prank, and discovered that no matter how people tried to delete it, it remained in cyber space, hiding. Ironically, once they thought they had voided it, no one looked for it again, and since he hadn't accessed it in a long time, like so many things hanging around in nebulous computer space, it was forgotten. He typed in another code. Pete started whistling, tapping a pencil as they waited. The minutes ticked out to twenty. On the twenty-second, the bank opened and Pete's whistle cut off in mid-note.

"How'dya do that? How's that possible? You can walk into protected files just like that?" Pete snapped his fingers, his eyes spread wide.

"Luck," Mark said quickly.

"Uh huh, sure! You know what I think? I think you coulda been one helluva a criminal."

"Oh, come on, Pete. It's just no one is paying attention to security. Why should they?" Mark said, trying to avoid the real explanation. It was better if Pete didn't know. "You and I both know they've backed this data up a million ways over so nothing can be lost. But we don't want to erase anything, we only want to put something in. Their confidence lets me walk right in the front door," Mark explained.

"Does that mean you could walk into your bank account, or mine, and add money?" Pete asked.

"Not without getting noticed! I promise, the banks have taken precautions against that idea." Actually, Mark probably could have done just that, but he had never been interested in money and still wasn't.

Pete drummed his fingers on the desk, cleared his throat and said, "Good try, bud. Now tell me the truth. How'dya break the code so easily? I'm more likely to believe you put a spell on the machine than that it was an accident."

He was caught. Pete was an old cop. He wasn't going to believe much short of the truth, but maybe Mark could get away with making it just a little short of the whole truth. "It started when I was a kid," he began, keeping his mind just ahead of the real story so he could edit it as he went. "One day I was looking for an e-book at the library and discovered the database entry was wrong. So I thought, *why not correct it?* I deleted one source and put the book into the right one. Sure enough, it worked. No buzzers went off, no one came after me. Nothing. But I was a good kid, and I got scared, so the next day I went back and restored the records to the original, if incorrect, status."

"Keep going."

"I was also a curious kid and couldn't leave well enough alone. The next week when I went to check out a CD, I wondered how many other book-mistakes there were in the data base. So I checked. There were a ton of books that had notations like stolen, or lost. I searched for some of those titles, cross-referenced libraries, and lo, a fair number of them had been returned to the wrong library and weren't lost or stolen at all. There were also bunches of books they still thought they had that were actually gone. Nobody had checked. They believed whatever the database told them. That's when I wondered, gee, could I get them to order some of the missing books that I really wanted to read? I figured out what file to enter and hacked in, but it was coded.

So, I fooled around and got lucky. Bingo, I was in and the library collection was restored, courtesy of Markham Perralt. Since then, I've tried breaking codes a few times. Sometimes, if the people who check the databases are complacent about it, I get lucky."

Mark had left out a pertinent item. It was better if no one else knew a code-breaker virus was virtually hanging, waiting permanently, out there in cyber-space. Fortunately, Pete seemed satisfied and laughed. "You are one very, very smart fellow, bud, and I bet I don't know the half of it."

Mark smiled. He never thought of himself as smart. He was just a guy, living his life, smart about some things, dumb about others, just like everybody else.

"Okay, we're in and it's your turn. Now what, Pete?" Mark asked, hoping to move past any further explanations quickly.

"Now, I call my friend to come over. But do me a favor. Don't tell him how you did that, okay?"

"Pete, is this guy trustworthy?"

"If you pay him enough, he's a mute."

Mark nodded. "What if someone else paid him more?"

Pete shrugged as he dialed a number. "Nobody ever said going underground was completely safe, but my guess is nobody's gonna catch on. They probably ain't gonna think to look for nothing. If our guy tried to sell the info to someone, they'd probably laugh him outta the country. I mean, who's gonna believe him? All this money for something no one can use?" He paused. "Hello, yeah? Okay. Midnight. So long," Pete said and put the receiver down.

PRINCES CHARMING

September, Back to School Issue

Mrs. Grimm   Prince Ahmed

Rapunzel's Prince   The Beast

Prince Valiant   Cinderella's Prince

Sleeping Beauty's Prince

MRS. GRIMM'S FOURTH GRADE

Twelve midnight came. Pete's contact came. Everything about him was incongruous. His arms were short, his hands were small, his legs were long. A thatch of conspicuously dyed-blond hair ran down the middle of his head, from forehead to the nape of his neck, and although the rest of his scalp was shaved, stray strands hung over the earpieces of his thick black-rimmed glasses.

"Seven kids, huh? New identities? Have you, uh, figured out how to wipe the old ones yet?"

"Come on, Bret, you know that can't be done," Pete said quickly. "Just draw up the papers like we agreed."

"What good are they gonna do you?" the man asked.

Pete lowered his voice connivingly and said, "Probably none, and then this guy here is paying you for zip." He pointed at Mark, who laid a stack of bills on the table next to the computer.

"Cash?"

Pete continued speaking in just above a whisper to Bret. "I told you, this guy just wants to see if it can be done. It's the challenge for him. He's bored. Not much he can't figure out. You know, a genius type! The pay is great, it's cash, no one can link you to him, so whatta you and me care if a rich guy wastes his money buying a few jollies?"

Bret looked at Mark for a long moment before he sat at the little computer and deftly typed in very official forms down to tiny numbers across the bottom of the pages. Then he inserted a font Mark had never seen used on anything. Mark watched carefully, committing each move to memory. His memory was his secret weapon. He remembered everything he saw and if he concentrated, he could extend it to what he heard. He had deliberately suppressed his hearing memory at one time because it had become an overwhelming noise. He never took his eyes off Bret's hands and, this time, he also memorized the sounds the keys made as they were tapped.

"Okay, there you go," Bret said an hour later. He reached out, scooped the bills off the table, stood, stretched, then scurried to the front door with Mark and Pete right behind him.

"Thanks," Mark said. "You did a superb job."

"Good, 'cause that's what you paid me for, wasn't it? I'm the best, but it isn't gonna do you any good, you know," Bret said, opening the door. "By the way, I don't know you, and don't ask me to do this again."

"Why? As far as we know, it isn't illegal just to fill in the forms," Mark said.

"Maybe not, but there's something strange about all this." Then Bret was gone.

"Whew, first I was afraid he was going to back out and now I'm afraid he's going to tell someone."

"He won't. He just got a lot of money for what seems like something useless to him. So why would he tell anyone? As far as he can see, nothing will ever come of it," Pete said. "The perfect cover for us."

"Are you sure?"

"Oh, he's gonna watch, see if he can make a buck off turning us in, see if a red flag goes up, but I doubt anybody's gonna be paying attention as the kids' names get added to the data bank. Just a new buncha newborns. I think we're safe, but keep those fingers crossed anyways."

"Do you think what we're doing is dumb?" Mark asked.

"If we get caught, but we gotta do something. Just wish it was something else."

Mark nodded to Pete and closed the computer just as Jack, Rollo, Elflet and Paul burst into the room, barefooted, pajama-clad, and sleepy-eyed.

"Mark, there's a truck outside!" Rollo said urgently.

"So?" Pete asked.

"With crates!" the boys screeched excitedly.

Mark raced out to the porch. The sky was a solid bank of whirling clouds reflecting a pink glow from the city lights. The wind was whipping up as two men lifted a huge box off the truck bed and carried it towards the porch. Mark rushed past them and straight to the driver.

"Uh, please, who hired you to deliver these boxes? I really need to know!"

"Yeah?"

"I'll tip you, handsomely," Mark said desperately.

"Sure," the man said, his hand out for the money. As soon as he got it he said, "Maypole's Web Store."

"What? You're delivering stuff for the house at this hour?" Mark exclaimed.

"Sure, whatcha expect us to be delivering?"

"Never mind," Mark said, shaking his head as he walked back to the porch. Within a few minutes the truck rumbled off into the night.

Mark hustled the kids back into bed and said goodnight quickly.

"No more kids?" Paul asked as Mark pulled up his covers.

"Aren't there enough kids in the house already?"

"Lots of kids still in the catalogs," the little boy said.

"True, but they can't all live here," Mark said.

"They waiting," Paul pointed out.

"Yes, I suppose," Mark said as he turned off the light, shut the door and sank down on the top stair step. He closed his eyes and took a deep, deep breath.

"Hey, Mark." Pete called up to him from the hall. "Come help me bring those boxes into the house."

Mark descended slowly. He was really tired.

"We might as well unpack them out there. If the kids want them for something, they can have them. Otherwise we'll tear them down and put them out for recycling."

"That play house of theirs is a real work in progress," Pete said. "I crawled into it yesterday. They've interconnected all the crates so it's one big structure," Pete rambled on as they pulled the packing tape off the first box. "They've cut out pictures from catalogs and put them up on the walls. A little furniture, and they're all set."

"Pots and pans? I already have pots and pans. They go back, don't even unpack them," Mark said as he unfolded the top of the box.

A card fluttered into his hands as he slammed the lid down. It read: "Thought you might need these, Love, Kate."

"Aw brother, I can't send them back. My sister sent them."

Mark pulled the pots out of their packing and stacked them while Pete cracked the next lid.

"Huh? Quilts, seven of them with a note from Elliot. 'The beds are coming!'" Pete read.

Mark laughed. Elliot thought everyone should have a bed and a quilt to go on it. Even though Mark had let Rollo and Elflet and Jack build makeshift beds for the kids that were pretty sturdy, Elliot hadn't been satisfied. Mark backed into another box.

"Do you remember them dropping off a third box, Pete?"

"Nope, but it has holes in it. Look on the sides," Pete commented.

"Oh boy, I hope no one sent us a pet!" Mark said. "That's just what I need to add to this menagerie. A dog! Something else to take care of."

"Mark," Mirabella said, standing in her bare feet in the doorway.

"You're gonna catch your death standing there in your nightie, young lady," Pete said. "Get shoes and a jacket."

She pointed to the box. It seemed to be wobbling, floating just an inch above the porch floor. Mark blinked and pulled off the packing slip. It read in big red letters: *Back Order.*

"Whatsa matter, Mark? You're greener than Traxon," Pete said.

Mark cut the tape around the lid. The instant he finished, the lid flew off and a slender boy flew right past them into the high trees around the house. He whistled and without warning, a puppy shot out of the box and joined him to perch on an upper branch. A dog and a boy! Mark knew his mouth was open and clamped it shut.

"Mirabella, can you please tell him I'll leave the front door open? He can come in when he's ready. I'm too tired to coax him inside. Come on, Pete, let's put the pots and quilts away."

"But, you can't leave him out there," Pete said.

"Don't worry. He'll come in. I told you someone was on back order. I guess it was him, but I don't remember a dog."

"He wouldn't come without his dog," Mirabella explained.

"My luck. One bed, one quilt short," Mark muttered to himself.

"Any more back orders?" Pete asked, catching up with Mark.

"Yeah, I think one more is all. Maybe I'll get lucky and the stock won't come in."

Mark felt dazed. He walked into the house, brushed a new pile of catalogs that tumbled at his touch, but he didn't blink. He walked to the mantel in the great room and absently looked at another pile of catalogs stacked there. He sat on the sofa suddenly and did nothing. It was too much. He couldn't handle eight kids. He couldn't! What if it turned out to be nine? He was only twenty-four. Getting rich was supposed to have made him carefree, gotten him respect, made girls like him, not have gotten him eight kids, an ex-cop, his albino grand-daughter and a frustrated personal manager.

Mirabella came in and patted his shoulder. She had an eight-year-old or so boy by the hand. *This is the new boy,* she thought at him. *He finally came out of the tree. I keep telling him not to be afraid, but he doesn't believe me.* "Oh, and here, this was taped to the box," she said out loud, handing him a now familiar looking envelope. Mark clutched it without opening it, his attention riveted on the child who glared at him, standing in what Mark suddenly realized was only his underwear.

Mark patted the sofa for the boy to come and sit next to him. No effect. The boy stood, watching him, watching very warily.

"What's your name?" Mark asked the child before him.

"Speedy," the boy said suddenly, and the dog barked.

"Speedy? That's your name?" Mark asked, a bit dismayed.

"No, sir. That's my dog's name. Here, Speedy, come."

The dog barked loudly from the porch.

"Let the dog in, Mirabella," Mark instructed.

A short-legged, black Scottish Terrier leaped on the boy, licking his face and hands, and then stood on all fours growling deep in its throat at Mark.

"Okay, now what is *your* name?" Mark asked the boy again, ignoring the little, snarling dog as best he could.

"Samuel," the boy said.

"Where are your clothes, Samuel?" Mark asked.

"In the crate, but they aren't mine. They made a mistake."

"What do you mean?" Mark asked.

"They had me dressed in the wrong costume. I am not Super Boy, but they gave me his red and blue body suit with the red cape. You know the one?"

"Uh huh. So?"

"So, I'm not him. I am Samuel Strong and I've got really strong muscles, but I don't have x-ray vision, and I didn't land on earth in a space ship," the little boy said.

"How did you get here?" Mark asked hopefully.

"You know. I came in the mail."

"Oh," Mark said despondently, as he watched a stringy little boy in his underwear making claims to really big muscles. If he wasn't so upset this would be funny, but he was too tired to laugh.

"See it says, *Samuel Strong, also known as a strong boy*, right there on my tag, and that means I'm strong!" the boy insisted, obviously waiting for a greater show of acceptance than an *oh*.

"I'm sure," Mark said wearily.

At that moment Pete reappeared. "Why is Mirabella still up?"

"She got the boy out of the tree for us," Mark said.

"I can't believe we got another kid! Where's his clothes?"

"They sent me with somebody else's clothes. I'm Samuel Strong, also known to be a very strong boy."

"Who?" Pete asked, looking skeptically at the skinny little kid in front of him. "Look, kid, just put back on whatever clothes you've got and I'll show you where you can sleep."

"No!" Sam said.

Pete grumbled something and then towered over Sam and said, "It's late, kid. I'm tired. I'm also bigger than you, so do what I say!"

In a movement too swift to be seen, Samuel Strong lifted Pete into the air above his little head. Pete made a strangled noise and squirmed as Sam tossed him into the air and caught him again as if he weighed no more than a feather pillow.

"Hey!" Pete exhaled. "Put me down and don't you ever do that to me again."

Sam dropped Pete with a thud. Snarling like his dog, the boy declared, "I'm not putting on those stupid clothes!"

"You nearly gave me a heart attack," Pete complained. "My heart is pounding," he said, stabbing his own chest with a finger.

"I can't hear it," Sam said unsympathetically.

"I'm telling you, it's pounding in there."

"Calm down, Pete," Mark advised.

"Easy for you to say, you weren't just thrown into the air by an eight-year-old!"

Sam stuck his tongue out at Pete, like any eight-year-old might, except this one was Samuel Strong, a very strong boy.

Mark felt his own heartbeat speed up. He couldn't look at the child. It was too much, all of it. He had to get away! He ran out of the house, sprinted to the corner and kept running until he reached a bus. He barely got on before it pulled away. Mark collapsed into a seat and hunched his head into his hands, panting heavily. Another kid, and this one could fly and pick up grown men and had a dog, but no clothes of his own! Enough was enough.

He spent the rest of the night and the next day in a daze, wandering downtown, window-shopping, sitting in the park, trying to think clearly, wandering some more, eating a hot dog without his accustomed mustard. At last, when he realized the light was fading towards dark again, he got on another bus to go home. He leaned his head against a window and closed his eyes. He felt as if someone had wrung him dry of all emotion and left a rag lying on a bus seat.

"Mark!" Lady A said out of nowhere. "You look awful! What on earth are you doing on this bus? Where are the kids?"

"Home. I should look awful! They sent me another kid and this one has a dog!"

"Another? Oh my!"

"It's my doom."

"What's that envelope you have in your hand?"

"Huh? Oh, I found it with the box they delivered Sam . . ." He stopped himself just in time.

"What's in it?"

"Here, you open it," he said. "I don't care what it says, I'm sending the boy back, and the dog."

He heard her tear paper. "It says here that the cyborg wind-up action figure you ordered will be arriving shortly. In fact, it says it is specifically *Castor the Cyborg*."

"No, no, no, no!" Mark groaned and sank into a seat.

"Mark, it's only some toy. What's wrong with you? Come on, let's get off and get some coffee."

She pulled him off the bus, but it wasn't until they were sitting on a little wall with Styrofoam cups of hot coffee in their hands that he looked at her.

"Lady A, you look beautiful," he said, his eyes locked on her. "I've never seen you dressed like that before."

She blushed. Her hair was clipped back with silver barrettes that matched a filigreed necklace hanging tightly against her throat. Her clothes were tailored in navy velvet and fitted perfectly to her body. She was exposed as lithe and willowy, not dumpy at all.

"Where are you going," he asked dully, "dressed like that?"

"To a party at my parents' home," she said, pouting her lip out a little. "And I'll never hear the end of it: 'No man, not even a date, no decent job, no decent house!' It's the same every year."

"Why do you go, then?"

"Obligation? Habit? I'm not even sure. Maybe to prove something, not that I ever do. It's stupid, and just to make this year worse, that creep who has been following me will be there."

"I thought he was gone. Why would he follow you, anyway?"

"Money," she smiled.

"Money? You?" he almost laughed, but didn't have the energy.

"No, not me." She laughed herself. "But my parents are filthy rich, you see, which I try to forget every day of my life. I am their greatest disappointment. All my sisters and brothers are rich and well-heeled. They belong to all the best clubs, have wealthy husbands and wives who are also well heeled, who all look at me like I am a — gee, I don't know what? But they will look at me that way when I appear forlornly unescorted yet again this year." She finally stopped and actually spit onto the sidewalk. "I had a bug in my mouth," she explained before she continued. "That was why I went on that date the other night."

"Because you had a bug in your mouth?"

"Of course not! So I could have an escort for tonight, but I couldn't stomach that guy even for one night, and now I can't get rid of him. He's my father's new wonder boy. Papa is probably egging him on."

"Well, if it's any consolation, Kate and Larry don't approve of me either." He stopped blankly for a moment before he said, "Did I tell you? I'm running away. Things at the house are out of control. Completely out of control!"

"Running away, huh? Well, if you want to see why I've been running away my whole life, just come to my parents' party," Lady A said, and nudged him.

"Are you trying to one-up me?" he asked.

"I don't have to," she said. "I win hands down."

"Want to bet?"

"Sure, but the only way one of us could win is if you come to the party and see for yourself," she laughed.

"Okay, I will come," Mark said.

"Uh, not dressed like that. They wouldn't let you in the door," she said, pointing at his jeans and tee-shirt.

"Fine, come on."

He yanked her down the street to Martin's Haberdashery. When they left, Mark was dressed in high-priced shoes, and a suit, a tie, a shirt and even new socks. The only thing left on him that he had started with was his underwear. The rest of the clothes he'd been wearing were stashed in a brown paper bag.

He hailed a cab and they arrived at the party only fifteen minutes late. The house was huge, enclosed by a gated stone wall. The cab drove down a long drive, surrounded by carefully-tended winter gardens and lined with low, berry-covered hedges.

"Wait, Lady A," he said, and pulled her to a stop just before they entered the house.

"Cold feet, Mark? Afraid of losing the bet?"

"No," he said firmly. "If I'm your date, I think you'd better tell me your first name."

"Oh, yeah. Ashley," she said and grimaced.

"I like it," Mark said. "It's classy."

"Well, I hate it, but thanks," she said.

"Ashley," he murmured as they were greeted just inside the door by an excited elderly woman in a bouffant, orange wig.

Mark leaned over and whispered to Ashley. "La Grande Orange!"

Lady A elbowed him as she said, "Hello, Aunt Margaret."

"Well, well, my dear Ashley, with a good-looking man on your arm!"

Mark repressed an urge to pull the big wig off the lady's head, and smiled politely.

"How long have you and our Ashley been keeping company?" Aunt Margaret asked nosily.

"Serious time? Months now. We spend quite a lot of time together," he said happily.

"Really?"

"Indeed," Mark said, and impulsively added, "after all, we have the children to care for."

"What? Oh dear, oh dear!" Aunt Margaret dithered.

Lady A grabbed his arm and pulled him away as Aunt Margaret rushed through the crowd to a dignified, barrel-chested man.

"How could you lead her on like that?" Lady A whispered.

"It's all true, isn't it?" Mark whispered back.

"Yes, but you made it sound like we're involved!" she said.

"Come on, Ashley, let's have a little fun."

She looked at him for a long moment before she grinned and said, "But no lying."

"Okay, but do we have to correct their misconceptions?" Mark asked as the man came up to them.

"Hello, Papa," Lady A said. "This is my friend, Mark Perralt."

"How-do-you-do, young man?" Papa said, eyeing Mark, sizing him up as they shook hands.

"I'm pleased to meet you, sir. I've been hearing a lot about you. I've been asking Ashley about her name for a long time now. You are Harold P. Anderson, Net magnate, aren't you?"

"Well, well. My little girl finally found someone in the know. Just out of curiosity, what do you do for a living, Mr. Perralt?"

"Work," Mark said, leaving the word in the air all by itself.

"Versus not working?" Papa Anderson asked.

"No, versus parenting," Mark said.

"And where might you work when you aren't parenting?" Mr. Anderson asked.

"For me, Harold," Mr. Cannady, said joining them. "Nice to see you, Mark. I didn't know you knew Miss Anderson."

"Oh, we have known each other for ever so long a time," Ashley said, hanging on Mark's arm. "He's such a sweetie, my Mark."

Simultaneously Mr. Anderson's eyebrows went down and Mr. Cannady's eyebrows went up.

"The children have drawn us together even more," Ashley continued. "It's such a bonding experience, a family."

"What kind of joke is this?" her father asked angrily.

"I thought you wanted me to find a successful man, Papa. Well, I have," she said, dragging Mark off to grab hors d'ouevres that were being passed by blue-garbed servants, as she waved to her father.

"Ashley, let's not go too far here," Mark said, starting to worry about how this all might snowball.

She smiled, reached up and kissed him, not a peck, not briefly, but a long showy kiss, which Mark suddenly found himself returning.

They were quiet for a few minutes afterwards until she finally said, "What agency did the kids come from, anyway?"

"I don't want to talk about the kids right now," he said.

"Come on, Mark. You should make that agency take them back."

"Ashley, you can't really mean that. After all, they brought us together."

"Let's dance. Come on," she said, uncharacteristically not following through on her curiosity.

She really was very lovely, he thought as he led her onto the dance floor. It was a fast dance, but they clung to each other, dancing to their own, slow melody. Mark felt like he was in heaven until Lady A whispered into his ear and reminded him it was all an act. "Are they watching us?"

"I don't know," he admitted, feeling his stomach shrink.

"I forgot to look, too," she admitted and Mark's stomach refilled itself, "but I hope that creep sees us. Maybe he'll finally leave me alone for good."

He didn't want the dance to end, didn't want to let go of the moment, but he knew he would have to. He had misled her about the kids and when she found out she would be furious. Who wouldn't be? He had to tell her the truth now.

"Ashley," he said, "I need to tell you about the kids, but not here, not now."

"Good. I don't want anything to spoil this moment."

They danced every dance the same way until dinner was served. They were seated at a table with two young stockbrokers and their wives.

"So, what do you do?" one of the wives asked Ashley.

"Why she runs Lady Anderson's," Mark said quickly. "I'm sure you've heard of it. All the best for your home. A wonderful place to shop! Give them your card, Ashley," Mark said, helping the game along.

"Oh, please, do come down," Ashley cooed, passing around her canary-yellow business cards.

"I don't recognize the address," one woman said, a perplexed look on her face.

"But you know the name, don't you?" Mark said smugly.

Lady A smiled broadly. "Do visit. I'm sure you'll be surprised at the quality of our goods."

The ladies all nodded and the men said, "Of course." Then one of them asked, "And you, Mark, do you gamble on the market?"

"No, never," Mark said.

"He doesn't play the market, but he does play roles quite well." Ashley smiled sweetly at Mark.

"You're an actor?" one of the women chirped.

"No," Mark said succinctly.

"What exactly do you do?" the first man asked suspiciously.

"The impossible," he said happily. "I work for Cannady's. Do you know the company?"

"You aren't Mark Perralt, are you?" one of them asked. "Cannady's secret weapon?"

"Not so secret, apparently." Mark almost groaned.

"Give us a tip," the other man said conspiratorially. "Really, what should we know?"

"Toys," slipped out of Mark's mouth. "Real toys, not computer games," he continued before he could stop himself, which also reminded him he should call the house. "Could you all excuse me for a moment? I need to make a call."

"Where are you, Mark?" Pete demanded. "I didn't know whether to be angry or worried about you."

"I'm having some fun."

"That's great, as long as you come back," Pete said.

"I'll be back. How are things?"

"Fine for the moment. Traxon is showing them how to play Stand-Forward or some such. Claims it's a game from Ardromini. Anyway, they're all playing. When will you be home?"

"When this party I'm at is over. Right now I'm having a grand time. Say goodnight to everyone for me, and a goodnight and thank you to you, too, Pete."

ROBOTA & AUTOMATA

KITS
With easy, clear instructions!
All tools included.

Special computer chips for:
Voice Intonation
Languages
Task Instruction
Skills
and
Moral Values

Robot Roller, 1950's, tin, extendable arms, wind-up key action, rare ....235.

Andrea Automata, e.21st c., realistic plastic skin, charming southern accent, solar powered ....350.

House Hold Harold, scarce, designed to clean homes, includes vacuum extension, brush tools ....645.

Superbot,19th c., limited edition, no special features, requires imagination.......................................200.

Intellibot, 21st c., excellent tutor, speaks 7 languages, 25 dictionaries in its memory banks................400.

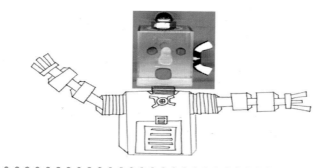

Mr. Cannady left the party with his wife as Mark and Ashley said their good-byes.

"It was a pleasure to see you, Miss Anderson. I hope to see you at Mark's party next week," he said.

"Well, if he invites me, Mr. Cannady, I suppose I might come," she said, pretending to having her feelings a bit hurt.

"Don't blame him. I was responsible for the guest list. Of course, Mark hadn't told me he had a serious other, but please do join us."

Lady A laughed gleefully as they walked slowly towards the bus. "Serious other?"

"Right," Mark agreed. "Silly! But now it's your turn to help me out. Be my date next week."

"Fair is fair, I suppose. So are you going home now?" she asked.

"Where else can I go? You don't know of any more parties, do you?"

"No, that was bad enough!"

"I had fun," Mark admitted. "I like putting people on."

She laughed. "And you're teaching the kids that skill, I noticed."

"What?" he said. He had no idea what she was talking about.

"The kids. The things they claim!"

"Uh, like what?" he said, feeling uncomfortable about where this was going.

"Oh, you know. This one is from outer space, that one is an elf, this one can fly."

"Fly? You know about him already?"

"Him? I meant Ailithe. None of the boys have claimed such a thing. Who are you talking about?"

"Oh, did I say him? I meant her," he said quickly.

"Mark, this is serious! Their imaginations are out of control. You need to teach them to tell the truth, and I think Elflet needs to be called by his real name."

"Thanks for telling me," Mark said.

"When they go to school, their teachers won't tolerate that stuff. You shouldn't either. It's unhealthy."

"Lady A, I mean Ashley, what is reality, anyway?"

"What? You want to talk philosophy? Forget it!"

"Oh, come on, Ashley. What are you afraid of?"

"You like challenges," she pointed out.

"So do you. I'm just throwing down the gauntlet. Now then, what is reality?"

"Come on, Mark, it is what is!"

"But how do you tell what is?"

"It's what you know for sure," she said impatiently. "What kind of game are you playing now?"

He stared at her for a moment before he said, "Your father, doesn't he base his life on a different perception of reality than you do? The way you've chosen to live your life is very different from the choices he's made."

"That's obvious. My father thinks people are happy when they're rich, and pitiful when they're poor."

"But you don't? To you that's unrealistic?"

"I don't think money buys everything," she replied.

"I think you're right, but he thinks you're wrong. You felt so strongly about your beliefs, you rejected your family's way of life. You wanted a different reality."

"My father wanted me to go to the same schools he had, to go into the same business, to be just like him, and I didn't want to. It was that simple. I left. And that was the one thing that was real, very, very real for both of us. But what does this have to do with the kids?"

"It galls your father that he can't control you. It shakes his faith in himself, doesn't it? He can't stand that you live on the edge of what rules his reality: poverty versus wealth. His world doesn't allow for shades of grey, but we know better because you and I have lived in both worlds."

"Yes," she said softly, "and I like the world I've chosen. It's familiar, comfortable, close to everyday people."

"But as sure as you are that you're right, your father is equally sure you're wrong. Well, have you considered that what the kids tell you might be their reality? And comfortable and familiar?"

"No, absolutely not. What they believe is impossible. Mark, Mirabella claims she can read minds!"

"Yes, I know."

"You know? You know and you don't do anything? You don't try and set her straight?"

"But, my Lady Anderson, if I did that, I would be just like your father."

"Mark, that is outrageous! It's a completely different situation. My father's problem is his set of values, not his sense of reality."

"But, Ashley, values make our realities. I think what I need to teach the kids is how to behave in public." He sighed. "But I'm afraid that's more easily said than done."

"Mark," Ashley said, suspicion creeping into her voice, "do you believe them?"

"My stop," Mark said cheerfully, avoiding an answer.

"Mark Perralt, you didn't answer me," she said angrily.

"Got to go. See you!" he said and started for the door.

"Oh, no you don't," she said, and in her hurry to catch him tripped off the bus into his arms.

"Hmmm, good catch I made," he said and set her on her feet.

She sputtered and pushed him away.

"The bus is gone! You made me miss the last bus home!" she yelled at him and pushed him again, this time with the palms of both hands. "You and your amateur philosophizing!"

"Sorry. Come back to the house with me for tea and cookies and I'll take you home later," he said.

"I don't have much choice now, do I?" she said angrily.

They were halfway home when he tentatively reached for her hand. She let him take it and he felt a juvenile thrill course through him.

"Maybe, just maybe, Mr. Cannady's assumption wasn't so silly," Mark said. "You could do a lot worse than a crazy, well-to-do individualist working for a money-grubbing corporation!"

"Yeah, but I could do better, too," she said, and took her hand back out of his. "You're reading too much into this."

They were at the house by then. It was two in the morning and every light was blazing out of the windows, casting hollow spaces onto the dark lawn where the light didn't fall.

"What the?" Mark said, racing up the porch steps, pushing past the boxes now shoved to one side.

He almost crashed through the door when it opened unexpectedly. Mirabella was waiting nervously.

"Do not panic," she said. "It's only a small glitch. The rest of your order came, but we, uh, well, it uh, appears to be, uh, deactivated."

"Dead," Elflet said from just behind her.

"What?" Mark said, racing into the great room. "Where is it? Where's the order?"

Fiona pointed up.

Mark dashed up the stairs, with Elflet, Fiona, Mirabella and Ashley on his heels. A boy was laid out on Jack's bed, corpse-like, his arms crossed rigidly on his chest, his head held stiffly, face straight up. Below the waist to the ankles, his body was still encased in packing cardboard. The skin on his hands and feet was pewter-finished, the nails on his toes and finger-tips golden.

"What is that?" Ashley asked.

"Castor," Mirabella answered quickly.

"I didn't ask who. I said *what* is it?"

"Oh," Traxon piped up, "a cyborg. He was delivered this afternoon."

Mark pulled the cardboard off the boy. The body beneath was naked, seamless, a single smooth sheet of pewter-colored skin.

"That's no toy. You ordered a wind-up toy cyborg, not that! What is that?" Lady A said again, pointing stubbornly.

"Castor," Paul repeated.

Lady A gave Paul a nasty stare.

"He's dead," Paul said somberly.

"You can't kill a cyborg that easily," Traxon pointed out. "We just can't activate him."

"Poor kid," Pete said.

"Where's his tag?" Mark asked.

"Tag?" Lady A said. "Tag? You mean one of those stupid things you hung on all their arms?"

"I'll look for it," Jack said as everyone ignored her question. "Come on, Rollo."

The boys ran off, thumping down the stairs. Mark heard them open the front door. Presumably they were looking through the crate Castor had been delivered in.

Lady A grabbed his shoulder and swung him towards her. "Mark Perralt, look at my lips." Speaking very clearly and slowly, she demanded an answer. "What is going on here?"

"It's a very long story, and I don't have time right now," Mark said, just as Rollo ran in with a tag clutched in his hand.

"It says to activate within eight hours of delivery!" he shouted.

Mark grabbed the tag, but half of it was missing. "How? It doesn't say how! It's missing that part. Look for a switch or a button or something. How long has he been here?" he asked Pete.

"We found him right after you called. That was about six hours ago," Pete said.

"Six hours! But you aren't sure when he actually came. Come on. Think. Ashley, help. Pete? What do we do?"

Pete shook his head, and Ashley stared at him like he was crazy.

"Button?" Paul said and poked the stiff boy with his pudgy thumb where a belly button should have been. "No belly button?" the little boy said quizzically.

No, but Mark heard a tiny click and Castor's eyes fluttered open.

"Good going, Paul," Jack said, giving the littler boy a bear hug and lifting him off the floor.

"Put me down," Paul protested.

"Hello," Mark said to Castor. "How are you?"

"Stiff, confused," a soft voice answered.

"Sorry. The directions for activating you were torn off."

The boy-cyborg sat up, straight from the waist, as if hinged. Maybe he was hinged.

"Would you like some clothes?" Fiona thought to ask.

"Yes, thank you," Castor said.

Mark noticed that his mouth was moist and pink. A human mouth, not the mouth of a machine.

"Do you bleed?" He hadn't intended to voice what had crossed his mind at the sight of Castor's mouth. "I mean, if you're a cyborg. . . ?" He stammered in the confusion of the moment compounded by the whole day. "What I meant to say was, you look like a regular boy, but cyborgs are part machine and I wondered which part . . ." He let the sentence trail off. He was still managing to say all the wrong things, but couldn't seem to put it right.

The boy picked up a pair of scissors and just as Lady A and Fiona screamed, stabbed his leg with them.

"No, no blood," the boy said, calmly observing his own leg.

"But you cry," Mark said, pointing out the tears running down Castor's cheeks.

The boy wiped at the watery drips. "Perhaps I should turn off my emotional circuitry," he said, "but I don't remember how."

"I don't think you can anymore, turn it off," Mirabella said. "We've all changed since we arrived here."

"From what? Changed from what?" Pete seized the opportunity to ask her.

"I don't remember," Mirabella said. "Just changed."

Mark, too, had changed since the children had arrived and he wasn't sure how, either. He had always been eccentric, that was a given, but the children had changed him in a new way. His reason had been overturned and he had easily accepted impossibilities as realities. The whole series of events was more like one of the games he had played silently, had silently acted out as a child, only in reverse. Now, they were reality and his other life a hoax. He had known his games weren't true, but had loved indulging in them privately. He had almost forgotten them, almost forgotten lying under trees and staring up into their branches, imagining anthropomorphic animals of immense proportions and power protecting him from evils he could just sense at the edge of his imagination. Slowly he had left the stories behind, outgrown them, buried the memories of them under new realities, until suddenly, impossibly, characters he would have once absolutely known were make-believe were in his house. Only make-believe was real now, and instead of being protected, he found himself in the role of protector.

Castor blew his nose loudly. "I wish they had left out the body-functions when they made me," he said seriously. "These nose blowings and cryings are such a nuisance."

Lady A was looking around the room, her eyes narrowed, her fingers drumming in impatience on the bed post. "Mark, what on earth is going on?"

He expelled a huge sigh. There was nothing for it now but to explain, if he could. He had no idea where the kids really came from. He had tried to apply logic to an illogical situation. He had hired an investigator, tried to trace the catalogs and shipping invoices. All to no avail. None. So what could he tell her?

Another sigh escaped him. "I'll do my best to explain, but my best isn't much." What else could he say?

Ashley laughed at him. "Come now, Mark, I'm sure you can explain how you trained these kids to be such good actors, but what I can't understand is why you would bother to do something like this."

"I didn't train the kids. I ordered them from the catalogs, they came, they weren't toys and that is all I know about their backgrounds, except that they're all versions of story characters. I wish I could explain it away to you, or for that matter, I could explain it at all," he said.

"Oh, come on! I knew you were smart, but not this smart. How'd you manage to pull off such a convoluted hoax? How much money did you invest in this prank?"

"Me? Why would I pull this hoax? On whom? I'm a victim here, Ashley."

"Right! And I suppose you don't have any idea how Traxon's toy works. I suppose you haven't thought to have someone analyze it, have you?"

"Ashley, I don't think he has a toy. I think it's all biological."

"What? Oh, okay, then take him to a doctor. That's a good idea. A doctor. Take them all. A doctor will tell you just how nuts you are," she said, hopping up out of the chair she had been anxiously fidgeting about in. "I'll call for appointments. Nine appointments."

"Ashley," he said, grabbing her arm. "This is not a trick, unless it's been played on me. The doctor isn't going to tell me what you want to hear. He can't. There is no logical explanation for what is going on."

She stopped, and shoved his hand away. "Let go. Everything, Mark, has a logical explanation. Everything."

"Ashley, listen to me. Please. Trust me, believe me."

"You want me to believe you? To trust you? Call a doctor tomorrow."

"I can't. I don't know what would happen if the doctor exposed the kids for what they really are," he said sadly.

"And what would that be? Come on, I want to hear this."

"I don't know, exactly, not yet. I'm working on it.

"Sure," she said. "Sure."

She slammed out of the house, her fancy party shoes snapping on the steps as she went down them quickly. He watched her go from the door. He thought he could hear her sobbing, but he wasn't sure. Or maybe she cried when she was mad or frustrated.

Suddenly, he was running after her, calling her name. He didn't want to lose her like this. He stopped. Nothing. Not a sound, not a word. She had vanished.

"Ashley, where are you?" he called.

Still nothing, but at the end of the street, a shiny cab pulled away and he thought he saw her face looking back at him.

PLAY STRUCTURES

ORDER THIS CUSTOM BUILT GINGERBREAD HOUSE

Cost appraisals based on materials selected.

When kids outgrow this delicious play house, no disposal required.
Just eat it!!
[Expiration date can be found on back of chimney.]

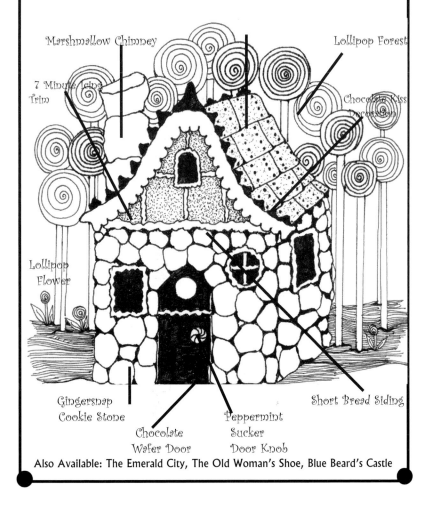

Marshmallow Chimney

Lollipop Forest

7 Minute Icing Trim

Chocolate Kiss Decoration

Lollipop Flower

Gingersnap Cookie Stone

Chocolate Wafer Door

Peppermint Sucker Door Knob

Short Bread Siding

Also Available: The Emerald City, The Old Woman's Shoe, Blue Beard's Castle

Someone was hammering on the door. Mark rubbed his eyes, trying to wake up. The banging grew louder. "Come on, Markham, open the door!" Elliot yelled.

He stumbled to the door and threw it open. Elliot practically fell over the door sill.

"What did you do last night?" Elliot demanded.

"What are you talking about?" Mark asked, bewildered.

"How could you get involved with Anderson's daughter? He is Cannady & Company's arch rival. There are rules against such things, and for good reasons."

"Like what?"

"Number one, it could give Anderson a chance to find out about, and to steal, our clients."

He laughed at the irony of Elliot's fears. "I promise you, Lady A is not a spy for her father!"

"Markham, this is serious. This is a very incestuous business. You've made a major mistake."

"Well, relax. We broke up."

"What? Wait, wait, wait! You can't do that."

"Now you wait, wait, wait, Elliot. I can, and I have, and you and Mr. Cannady have nothing to do with it or to say about it. Besides, I thought you just said you didn't want me to be involved with her."

"Anderson will be after Cannady's so fast you won't be able to blink if he thinks you dumped his daughter. We won't even feel the pain, it will be so quick." Elliot moaned, as he slit his finger across his throat.

"Not to worry, Elliot. She dumped me," Mark said, feeling a little gloomy at the thought. Actually, she had stopped the relationship before it had really gotten started. "Anything else, or are you finished?"

"Oh, there's more. A whole list. You've been coming to work disheveled, your suits hanging oddly, your shirts crinkled," Elliot complained.

I've lost weight, Mark thought.

"Your hair is too long."

I'm growing it, Mark thought.

"You've taken too many sick days."

I'm sick to death of that place, Mark said silently.

"The first meeting about the new toy you're working on is Friday of next week and you aren't ready, are you?"

I guess I've blown this one. Mark smiled to himself.

"Your party is Saturday."

"Saturday?" Mark said out loud. *"This* Saturday?"

"I figured you had forgotten. And from the look of things, you aren't going to have the house ready," Elliot said. "Markham, are you trying to get fired?"

Mark sat down and put his head in his hands. "I don't know," he said truthfully.

"Markham, you are dependent on this job. You've bought a house, you've got a new car, new furniture, new clothes. You need this job."

"That was all stuff the company thought I should have, not me," Mark said.

"You haven't saved any money, have you?" Elliot half-asked, half-stated expectantly.

"Some."

Actually it was a lot. He couldn't spend it all even when he tried, but Elliot chose to interpret his *some* to mean not really.

"See, you do need this job. You have responsibilities," Elliot continued his lecture.

"You could say that, yes," Mark said, thinking of the kids.

"To the firm," Elliot said.

Mark laughed. "To nine children," he said in a chortle. "And the company should be grateful, or maybe I would quit."

"Nine? Nine!! How did it get to be nine?" Elliot yelped.

"It is a long, long, story," Mark said.

"Send them back!"

"No," Mark said.

"Why not?" Elliot asked as he pulled on the hair at the nape of his neck.

"Don't do that, Elliot. You'll pull out all your hair."

"You're changing the subject."

"No, I'm just finished with the previous topic. I am not sending any of the kids back. Now then, about the party . . . "

"If you won't return them to the foster care agency they came from," Elliot said stubbornly, "will you at least make sure they aren't in the house during the party? Send them somewhere. You can't afford to have them ruin the affair."

Mark knew that was a reasonable request, probably a good idea, but where was he going to send them?

We could spend the night in the play house, said a voice in his head that he knew was Mirabella's.

Do you always have to listen in? he asked back without speaking.

No answer.

"Okay, I've thought of a place I can send them for the night," he replied out loud to Elliot.

"Good, good. Now then, the caterers will arrive at five and the party starts at seven-thirty. I've made a schedule for you and a list of what you need to do," Elliot said. "I sent it to your computer, so print it out."

"Lists, lists, lists! Yes, Elliot, I will read your lists. Truly, I will, because I never ignore your lists," Mark said.

Elliot gave a little snort. "I haven't really noticed that, but seriously, Markham, the rumors are growing about how long Cannady will put up with you. Perhaps you are too unpredictable for the firm. That's what is circulating."

"But that's my brilliance, isn't it?" Mark smiled broadly.

"Probably. I'll see you tomorrow," Elliot said. Mark thought he heard him add, "Unfortunately."

Too imaginative might have been a better word than unpredictable. Maybe that was worse. Imagination was almost a curse word. Dreamer. Loon. Nut-case. He had heard all those names slung at him like bullets on the playground, until he had finally subdued his imagination and turned his mind to facts and technology and practicality. But, apparently, imagination wasn't something that could be purged that easily. It had emerged again after high school and led him to be a fix-it man. Until the reunion. Then he had tried to subdue it again with this job, but no, it was still a problem. He shook his head, trying to break his own train of thought.

He looked around in an attempt to change the path his mind was on by concentrating on the party, but before he could stop himself, he was back on the same track. He had gone to Cannady's to show the world he wasn't a freak and a failure, and just when it looked like he might succeed, along came the kids. It wasn't fair, but the kids had exposed the truth. He could not resist his own drive to create. Elliot viewed his work at Cannady's as unpredictable, but that was a farce. At places like Cannady & Company or Anderson, Incorporated, they pretended to want unique products, but only if they were easy to recognize and easy to market. If someone actually hit the jackpot with a truly new idea, every company that could slapped its own label on the product, stuffed it into new packaging and flooded the market with it, until it was just another of many.

Once, Mark had bought seven disk players. He had taken them out of the packages and for his science fair project, measured the quality of their sound, their reliability, et cetera. They had all come out the same. He took the innards out of the machines and examined them, too. They were all identical. The only difference was in the pricing and packaging. He had titled his project *The Great Sameness Scam*.

He plucked a few catalogs off the floor and dumped them on his bed. He thumbed through them. The catalogs were out of character with the commercial world. He had yet to find two identical products advertised in any of them.

He picked up another one of them and fingered its cover. They were cleverly constructed, some with pages getting progressively smaller, others with fold-outs, fold-downs, pop-ups. Some had card covers, some soft paper. One even folded out into a poster, while another was made up of lots of little books bound into a bigger one. For the first time he realized the beauty in their variety.

He sat back into the pillow on his bed and thought, and slowly silence crept into his mind. It was too quiet. Where were the kids? He dropped the catalog in his hands and darted up the steps. They were all together in Fiona's and Mirabella's room, each one doing something: playing cards, drawing, or in Paul's case, eating.

"What's going on, guys?" Mark asked.

"We're practicing," Elflet said, "to show you how quiet we can be during your party, so you won't send us back."

"I will never send you back. Not ever!" He paused. "Would you guys like to have your own party out in the play house Saturday night?

I'll buy you each a sleeping bag and you can pick what you want to have to eat, too."

"Food?" Rollo asked.

"Food," Paul said.

"Yeah," Jack said. "That'd be so cool!"

Nine heads nodded up and down.

CLASSICS

"**A**shley Anderson? This is Elflet, please come back tomorrow," Mark heard the little boy say.

He peeked around the corner and saw the child on the phone.

"We need you! Please," Elflet pleaded.

Mark took the phone from the little boy and said into the receiver, "Ashley, please listen to me! Just let me talk to you."

She hung up. Mark gave the phone back to Elflet. Pete was watching *Sports Arena Side* on television with Jack and Traxon. Paul was napping in Pete's lap as the show droned on and on. Mark wandered outdoors. Nobody was out. He could tell when the show was airing: no traffic, no lawn tenders, no noise outside.

Mark stepped back into the house and called, "Watch the kids for me, Pete. I have to go out. When I get back, we need to talk."

"Sure, sure," Pete said, his eyes never leaving the screen.

Mark drove down the rutted road that led to Lady Anderson's. It was unlikely she'd have many clients while the sports shows were on.

The shop was deserted, so he rang the bell and when she came into the front of the store, he launched in instantly, talking as rapidly as he could.

"I don't have many friends, Ashley. I don't want to lose you. Please, please, let me explain about the children."

"It's easy to see why you don't have friends and, particularly, why you don't have a girl friend."

"Ashley, I truly want to explain what is happening, and I know it sounds crazy, but I really did order toys from the catalogs and got children instead. And even if I wanted to, I have no idea who to return the kids to."

"You could trace them through their universal ID's," Ashley said.

"They didn't have ID's."

"Give me a break, Mark. You need help. I checked the computer registry and the kids all have identity papers."

"That's good," he said, afraid to tell her they were forged.

"So, you were and are still lying to me?"

"No, no. I am not lying. It's hard to explain."

She waited.

"Okay." He paused. "Pete and I forged the papers for their ID's. We had to. In fact, you were the one who made me realize that when you wanted to register them for school. Remember?"

"So now you want to make me responsible for your insanity?"

"No, no. Look, I hired Pete to help me track down where the kids came from and when he couldn't, I paid him a lot of money to help me forge those papers. I originally wanted to send the kids back, all of them. Now I just want to know where on earth they came from."

"That's it? That's your whole story? You, the great genius, Markham Perralt, couldn't come up with anything better than that? Come on! Admit it, they are everyday children who happen to be just a little quirky, but we both know they didn't suddenly step out of the pages of a story book. As to papers, no one can forge fake ID's without setting off some serious alarm systems. So stop the lies! All I want from you is an explanation of why you would pull this hoax? What's the point?"

"Okay, okay, forget about the papers for the moment. Concentrate on the kids. How do you explain what they can do?"

"It's a trick of some sort!"

"Ashley, try, for a few moments, to accept that they arrived on my front porch in crates and boxes after I put in an order for toys of similar descriptions from some of the catalogs. Ask them and they'll tell you they have no memories of anything prior to being in those crates. What explanation do you have for that?"

"Just leave me alone! Stop trying to perpetuate this bizarre gag." She scowled and threw her hands in the air.

He waited without saying a word.

Finally, grumbling under her breath she said, "You are incredibly frustrating. Okay, here is a neat little explanation that makes as much sense as what you're trying to sell me."

"Good, I need an alternative."

She almost snorted as she said, "There's an evil magician out there who cursed you because you're so weird!"

He smiled. "I actually considered that myself."

"Yeah, really? And you discarded it for the baloney you just tried to sell me?"

He lifted his shoulders and let them drop in defeat. "What can I say? We've been trying to solve this for weeks. No luck so far."

She cocked her head at him and said, "What's the rest of it? There's more, isn't there? Come on, just spit it out."

"A bit. Not that it will make you feel better. Someone has been sending the catalogs out for the last fifty-two years. And these mysterious entrepreneurs, whoever they are, have found a foolproof way not to be traced by anyone."

"How is that possible?"

"I don't know."

"So you're claiming to be an innocent in all this?"

"That's right."

She made an odd noise in her throat and stomped into the other room. He almost followed her, but stopped. What was the point? He wasn't convincing her of anything.

"Ashley, do you think my house could be the only one that gets these catalogs?" Mark called after her, hoping to prevent the conversation from dying.

"I'm sure they are delivered somewhere else," Ashley said, sticking her head through the doorway, "but what kind of kook would order any of the junk in them?"

He pointed to himself.

"Even if someone else has ordered from them, do you think they would admit it? I doubt it," she said.

"Okay, so I ordered what most people would think was junk. But I didn't get what I ordered. I got nine, living, breathing kids. What am I supposed to do with them? Hide them in the playhouse, lock them in the towers?"

"Right, nine children! You got nine children instead of toys! You are really pushing it," Ashley said angrily. "You claim the kids have counterparts in stories?"

"Yes, that's what it looks like."

"Then why haven't I ever heard of a Rollo Wiz or a Sam Strong? I'll tell you why, because there aren't any such characters. You should have kept it simple, instead of tangling yourself up in such complex lies."

"Look, before the kids came, I found an old Mother Goose book. I loved nursery rhymes when I was little, but do you know any children who are still familiar with them?"

"No, I don't," she said crossing her arms across her chest, clearly humoring him, "but then, I don't know any nursery rhymes, either."

"That's what I thought, but it doesn't mean that they never existed, just that they're almost forgotten. I'll show you the book and then maybe you'll believe me."

She shook her head. "You're crazy, you know."

"It may sound that way, but please Ashley, don't leave us. The kids need you. I need you. Don't desert us," he begged. "Maybe the kids aren't who I think, maybe I am just going insane, but what if I'm not nuts? Then what? Aren't you even a little curious? You can't deny that the kids are peculiar, can you?"

Shaking her head, she said, "Okay, I must be crazy, too, but I'm only coming until you can find someone else. By the way, call me Lady A, not Ashley. It turns out I don't know you well enough, after all."

"Oh, one more thing," he said sheepishly. "Are you still my date for the party?"

She hissed through her teeth. "A promise is a promise. I'll be there for that, too."

It made him feel ecstatic that she was coming back. On the way home, he stopped at the Book Stop. A prim, thirty-year-old woman was tending the store. She glanced at him and went back to her paperwork as she said, "Can I help you?"

"I hope so. I want to buy every book you have on fairy tales, myths, legends, fables, nursery rhymes and the like, as well as all the old storybooks and anything you can find on superheroes!" He expelled it all in a rush and waited for a response.

The woman looked up very slowly and gave him a hard, skeptical stare. "That would be quite expensive," she finally said in a controlled voice.

"I realize that. You gather the books and I'll be back later to pick them up with cash in hand, if that's acceptable?"

"I am unsure how much we can provide you with." The woman's voice was icy.

"I want whatever you have, and here, I'll give you a deposit to reserve whatever you acquire in the future. How much would you like for that?" Mark asked.

"I have no idea," the woman said.

"Perhaps five-hundred?" Mark suggested, not looking at the woman's face, guessing the dismay he would see etched there.

"Why on earth do you want such junk?" the woman asked, with ineffable disdain.

Mark ignored the question as he scooted out the door, calling out, "I'll be back this afternoon."

He wasted an hour looking at dishes and finally chose a very plain service for sixteen of pale blues edged in even paler blue with cats in the middle. Then he went to the flower shop and ordered a bouquet of lavender and pink orchids to be delivered to Ashley at the house the next morning after he had left. He regretted that he didn't think she was the yellow and red type.

He had lunch at a small restaurant near his bank, sipping tea and eating a delicious lobster salad that he never would have been able to afford before he had taken his new job. He went to the bank and withdrew a sizeable sum of cash and headed back to the Book Stop. It was getting late and the sun already hung low in the sky. Across the street from the store, two cops were munching on sandwiches and gingerly sipping from thermos tops that sent spirals of steam into the air as they leaned lazily against an out-of-use traffic light.

He ducked into the shop. The woman looked up at him without a smile and barely a greeting.

"Ready?" she asked. "There is what I found."

There were five medium sized boxes neatly taped shut and stacked in a corner.

"That's great," he said. "How much?"

"Fifteen hundred," she said, eyeing him.

"Fine," Mark said and counted out the bills.

"If you like, you can use the dolly, there, to take them to your car," the woman offered a little more generously as she put the bills away.

"Thanks," Mark said, piling the boxes onto the dolly and trundling them out to his car. He hefted in three boxes and reached for a fourth.

"Need some help, mister?" one of the cops asked, lifting the box into the trunk.

"Thanks, but I'm okay," Mark said. He felt the hair rise on his neck. Police were rarely friendly to him.

"You bought a lot of books?" the cop asked.

"I'm working on a project for my company," Mark said quickly.

"You got a company-type car here," the cop said with a wave of his hand, "but you don't look very company."

"It's my day off," Mark said. "Is there some problem?"

"Mind telling me the name of the company you work for, mister?"

"Cannady & Company. You can call this number to verify that." Mark scribbled the office phone number on a scrap of paper.

"Yeah? Why don't you just tell me what project you're working on instead?"

"Pardon me? Mr. Cannady would fire me instantly if I gave out that information."

"Yeah? Well, not answering could get you arrested."

"Are you threatening me?" Mark asked nervously.

The cop didn't answer. Instead he put the last box into Mark's car before saying, "You know, mister, you shouldn't go around forcing people to sell you books they don't wanna sell! That's called harassment and it ain't legal."

"What?" he asked dismayed. "I didn't force her to sell me anything. She was happy to take my money."

"That ain't what the lady says. Stay away from her, got it?" the cop said boldly and walked away.

Mark hopped into his car and sat there a minute. The woman had called the police about him, had lied to them about him. His hands were shaking so badly, he wasn't sure he could drive. Why had she reported him, what had he done? She hadn't objected when he had asked for the books. He had paid her. He wasn't doing anything illegal, to his knowledge. Suddenly he was mad instead of frightened. He stepped on the gas and took off.

What was going on? All he had done was buy a bunch of old books. It didn't make any sense. He left the books in his car and walked unsteadily into the house.

"Hey, what's wrong with you?" Pete asked as soon as he saw him.

"You were a cop, Pete. Is there a law that would prohibit me from buying old books?"

"None I know. What kinda old books didya buy?" Pete asked.

"Fables, storybooks, nursery rhymes, that kind of thing."

"Nope, no law against it," Pete said.

"They're only children's books, for goodness sake!" Mark protested, still angry and confused.

"That's all."

"Then why? Why did the sales lady sic the cops on me?"

Pete rolled his eyes. "Look here, bud. You go into this store and flash a wad of money, right?"

"What's wrong with that?"

"Nothing, except, it's a bookstore. People don't buy many books no more. So here you come with all that money. It attracts this lady's attention. She probably squints at you, like so?" Pete tipped his head and bunched his eyebrows together.

"Sort of, like that," Mark admitted.

"So you got her attention 'cause she don't get many big spenders in her store. She's almost licking her lips and then you go and say you want books on certain stuff that makes her nervous."

"Certain stuff? Pete, that *stuff* is eating my food, and messing up my house and playing in my backyard!"

"I know that, but she don't. She musta wondered why you'd want kids' books. You don't look old enough to have kids. Makes her even more nervous. Besides, she might not have the books you want and she wants that money. She feels thwarted, angry. Still, she's drooling over the cash you undoubtedly plunked down on the counter, knowing you. She don't wanna lose it, and she don't want you coming back after she gets it from you neither 'cause she doesn't like the kinda books you want. Only weirdos want stuff like that."

"*Stuff* again?" Mark remarked.

"Uh huh, that's right. Stuff. So, she calls the cops in, claims you're harassing her and just to be absolutely sure you won't be back, pays them to scare you off."

"Why didn't you warn me, Pete?"

"'Cause I didn't think you'd go buy up everything you could find about the topic and make a spectacle of yourself," Pete pointed out rather calmly. "I mean, you're the one that keeps talking about discretion. What'd the cops say to you, anyways?"

"They warned me off from coming back."

"See, it fits. I don't think we need to worry too much if that was all. Cops nowadays are a little bored. They gotta make their lives interesting and this lady went and paid them to do it." Pete smiled, trying to reassure him.

"It was only some innocent books," Mark said sadly.

"I know. Go figure!"

"It was only some books," Mark repeated inconsolably.

"Mark, I'm gonna tell you a story. My grandpop was a little eccentric, see. He used to harangue my mom and pop 'bout how my brother and me oughta be reading more. My brother and me would listen to them argue, but we couldn't figure out what they were talking about back then."

"So, what has that got to do with what happened today?"

"You ever heard of *Grimm's Fairy Tales* or *Aladdin and his Wonderful Lamp* or *Hansel and Gretel* or *Robin Hood*?"

"Robin Hood is for sale in one of the catalogs."

"How 'bout King Arthur, or Ichabod Crane or anyone from *The Ramayana Tales*, are they in the catalogs?"

"I'm impressed. I never would have guessed you were so well read."

"Why, 'cause I talk uneducated?" He grinned. "Anyways, my grandpop finally got so mad at Mom and Pop, he decided to read what he called 'real' books to me and my brother. Whenever we were coming over to his house, he'd go to the library and come home with a big stacka books to read to us, or he'd buy up a stacka old comics. We made fun of it at first, then looked forward to it and finally loved it. He was a stubborn old man, my grandpop."

"So he was right?"

"Yeah, we came to love those books so much we still got them from the school library after he died. Our buddies laughed at us, so we hid the books in our backpacks and only read 'em at home, but we read 'em. Until the day we went to get books, and the shelf marked Myths and Legends was bare. So was the one labeled Classics. *The Count of Monte Cristo, The Knights of the Round Table, The Last of the Mohicans*. All gone. We thought they musta been stolen, but the librarian was perfectly calm. She'd purged them over a long weekend. We yelled at her. She said they needed the space for more computers.

We yelled some more. She said no one read those books. 'What about us?' we screamed. She sent us to the principal. You know what he said? I never forgot. I remember his exact words. 'It's better if you boys just forget about all those books. Nobody needs them anymore.'"

Suddenly, as if a recording had come on in Mark's mind, he could hear a chant. His auditory memory was playing back his father's voice. *"Ev'ry giant now is dead—Jack has cut off ev'ry head. Ev'ry goblin known of old, Perished years ago, I'm told. Ev'ry witch on broomstick riding, Has been burned, or is in hiding. Ev'ry dragon seeking gore, Died an age ago or more,"* his father chanted. "L. Frank Baum wrote that, Markie. Will you remember it?"

"I promise, Daddy."

Pete's voice reached him from down a long tunnel, interrupting the memory.

"What gave you the idea to go looking for all these books, anyway, Mark? How'd a kid your age know about them?"

"When I was about eight, I found a bunch of books hidden in the attic. I sneaked them out one at a time and read them under the covers with a flashlight."

"Lotsa kids do that," Pete said.

"One day Kate must have tattled to Mom because when I went back to the attic, all the books were gone. My mom had thrown them out. Then the other day I saw Tarzan in a catalog. I had read *Tarzan of the Apes* three times in that year I was eight, and here was Tarzan, so I wondered if I might find some more leads to the kids in books. I didn't know where else to start. I couldn't think what else to do. And I thought maybe I could prove something to Ashley, too."

"Yeah, well, it wasn't such a good idea."

"Now what, Pete? Where are we going to find what we need to know?" Mark asked.

"I dunno."

He couldn't think of anything else to say. "I've got a headache, Pete. Could you get the books out of the car?" Mark asked.

Pete came back in a few moments and plunked the boxes in front of Mark. He snapped the tape apart and started pulling out volumes. "Will you look at these titles? *Giovanni, Bard of Larimore, Under the*

Flame Trees of Bangkok, Tracing The History of the 57th Congress!
How about a trashy romance? Here's an Almanac, thirty years out of
date and a college textbook on a long-lost computer language." Pete
screwed up his face and suddenly erupted into laughter. "That lady
sure stuck you with a whole lotta junk! You only got eight or nine
kid's books in the lot. She got you good, Mark!" he said, trying hard
not to chuckle.

Mark laid his head in his hands and groaned. He looked up and
he frowned. "Now I am mad. Put all the books, except for the kids'
titles, back and seal the boxes up. Then get Traxon down here." A
red fury swam in his head.

"Whatcha thinking about? I don't wantcha to do nothing rash here,"
Pete said.

"So I won't tell you my plan. What you don't know can't hurt you."

"Mark, that was the motto of the book banners."

"Well, that is ironic. Go get Traxon," Mark said again.

Pete left shaking his head and muttering about how he should
have stayed a solo operation.

Mark washed his face, combed his hair, slipped into his business
clothes and shiny shoes. He tied his tie neatly and put on his old wire-
rims. He looked in the mirror and saw the perfect disguise. The new
him, except for the glasses which were the old him.

Traxon came to the door, his face dirty, his hair unkempt.

"Go wash your face, comb your hair, get a jacket. We're going out."

"Where?" the boy asked.

"Just come," Mark said. "I'll explain as we go."

"Can I come, too?" Mirabella asked. "I'd be most useful to your
plan, and please, tell Traxon to look for a book about Atlantis."

She already knew what he was planning. He smiled and added
her into the equation. Mark would walk back into the store and rant
and rave about being cheated, and while he held the clerk's attention,
Traxon, in an invisible state, of course, would sneak into the stock
rooms and exchange the books they had given him for the topics Mark
had really wanted. Mirabella would be their link, would keep them in
touch and warn them of any danger. It was the perfect plan, the simple
plan. He was lucky because Rollo had taken him at his word, and

taught Traxon how to read English. If there was a question or a problem, Traxon would be able to relay it through Mirabella. Traxon was to transport the books within his screen and deposit them in the car, which they would park around the corner from the store front so the clerk couldn't see it. The perfect plan!

Mark didn't care if it was a fair monetary exchange. The store would probably still owe him money, but he didn't want it back as long as he got titles he wanted.

The closing time painted on the door was fifteen minutes from when they arrived. Mark noticed there were no police casually hanging about, but then he wasn't expected. He walked in with Mirabella and held the door for her and a certain invisible person.

"Yes, sir? Can I help you?" the woman who had waited on him earlier said, clearly not immediately recognizing him.

"I hope so. I've come for an explanation." He dumped the first box of books she had sold him on the counter, then pulled in the rest from where he had stacked them by the door.

"Oh, it's you," she said.

"Me, and I didn't much care for the trick you played on me earlier."

"You are not welcome here," she said indignantly. "Leave, please."

"You cheated me and put the police on me. Now I want some recompense," Mark said loudly.

"You should have checked the merchandise to make sure it was what you wanted," she replied haughtily. "We are closing now. You must leave."

"No, but do close up so we can settle this without interruption," Mark said.

She is going for an alarm key, Mirabella said silently.

Mark shook his head at the woman. "Please, don't do that. Why don't you check and be sure I've returned all the books you 'sold' me?"

Mark felt Traxon pass by him, and the door jingled as it opened.

The teller looked up. "Don't play with the door, little girl," she said to Mirabella.

"And then, I want you to give me the books I paid for," Mark demanded, ignoring the bell.

"No sir, I don't carry such books. Nobody would waste their time reading them, so I don't waste my stock space on them!"

"I don't care if you think I'm wasting my time or not, but decent people don't cheat other people. If you didn't have the books I wanted, or didn't want to sell them, why not just say so? The lady who was working here several weeks ago didn't mind selling them to me."

"I am one of the new owners and we are reputable people. That's why we fired her on the spot," the woman replied smugly. "We do not sell trashy merchandise."

"But you do cheat people!" Mark said.

The door bell jingled again.

"I said, don't play with the door, little girl!" the woman said irritably. She stopped and frowned as she noticed that Mirabella was nowhere near the door.

"Maybe it's a street vibration," Mirabella suggested sweetly.

"I'm going to call the police," the woman said.

"Be my guest," Mark said. "I'd like to talk to them about you. There are laws that protect people from being cheated."

"Why don't you just leave?" the woman said, barely keeping her voice even.

Jingle.

She walked around the counter, looking very flustered, and opened the door to show them out.

"Sorry, but we are going to settle this now," Mark said.

He closed the door and pulled it firmly.

"Just to be sure it doesn't jingle," he laughed.

The woman backed around the counter to put it between Mark and herself. "I don't have any books for you. I threw them all out when I bought the place."

Not so, Mirabella said silently. *Traxon has found quite a few.*

Jingle. The door opened and closed as the woman watched. Her eyes bulged.

"Did, did you see that?" she stammered.

"What?" Mark asked.

"What's going on here?" the woman bleated, obviously terrified now.

"Nothing as far as I can see," Mark said honestly, since he couldn't see Traxon. "Are you going to accommodate me or not?"

"Not," the woman said stubbornly. "I have a right to choose what I want to sell."

"Then I expect a refund, or I'll be calling the police this time," Mark said. "I'll return for my money tomorrow morning."

The door jingled once more before they got to it and the woman practically jumped out of her skin.

As soon as they were to the car, Mark said, "How much did you find, Traxon?"

No answer.

"He's still inside," Mirabella said.

"What?"

"He is making one last search," she explained.

They could see the woman moving about through the windows. They stood in the shadows on the sidewalk, waiting nervously. The woman moved towards the door just at the moment Traxon came out. The door jingled as he slammed it and Mark heard him say, "Come on, let's go, quick."

They piled into the car and sped off.

Traxon materialized hugging a small box. "It took me a long time to find the stuff. They were all up on the top shelves in real dingy boxes. I already put three boxes in the trunk. This was the last of it."

"Good job and thank you both," Mark said.

"I think she would have called the police except she was afraid they would think she was crazy," Mirabella said. "Were you scared in there, Traxon?"

"Naw," the boy bragged.

He was, Mirabella said to Mark.

"I like being able to help you, Mark. You do so much stuff for us."

Mark slowed the car and parked in front of a small dessert shop. "Come on, how about a treat?"

"I can't eat sugar," Traxon reminded him.

"Well, what about a cup of mulled, hot cider? No processed sugar, so that should be okay," Mark suggested.

"Yum!" both kids said.

They sat near a fake fire and sipped from the spicy drinks. Traxon seemed to glow a tad greener and Mirabella sank deep into her seat.

"This is nice. So warm. The cold is finally gone," she said.

"What cold?" Mark asked.

"The cold from storage," Traxon murmured. "Finally gone."

They sat quietly until Traxon looked up and said, "You won't send us back into the cold, will you, Mark?"

"No, never. Do you remember anything other than cold?"

"It was damp," Mirabella added. "And I heard minds, but they were distant. Sometimes they seemed to be bickering."

"I don't remember anything like that. Maybe damp, but no voices," Traxon said.

"Maybe we weren't in the same place. So nice, so warm here," she said again.

"Let's go," Mark said. "I want to get home and see what books we got this time."

The children smiled, gulped the last bits of cider and gathered themselves up.

"Mark, am I really from another world?" Traxon asked.

Mark wished he had an answer, but he didn't.

FICTIONS

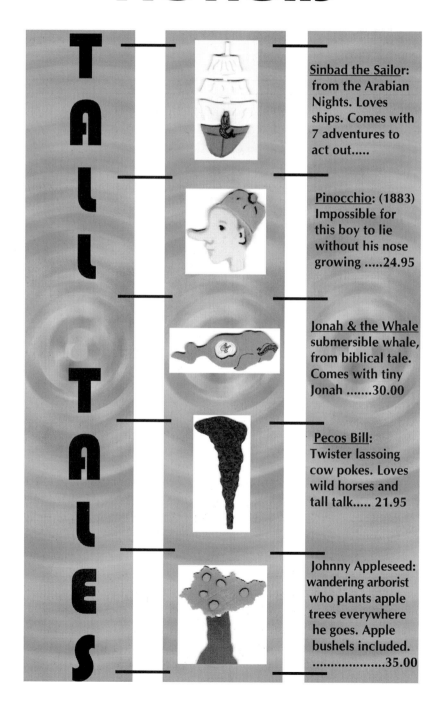

TALL TALES

Sinbad the Sailor: from the Arabian Nights. Loves ships. Comes with 7 adventures to act out.....

Pinocchio: (1883) Impossible for this boy to lie without his nose growing 24.95

Jonah & the Whale submersible whale, from biblical tale. Comes with tiny Jonah 30.00

Pecos Bill: Twister lassoing cow pokes. Loves wild horses and tall talk..... 21.95

Johnny Appleseed: wandering arborist who plants apple trees everywhere he goes. Apple bushels included. 35.00

Sunrise, the alarm, and a slow opening of his eyes into November morning gloom. The clanging discordance of the alarm again, telling him to get up, get out of bed, to move it. The same scenario greeted him every morning.

Mark padded into the bathroom. His hair was growing out, curling into unruliness again. His eyes were puffy, unready for the day. His face looked thinner. No, that wasn't right. It looked older, more angular. He would be twenty-five in another two months. He grinned and made funny faces in the mirror, brushed his teeth, scrubbed his face and decided to let the stubble turn to a beard.

The house was still, filled with a silence he knew was the quiet of sleep. He liked these moments when the house was his, the air surrounding him filled only by the noises he made himself.

He picked up a book out of one of the boxes they had lugged into the house the night before. The spine was mended with cracked and yellowing tape. It was called *The Fabled Cities of Athens, Rome and Pompeii*. Obviously Traxon had been hoping for Atlantis but it wasn't mentioned in the index. He put it down. The next book was a comic book, *Boy of Wonder and the Invaders from Outer Space*.

A copy of *The Wizard of Lost Land* in a green cover with simple line drawings proved to be water logged. He scanned it quickly before he dropped it in the trash can. There was no mention of Rollo Wiz or the Wizard's boyhood. The book was a very thin abridged edition and added nothing to the version they already had anyway.

He munched on a raisin muffin as he looked through another box. *Strong Man and His Amazing Side Show* caught his eye. The stuff was fun. Sam Mann had a secret identity. He worked as a strongman in a side show. A stick-on handlebar mustache hid his true identity as Strong Man, a pure-of-heart hero. Strong Man's telltale superhero symbol was a birth mark on his chest, which could be seen through a cut-out in his black muscle shirt that he wore when on missions. He also wore black tights and steel-toed, black leather boots, which put him a little off balance when he flew, but really made it hurt when he kicked a nemesis. He didn't seem too bright to Mark. In fact, he just seemed to take advantage of his physical attributes to solve everything. However, Mark had to admit that the strongman loved to put on a good show for his audiences, both at the side show and while on his super missions. Mark noted that Sam Strong and Sam Mann, also known as Strong Man, had oddly similiar names, could both fly and were both unusually strong. Sam was going shopping with Pete tomorrow and the comic made Mark wonder what kind of attire for the boy they would come home with.

Mark looked at his watch. Whoops, he'd be late if he didn't hurry. And he wanted to have a little time to nourish an idea that was nibbling around in his mind before his meeting with Mr. Cannady.

He practiced, speaking out loud in the privacy of his car as he drove to work.

"I have an idea for the game. How about super-hero games? I know it's been done before, but not with the new technology. Okay, okay, I know it needs a hook. I'll work on it," he admitted to himself and the imaginary Jerome Cannady. He tried several more times.

By the time he got to work, he could sense there was a beginning, at least. He was headed towards something. He went in his office and closed the door. He took out a sheet of paper and began a chart. It was how he developed his best ideas. It was a pyramid of sorts. Along the bottom he wrote:

Super heroes of story and myth.
Adventurers who save the world.
Lost knowledge.

Knowledge was very important in a technocratic world, but what kind of knowledge would kids want to save? He began again.

Super heroes of legend and myth,
Save the world's machines from villainous . . .

He mulled on what could be important enough to require people to call for superheroes when they denied their existence to begin with.

Save the future.
from villainous plunderers,
Who are erasing the past.

Mark scribbled in the corner, *No past, no future.* He hatched the idea out. Time issues were dubious. Okay, what about the next one? He jiggled the pen back and forth in his fingers, put the point to the paper and wrote:

Be a techno-detective
Find out who is stealing DNA identities
Solve the mystery, find the keys . . .

His mind clicked along and then stopped, and he began once more.

Be a techno-detective
Solve the impossible!
Find out the technological secrets
To how super-heroes, nursery rhymes,
Myths, legends and tall tales are coming to life.
Be the first to find the scientific solution to an obvious hoax.

"Right," he wrote to himself sarcastically and laid his pen on his desk. He was way off, on the wrong track altogether. He had just encapsulated his own dilemma. It wasn't a game, it was his life. He shredded all his scribblings, except for the last one which he slid into his desk drawer to take home as a guide for his personal mystery. He stood and stretched his long frame. What he really wanted to do was go read all the books they had brought home the night before. He stretched again just as Elliot knocked on the door.

"Mark, how are you?"

"Fine. What's up, Elliot?"

"Nothing much. I'm just nervous about Saturday night."

"Don't be. Lady A and the kids are presently putting spit and polish on everything and straightening up."

"Good, good," Elliot said. "Now, here is your list for the week and what is that on your face?"

"Beard. Do you like it?" Mark said proudly.

"I'll arrange a shave and a hair cut for, let us say, one o'clock," Elliot answered.

"I'm growing a beard. Why would I want a shave?"

"Mark, this is not going to help your cause around here."

Mark put his mouth close to Elliot's ear and said conspiratorially, "Okay, at one o'clock." It didn't make that much difference to him and Elliot was probably right. "Now let me work."

He pulled his last idea out and put it on the corner of his desk while he pulled out a fresh piece of paper. He tapped his pen absently on his desktop. So many games already existed. Maybe something new in the field was an impossibility. Could there be a limit to imagination? Or was he being too picky? Maybe he could dress an old idea in new clothes, but that wouldn't be any fun. He doodled decorative figures on the papers with kids' faces around the edge of the page, then rotated the pen around in his fingers.

He was just admitting that he was stumped when the phone rang.

"What's wrong, Kate?" he asked as he heard her frantic voice.

"It's Milly. She's on the roof of your house. We came over to see the kids. They were playing happily and suddenly she was on the roof of one of the towers! She says Sam flew her up there. I don't know how to get her down!"

"Call the fire department," Mark said.

"I did, but they're tied up and I'm scared."

"Is Pete there?"

"No, he's out. What should I do?" his sister said tearfully.

"Get Sam to fly her down," Mark said without thinking.

She screamed at him hysterically. "Mark, this is serious!"

"Calm down, calm down. I'm on my way, but until I get there, ask Sam to help you," he said, modifying his approach.

He hung up and ran out of the office. He screeched into the driveway, flung himself out of the car, expecting to see a crowd, but the lawn was clear and when he squinted up through the sunlight, he couldn't see Milly or anyone else on the roof.

They were in the great room, Kate, Lady A, Milly and all the kids.

"What happened?" he asked, breathless by now.

Kate stood up slowly. "What happened? I'll tell you what happened! Sam rescued Milly. He flew her off the roof before the fire engine could get here," she said in a dazed tone. "I saw him do it." Her voice was drained and flat, her eyes unfocused.

"It was fun," Milly said happily.

"Fun?" Mark said, looking at Sam sternly.

"What is going on here?" Kate asked dully.

"I'm not sure myself. I'm trying to find out and I'll let you know when I do," he said gently to his sister. "Okay?'

Kate nodded *yes*. "Sure, whatever you say, Mark."

She held her hand out to him, offering him a sheet of paper.

"It's a bill from the fire department. It's for you. They give them out to pranksters." Her voice was still expressionless.

She took Milly's hand and left.

"Bye, Uncle Mark," Milly mouthed and waved a little wave on the way out.

Mark shook his head.

Lady A shook her head, too, making a shadow motion of his own movement. "I hope your sister thinks it was all a hallucination, I really do hope that."

"But?" Mark said, prodding her to go on.

"But? But, I'm terrified it wasn't. Was it, Mark? A hallucination? A dream? Or was it real?"

"Real."

She stared at him a moment and went off swinging her head from side-to-side, making her curls fly. He hoped she was okay.

"You mad at me?" Sam asked.

"No, I guess not. It was bound to happen one day."

"I'm sorry. I just wanted to make Milly happy. She said she liked the way birds could fly. Then she said she wished she could fly to the roof like the pigeons do, so I took her there."

Mark patted Sam's head. "I have to go back to work, but guys I seriously want you to practice being normal."

"What does that mean?" Ailithe asked.

"Get Lady A and Fiona to explain it to you sometime soon. The sooner, the better. Normalcy, or at least a semblance of it, would be a real blessing around here."

He left and drove slowly back to the office, almost looking forward to the structure and everyday routine of the job. On his desk was a message: *Mr. Cannady wants to see you immediately. Elliot.*

He straightened his suit, tucked in his shirt and obliged his boss.

"Well, Mark, is your emergency at home resolved?" Mr. Cannady greeted him.

"My niece was in a bit of trouble. She's six and there was an accident at my house, but everything is fine now."

"Good, good. Now then, I'm delighted with your game proposal!"

"Pardon me? I haven't submitted anything yet . . . ?"

"Elliot found it in your desk while you were gone. What a clever idea. I think with a little more work, it'll be fantastic. You never cease to amaze me. What ideas you manage to come up with!"

Mark was blank, but Mr. Cannady was shaking his hand heartily. "How soon can you work out more details?"

"Uh, I don't know."

"Well, make it quick, my boy. Here's the original back. Go to it!"

Mark glanced at the paper in his hand. It was his last pyramid based on the kids. He had to think fast.

"Uh, Mr. Cannady, I'm not really sold on this idea. That's why I didn't submit it myself. I think I can come up with a better one."

"Better, Mark? I always like better, but this is pretty good. Still, better is always better." He chuckled at his own joke. "I'll wait to make a decision until I hear your other suggestions."

Mark folded the paper and put it in his pocket. He couldn't let them use this idea. It would be too dangerous. What a fool he had been to write it down to begin with!

By the time he got home, the kids were in bed. Mark and Pete sat together in the after-bedtime-silence, heads in their hands, thinking, throwing ideas into the air, shaking their heads at their own thoughts and starting over again. Mark's carelessness had given an edge of urgency to the search, had raised the stakes so that either they had to solve the mystery of the kids, or he had to come up with one amazing idea for a different game. He couldn't tell which was going to be harder.

"How can a post office box be untraceable? Everything is registered these days down to the color of toenail polish a woman uses." Pete mulled it over out loud for the thousandth time.

"Registered," Mark repeated. "On computers," he mumbled, going back to a previous discussion.

"Wait, wait just one dang minute!" Pete said excitedly. "It's so simple. How've we been so dumb? Whoever's sending out the kids didn't transfer the information into the computer, that's all. So simple! So obvious!"

"Come on, Pete, that can't happen!" Mark said.

"Course it can. You said so yourself. Remember your story about the library books?"

"But it's the law that everything has to be registered."

"Yeah, we all know that, but who's checking?"

"You're serious. You're saying these people just ignored the law."

"Uh huh. And nobody knew the difference."

"If you're right, it's nice to know we're not in the middle of a surrealistic nightmare," Mark said, rubbing his forehead.

"Yeah, but it also means our search is probably gonna turn up zip."

"Pete, we can't give up now. We need to look at this differently. Maybe we need to go back to when the catalogs started coming."

Mark thought about Mr. Bill Henley's clippings hanging on his refrigerator, but before he could follow the chain of thought he had set in motion, Elflet pattered into the great room where they sat, his eyes glowing slightly with night vision. Mark slipped his feet quickly back into his shoes.

"The closets are locked," Elflet said plaintively.

"I locked them. You can't keep demolishing our shoes, Elflet," Mark said as gently as he could.

"Then send me to Cobbler's School. Please, Mark."

"Elflet, shoes are made by machines and robots now."

"Robots like Castor?" he asked.

"No, Castor is a cyborg, that's different," Mark corrected.

"How?"

"A cyborg is a combination of a human and a robot."

"That book you got says robots don't feel stuff," the little boy said.

"Which book?" Mark asked.

"The fat one with the paper cover. It says robots have to take care of people, but they don't have feelings. Does half of Castor feel and half not?"

"Listen to me, Elflet. Castor cries, he hurts, he laughs, he's alive. He is a people, one hundred percent people. Is anyone else awake?"

"Rollo is making something,"

"What?"

"Something to make us look scary if anyone ever comes to take us back. So we can scare them away!" he said, his little head going up and down.

Mark grabbed Elflet's shoulders gently. "Take you back to where?"

"To the cold."

Mark hugged the little boy and whispered, "No one will take any of you back. No one. Okay? You're staying with me. Forever. Where are you going now, Elflet?"

"To tell everyone you're our daddy."

"Elflet, go back to bed and tell Rollo to go to bed, too."

The child padded off. Mark turned back to Pete with a sinking sense of desperation mixed with defeat.

"Pete, if we don't find the answer to all this, the kids will never feel like they belong anywhere. Eventually, someone is bound to get supsicious and then what?"

"I'll do my best, but it don't look good, Mark."

Mark sighed and put his head back into his hands. "I'm tired. I need a break from all this, but no chance of that with nine kids calling me *Daddy* and a party to give."

Pete patted his shoulder.

Mark shook his head, trying to clear it. "I have to stay focused here, keep my mind on the party or else I'll disappoint Elliot."

"Go to bed. Get some rest. I'll clean up and we'll work on this again tomorrow."

"Rest! That would be good, but, Pete, all I can think about is how the kids got here. Who are they? What are they?" Mark said with a deepening sense of despair.

"Stop frowning. You're gonna give yourself permanent lines on your forehead and it ain't gonna help nothing. I'll see you in the morning," Pete said, turned out the light and went to bed.

Mark sat in the dark room, his mind darting about. He had to solve this before it swallowed his whole life. How had this happened? Was it a miracle or a nightmare? Was it science or otherworldly powers at work? Either way, was there any purpose to it? His thoughts bounced off invisible walls, unable to penetrate the fog that seemed to envelop and surround his mind. He had always considered himself a creative realist. It was how he had moved so easily into the corporate world from the junk world. But now, he had to wonder if he was dreaming. Would he awaken in the cottage or even at home with his mother and Kate, or maybe his father?

He pinched himself. It hurt. He pricked his finger. He bled, salty red blood which he sucked. There had to be a real answer, a real reason, a real explanation. There had to be. He was just missing it.

He awoke on the sofa. He was so stiff and cramped it took him several moments to sit up. A clock glowed *3:30 A.M.* He put some water on to boil and tried to stretch. He wondered again if anyone else got the catalogs? He made his tea and sat down to think. It was a good question. He could post an innocuous inquiry on some net bulletin boards, and see what responses, if any, he got. Maybe someone else, somewhere, would admit to receiving the catalogs. If anyone answered, then he could ask if they had ever placed an order. Maybe he'd get lucky. He sipped the tea and let its soft aroma soothe him. He stepped onto his front porch. Light clouds whitened the night sky and blocked both moon and stars. The air was suddenly wet and balmy with a recent rain that had driven the cold back, had suspended the weather in mid-season, slowed and held it there, much as his life seemed caught between two worlds. He took a deep breath of the fresh, sweet air and held it in his nose, his lungs, his mouth before he reluctantly released it and went back inside. On a whim he threw open the windows and let the freshness of the air into the house.

He logged onto his computer and opened an e-mail account at Bingo. He wrote a simple message: *Do you, too, get unusual toy catalogs through your mail slot? If so, respond to* errant@bingo.com.

He posted his question on sixteen message boards, shut off the machine and went to bed. He slept soundly this time.

BECAUSE OF MAD SCIENTISTS

SPECIALS FROM THE ISLAND OF DR. MOREAU

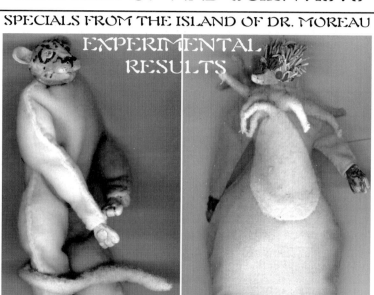

EXPERIMENTAL RESULTS

YOUNG TIGER: 150.00

YOUNG ECHIDNA: 150.00

YOUNG FROG: 150.00

Other products: Frankenstein's monster, The Fly, Mr. Hyde, The Invisible Man, Bionic Apes.

The temperature dropped during the night and by morning the house was icy. Mark danced on bare feet across the cold floor, slamming windows shut.

Pete came downstairs hugging his arms and shivering. "What happened?"

"I opened the windows and it got colder," Mark said, prancing in place to keep himself warm. "I'll turn on the furnace."

Except it didn't come on. Nothing, not a single breath of warm air.

"I'll start a fire in the fireplace," Pete said.

Mark bundled into double layers of clothes. "Where are the kids?"

"Dunno."

Mark trotted upstairs. They were all huddled under covers and quilts in Elflet's and Paul's room.

"Come on, we've built a fire downstairs," Mark said.

They just stared at him.

"What's wrong with you guys?"

No answer, until finally Castor breathed in deeply and said, "The cold. It has come for us."

Mark felt his eyebrows rise. "Nonsense. This is normal cold. It comes every year, and passes every year, and we are all still here when the warmth comes again."

"It's coming," Elflet said, his teeth chattering.

"No, it is not! Come on, we'll roast marshmallows, we'll drink hot chocolate, and you'll be warm again in nothing flat."

"No," Rollo said. "The cold will come and take us. We won't have anything except cold again."

"No, no. I promise. Come here, to the window." Mark beckoned them. "See, everyone is wearing coats, but they are all still out and about."

"The sky is real dark," Jack noticed. "Real dark. It was dark in the cold, too."

"It was grey in the cold." Mirabella nodded. "Murky, confusing, cold, lonely."

"Bone-piercingly cold," Traxon warbled. "Have you ever been the cold itself, had it in your cells, coating your hair and layering itself through your bones? So very cold!"

"Lonely," Paul said simply.

Mark picked Paul up and hugged him, then started to carry him downstairs.

"No!" Traxon shouted. "You can't take him!"

"Traxon," Mark said calmly. "None of you will be cold downstairs. Come now, all of you."

Fiona came to the door of the room bundled in a coat. She took Mirabella's hand and pulled her to her feet. "It's okay, guys. It's nice and cozy down there. Lady A just came and she has pots of tea and cocoa steaming for all of us."

Sam got up, hesitantly took Fiona's outstretched fingers and pulled Elflet up with his free hand. Slowly, linked by a chain of hands, they made their way into the great room. The fire flames roared and snapped. The smell of fresh baked muffins and oranges wafted to them.

"Yummy," Paul yelled, grabbing a muffin in each hand, his hunger overwhelming his fear.

Ashley smiled as the children dove in to claim their shares.

"I called a furnace man. He can't come until tomorrow," she said.

"The cold will get us before then," Traxon predicted gloomily.

"Mark, you'd better hurry or you're gonna be late to work again," Pete said. "We can handle things here. Get going."

Mark worried between meetings and deadlines. The kids, one and all, had an inordinate fear of the cold. Something rattled around in his brain, scratching to get out.

"What are you scratching your head for?" Elliot asked, putting final plans for the party into his hands.

"I always do that when I have something I can't solve."

"And what is it that you can't solve?" Elliot asked.

"Elliot, do you know much about genetic engineering or cloning?"

"Not much, except I don't like it!"

"Is anyone using it?" Mark asked.

"G-engineering. You know, to filter out disease-prone genes, to determine hair color, maybe a kid's sex, but nothing else that I know of. And if anything more is going on, I don't want to know about it! Is this for your game, because if so, it's a bad direction," Elliot added at the last minute.

"It's just for background. To make a good game, I have to know everything about the world it's set in. And I need this information."

"Then call up the sec-files. I'll have Sandra send the code through."

"What are the sec-files?" Mark asked, perplexed.

"Do you think Cannady's can stay on top without some way to access more or less otherwise inaccessible information? If you need obscure information you tap in the code for the security files plus a project number. It costs a lot, so be absolutely sure it isn't already available."

Mark knew he should say no, should back out right then, but gene engineering was related to the game proposal Mr. Cannady had liked and at the moment it was still his only idea. If it happened to overlap with his personal needs, who could fault him?

The code came through the next morning. It wasn't anything much until he typed it in and then he had to clear one-hundred-and-three security levels that popped consecutively onto the screen. By the time he got to the last one he was surprised to see he was back to level one. There was no way to skip a level, and the program carefully informed him that upon his next entry to the file, the levels would appear in a different order. He wondered if even his hidden code-breaker could handle this?

Before him was an index to a plethora of information. He hit a key for recording his requests and went on. The headline from Bill Henley's old clipping flashed in his memory: *Genetic Map Misused – Case Made Against Scientists.* He felt himself flip into a new gear, his mind beginning to rev faster.

Incidences of Genetic Engineering: Answer, 34,001 this year
How many of these were officially authorized: 25,222
Mark stopped, before he typed in his next question.
What groups are pursuing gene engineering?
A list of corporations came up on the screen, including Anderson's. He kept going.
Are there any consequences if the unauthorized companies are caught: A penalty of 5% of the profit margin.
He felt his stomach drop. There were virtually no consequences. A measly 5% penalty was all it took to get the government to look the

other way. It made him feel sick, made him shake. Where were the subjects of the unofficial genetic engineering? What had happened to them? He asked the computer.

No information available.

He could feel his heartbeat speed up. Either no one was monitoring the results of the experiments or else no one was recording them.

Mark took a deep breath, then another. If there was genetic experimentaion being pursued which the government was happily ignoring, why couldn't there be an underground of people pursuing g-engineering, people that neither *legitimate* companies nor the government knew about, people who might have gone beyond anything anyone else could have imagined?

He left the topic. It made him nervous. He wasn't sure how safe it would be to ask too many questions of the system. Still, he wasn't ready to stop yet.

Second topic: Clones.

Is cloning of humans possible: Yes.

How often has it been done in the last 10 years: 0 came up in bright red letters.

Is it only theoretical: No, 37 cases are recorded.

What happened in those 37 cases: All the labs where experimentation took place were closed down immediately. The scientists were removed from their jobs. Fifty-two of the seventy were found guilty of illegal scientific activity and sentenced to life terms in prison. Eighteen disappeared.

Could these have been the scientists in the article from fifty-two years ago?

Are any of the imprisoned scientists still alive: No.

So gene engineering was secretly condoned, but the line was indelibly drawn at human cloning. For a minute he felt relieved and then he typed in the next question.

Could there be unrecorded cases of cloning: Possibility is 1 in 500.

That meant there could actually be any number of unrecorded cases. The statistic was only that – a guess based on what was known. What about what wasn't known? He leaned back in his chair and wondered if he dared ask the next question.

Is there a possibility of using gene-manipulation to successfully create new life forms: Possible if used in combination with cloning.

Has it ever been tried: 20 such experiments were sponsored more than 60 years ago by the government.

For what purpose: That is classified.

Were they successful: That is classified information

Were these twenty experiments performed by the scientists who were arrested for cloning?

Two little blue stars blinked when he typed in the last question. It was time to move on to a new topic.

Explain the process of cloning: The answer is quite long.

Proceed: Pure cloning involves cells being taken from host organisms and suspended in...

The explanation took ten screen changes. A yellow warning light about time went off. Mark changed the default.

He found Suspended Life Forms in the index. His heart was pounding as he typed in his questions.

Define please: In theory, life forms may be stored in cold liquid tanks ...

The explanation went on and on, but the word cold had registered in Mark's mind, echoing over and over. He caught that it was a form of storing living cells, and possibly higher organisms, but that it was forbidden and had been for more than fifty years.

He hit the word "print."

No record of these conversations may be printed out. When you sign off, all recordings will be scrambled and erased. Only the record of use-time will be logged. Thank you.

Mark smiled. He didn't need a printout anyway. His memory would serve. He hit the delete and exit buttons, and sat back.

"Suspended in cold liquid," repeated itself in his mind.

GHOSTS

THE SPIRIT OF THE CASTLE (1800): AVAILAVBLE
IN BLACK, WHITE OR RED.........../......25.00
THE CANTERVILLE GHOST (1887): A FRIENDLY
AND UNEXPECTED HAUNT..........30.00
GHOST OF JACOB MARLEY: COMES IN DREAMS
BUT WITH GOOD INTENTIONS........25.00
BANSHEES: EXCELLENT SCREAMERS, SO COMES
WITH EARPLUGS................20.00
THE HEADLESS HORSEMAN: A BIT FRIGHTENING,
BUT DOESN'T STICK AROUND LONG .....:20.00

Mark slapped Mr. Henley's article down on the table at what had become their nightly meeting time and announced, "Pete, I think someone has cloned and gene-manipulated these kids, grown them like vegetables, harvested them and suspended them in cold liquid storage until someone puts in an order for one of them."

"Aw, come on, Mark, that ain't possible."

"Yes, it is. More than possible."

"Naw, no way! No one could get away with it."

"Did you ever read this article?" he said, tapping it with his finger nail. "The scientists in this article were prosecuted, but I did some research and found out some of them vanished. I think they might be the ones doing this."

"It'd be illegal, and nobody's getting away with nothing illegal no more."

"Well, someone is most certainly getting away with this."

"You're serious, aren't you?'

"Absolutely."

"Mark, someone would know!" Pete insisted again.

"We know."

"Know? Know? We don't know this! We're speculating. We don't know nothing," Pete reminded him.

"It's got to be!"

"Why?" Pete asked.

"I know it in my gut, Pete. It fits. Tell me it doesn't. Come on, Pete, tell me."

No answer.

"They g-engineered clones for specific features, and then suspended them in cold storage for years. Maybe for more than half a century! Pete, they've done it. I know they have."

"Who is they, Mark?"

"I told you who I think it is," Mark said.

He waited for Pete to protest again, but he didn't.

Instead, Pete said, "Okay, yeah, it fits. I agree."

What was it about Pete's response that was wrong? He wasn't sure, but something was definitely out of character.

"Pete, I expected a counter-thought, a realistic alternative, something grounded from you. You're supposed to be a voice of reason."

Pete sighed. "Geez, I can't pretend no more."

"What do you mean?" Mark asked suspiciously. "You're not a spy, are you?"

"Spy? Me? No, no. I never coulda hidden that from Mirabella. I'm no spy."

"She told me you were hiding something, something you didn't want to think about."

"It's all I could think about from the moment I met you. It took constant reminders to myself: *don't think about it, don't think about it.*"

"What are you talking about? What were you hiding?" Mark said nervously. "Tell me now."

"Okay, okay. I bet everything on you. I figured you might just be smart enough to figure it all out, and it seems like I bet right. Listen, Mark, I used to live around here when I was a kid. Not here, not in a fancy neighborhood or nothing, but not far away. And I knew this house. A friend of mine lived here when the catalogs started coming."

"Charlie Rich?" Mark asked.

"Yeah, Charlie! How'd you know about him."

"You and Charlie and Billy Henley? You were all friends?"

"Yeah? How'd you know?"

"I met Bill Henley. He moved away just before you moved in here. He told me about Petey, Charlie and Billy."

Pete smiled. "The Three Musketeers." He shook his head slowly before he spoke again. "Charlie used to give some of the catalogs to us, to all the neighborhood kids. When he moved away, I took a boxful with me. It got stashed in the attic of our house until my dad died. My daughter and I hadda clear out his stuff. What a nightmare! He'd saved everything, including old magazines, some of which were valuable. So we hadda sort them. My daughter found the catalogs. 'Hey Dad, these look interesting. Can I have them?"

"'Sure,' I said. I mean, why not? So, she went off with them and I forgot about them again. Until the day she called me and said excitedly, 'Dad, I ordered a toy from the catalog for Amy.' Amy is my other granddaughter. I didn't know what she was talking about at first, and when I figured it out, I also figured it couldn't matter. The catalogs were so outta date, I was sure nothing would ever come. Still, for no real good reason, I felt a little nervous. A coupla days passed and my stomach finally settled down and then the second call came. 'Dad, please come over right away!' We'd just had a blizzard visited on us, but I slogged through foot-deep snow as fast as I could."

"A toy had come, right? In a crate?"

"Yep, that was it," Pete said.

"Fiona?" Mark asked, suddenly putting things together.

Pete sighed. "Yes. She was only about one when she arrived, and so white. She clung to me as I lifted her out of the crate. Such a slight thing, almost transparent."

"Like a ghost?" Mark asked.

"Yes, just like a ghost. We never told her. She became our albino instead. Oh, my daughter and her husband had me try to find the company who had sent Fiona for a while, but I didn't get nowhere then either. When they couldn't return her, my daughter and her husband tried hard to love her. They raised her, home-schooled her so she didn't need no papers, and watched her grow up. We pretended until we believed she was real, and really an albino. Remember the day I dropped you off and saw the crates? I knew exactly what they were. Oh, they weren't the same size, but they were exactly the same construction. But so many of them! I couldn't figure out why there would be so many. Then you sorta offered me a job and that's when I set my plan in motion. By then my daughter and her husband were divorcing and blaming it on Fiona, who was in and outta trouble all the time. She wasn't a bad kid or nothing. She just made people uneasy wherever she went."

"So you took the job and brought Fiona here."

"Yes, where she could be safe."

"That's why she wanders at night in that ghostly way?" Mark asked as discreetly as he could. "Pete, do you know what this means?"

"That my granddaughter is a ghost?"

"It means that other people have ordered from the catalogs."

"I guess it does. But what I can't figure out is how or why the catalogs could carry the same merchandise for so many, many years," Pete said.

"How do you know they do?"

"Because I saved the catalog Fiona came from and here's its twin," he said, holding up an obviously new catalog next to a yellowing one.

"And it's identical?"

"Almost, except for its age and the fact that Fiona and some other items ain't in the new ones no more. Guess they got ordered, too, but nothing new has been added."

Mark felt a chill move through every inch of him. His stomach lurched. "It really does fit, Pete. It fits!" He waved his hands in the direction of a stack of catalogs near the door. "The rest of the merchandise must still be in cold storage." He felt the cold, a piercingly real cold. "Why would anyone do this?"

"I dunno, but their technology ain't sound. Their tinkering is screwy. I spent the day reading your books. I found ghost stories, and if they engineered Fiona to be a real life ghost-child, they blew it. She ain't invisible. She only startles people by accident, not on purpose. She can't pass through walls even though she can squeeze into extra-small spaces. About the only traditionally ghostly thing she does is, if she walks by chains, she reaches out and rattles them loudly. Some ghost!"

"Defective merchandise," Mark said.

"You got that right!"

"The mystery deepens every time we take a step forward," Mark said. "Why would anyone do this? What's the point?"

POORLINGS

LOOK INSIDE FOR:
Jean Val Jean
Mahatma Gandhi
The Little Matchgirl
The Little Princess
Cinderella

OLIVER TWIST   HUNCHBACK OF NOTRE DAME

Friday morning came and Elliot arrived at the same time as Lady A and the furnace man. The kids were enthusiastically toasting marshmallows for breakfast in the fireplace, except for Traxon who was toasting bread.

"What are you doing here, Elliot?" Mark asked.

"It's freezing in here!"

"That's why the furnace man is here," Lady A pointed out.

"Good, good," Elliot said.

"Not good. You people need a new furnace, and one that size has to be special ordered. It'll be Monday before I get it installed," the furnace man said.

"What? No!" Elliot cried out. "That's too late!"

"Too cold," Mirabella said shivering a little.

"You can't do that," Elliot cried again. "The party will be ruined."

"You better worry about the temperature in here," the furnace man said. "I hope you have a lot of wood for that old fireplace."

"Actually, no," Mark said. "I guess we'll go get some. Pete, can I borrow your truck?"

"Sure, go ahead."

"Markham, Markham, please, what should I do about the party?" Elliot asked.

"Call Mr. Cannady and ask him what he wants to do. It's his call."

"I bet I can fix the furnace," Rollo piped up.

"Sure, sure," the furnace man said patronizingly as he handed Mark a work order. "Go for it. At least you can't break it."

"Elflet, Fiona, Jack, will you assist me?" Rollo asked formally.

The four children marched down to the furnace, the furnace man left, and Mirabella, Traxon, Sam, Ashley and Mark piled into the truck.

"Why can't we bring Castor and Ailithe?" Sam asked.

"Mark is afraid they would be noticed," Mirabella explained. "Mark doesn't think it would be safe."

"Then how will they go to school with us?" Sam asked.

"I don't know yet," Mark said exactly at the moment Mirabella said, "He doesn't know yet."

"Salt and pepper," Mark called.

Poor as church mice, Mirabella said in her silent way.

"It's coming," Ailithe said, like a misplaced thought.

"What is?" Lady A asked.

"The wind. Cold, harsh mistress wind, this. She is bringing ice with her."

Lady A looked at Mark, who nodded.

"When, Ailithe?" he asked the child.

Her whole body shook. "Not today," she said.

"Good," Fiona said. "When the wind howls, hauntings come to mind."

"Enough, that is simply enough from both of you," Mark said firmly, trying to sound authoritative. "We have work to do for this party. Everybody, clean up your rooms. Lady A, it's time for you to go home. Pete, you and I need to make bagged dinners for the kids for tomorrow night. Hop to it, guys."

Everyone dispersed, except Lady A.

"You are a special person, Mark Perralt," she said softly. "I'll see you tomorrow evening."

"As my date?" he asked.

"Of course. I promised, didn't I?"

THE JACKS

TABLE OF CONTENTS

Saturday the party hovered over them all day. Mark inspected as the kids cleaned their rooms. Under Elflet's bed he found all the shoes in the house. Back they went, redistributed to their owners. Traxon's and Rollo's room was too good to be true. Rollo had created an artificial invisibility screen which had carefully blocked out the mess. Mark shook his head, and the two boys went back to cleaning. Castor's and Sam's room was orderly to a fault.

"Castor won't quit cleaning up," Sam complained.

Mark sent Sam off to help Pete pile wood, and then sat down on the bed with Castor.

"Let's get one thing straight, right now," Mark said.

"What, sir?" Castor asked.

"You cannot spend your life straightening up after other people."

Castor rotated his head, machine-like, and said mechanically, "It is my duty, sir."

Mark took him gently by the shoulders. "Stop. You're a person. You are not some machine or mechanical man."

"You are wrong, sir. I am clearly a machine. I do not even bleed."

"I am not wrong! You are not a machine! You don't have nuts and bolts holding your joints together, do you? You aren't made of metal, are you?"

"I'm the color of metal."

"You cry, you laugh, you feel fear. Those are human attributes. You are a boy, a real live boy."

"I am?"

"Yes! Now stop cleaning. Go read a good book," Mark said and pushed the boy out into the hall.

Ailithe was leaning against the window, her cheek flat against the glass. "It's the cold. She is coming with her winds and icy fingers." The child breathed and the window frosted over.

Mark pulled her away and sent her to the kitchen for a warm cup of cocoa.

"Ten kids is a lot, isn't it?" Fiona asked him from the doorframe of her room.

"Yes," Mark said.

"I'm one of them, you know," she said.

"Why do you say that, Fiona?"

"Because I just am. Don't tell Grandpa Pete. He doesn't suspect. He thinks I'm a real person."

"You are," Mark said.

"No, I'm not. I'm one of them. I'm a ghost," she said plainly and then trotted downstairs.

Mark sat on a step. He was exhausted. He wanted to be young, to be twenty-four and young, and instead he was fathering ten odd, impossibly real improbabilities.

"Hey, Mark, Lady A is here," Rollo called.

"Lady A!" Paul bellowed right behind the first call.

Mark couldn't take his eyes off her as he met her in the hall. She looked gorgeous in a clinging yellow gown with long sleeves that flared at the wrists. Her hair, sprinkled with bits of jewels, cascaded over a cut-away back. The bottom of the dress was embroidered with yellow-on-yellow patterns, and flared out in an echo of the sleeves. He couldn't think what to say.

Finally, he stumbled into, "You're early, Lady A."

"I don't think I'm early, Mark. I think you're late. You'd better go get ready," she said.

"Oh!" He glanced at his watch. "Maybe you're right."

"The wind, she comes, bringing her icy fingers," Ailithe chanted once again.

"Quit that stuff, Ailithe! Right now!" he said irritably. "Go wash the chocolate off your mouth."

"Mark, it is cold and windy out there, and the air does smell of a storm," Ashley commented.

Castor wandered by, his face hidden behind a catalog.

"Castor, I said read a good book," Mark said.

"Uh huh, I know, but I like the catalogs and this one is full of Jacks. Our Jack will want to see it, won't he?"

"Go, Mark, get ready. I'll watch the kids." Ashley said.

He slipped into his best suit and tie. His shoes were neatly polished. Something bright yellow caught his eye just under his bed. His tennis shoes! Shiny-new and neatly laced with bright red laces. Elflet had fixed them or else bought him a new pair.

He looked at them, untied the freshly polished black ones on his feet and slipped into the tennis shoes. They fit like a glove, soft, already perfectly molded to the shape of his feet. He laughed and walked downstairs.

"Don't say a word. I'm wearing them," he said to Ashley quickly.

"You're serious?"

"Yes," he said.

"Good," she said, and, kicking off her own high heels, walked about barefooted. He smiled as her yellow nailpolished toenails blinked in and out from under the hem of her gown.

Caterers arrived, huffing puffs of frosty air as they carried in platters and paraphernalia. Elliot hustled in, bundled in a down parka, his wife Laura following timidly behind him.

"It's freezing out there," he said.

Ailithe wandered past and started to speak, but Mark put his finger to his lips. A wisp of wind escaped her mouth, but she didn't say a word.

Traxon tramped by, holding Paul's hand and stopped. "Too cold for us in the play-house. We'll stay upstairs, really quietly."

"Oh, no!" Elliot groaned.

"I'll be with them," Pete said. "Enjoy yourselves, and don't worry. Now upstairs, all ten of you."

"I still can't believe you adopted all those kids," Elliot said.

"Believe it," Mark said just as the doorbell rang. Mr. Cannady and his wife stood at the door, the wind whipping their coats about them, their hats dripping droplets of rain off the brims.

"Rain?" Mark said questioningly. "Isn't it awfully cold for rain?"

Lucy Cannady, who had been almost hidden behind her husband, stepped into clear view now. "Jerome always insists we leave our house early," she said apologetically, as she patted Mr. Cannady's arm. "He likes to be sure to be punctual."

"It's fine, come in, come in."

"What an interesting home," she commented as her eyes scanned the entrance hall and glanced into the room beyond.

Before Mark could answer, he felt Traxon rush by.

"Excuse me for a moment," Mark said. The fire was blazing in the fireplace, and pieces of wood were magically floating over the hearth.

"Traxon, stop," Mark whispered. "Go upstairs right now and remain visible."

He hissed from his invisibility. "Ailithe says ice is coming. I want to be prepared."

"It's only cold rain. Go upstairs."

Mark felt the boy rush by just as Mr. Cannady and his wife entered the room.

"Oooo, what a lovely fire. I haven't seen a real fire in probably twenty-five years. Where did you get the wood?" Mrs. Cannady asked.

"For heaven's sake, fire is for the poor," Mr. Cannady said.

"Oh, hush, and enjoy it," his wife said. "Now, where did you find the wood?"

"Oh, you know, we scavenged it up here and there," Ashley said as she joined them and slipped her arm through Mark's.

"You two had better finish getting ready," Mr. Cannady said, looking down at their feet.

"We are ready," Mark said happily. He liked having Ashley clinging to his arm.

"Uh, haven't you forgotten something?" Mr. Cannady pointed down to Ashley's bare yellow toenails and Mark's bright yellow tennis shoes. Mrs. Cannady was trying to hide a smile.

Too late. The doorbell rang again and Mark went to let in the guests. Elliot was already there, greeting people, so Mark padded back into the great room. Mr. Cannady was examining the bookshelves.

"An odd assortment here. And all hand-held books. Unusual," he noted. "Must have cost you a pretty penny. Pretty much only a collector's market anymore. And what are all these old magazines?"

Mark felt his stomach drop as he realized the kids had filled part of the shelves with the catalogs.

More guests arrived and Mark said quickly, "Could you introduce everyone, Mr. Cannady?"

Mr. Cannady moved away from the bookshelves and the catalogs and began a round of introductions.

"What a night!" Carl Ellerby said. "It's starting to ice up out there."

"The weather predictions are never right. They were only calling for cold rain," his wife commented.

The caterers served the appetizers, strutting like silent penguins, facial expressions frozen into non-seeing masks. The party pattered on. Mark smiled to himself as he caught phrases of conversation.

"I have the most advanced phone available today. Fifteen stations to any line in the world. You can access your e-mail, see the person you are speaking to, get onto the World-Wide Web, and it all fits on your key chain," a double-breasted-three-piece-suited man bragged.

"Let me give you some market advice – toys, real toys!" someone said, and Mark chuckled. Rumors were wonderful things, and so easy to start.

"I have just hired the best tech-tutor available for my seventeen-year-old. Brilliant boy, brilliant. Great future ahead for him."

The wind picked up outside. People relaxed and got louder as they picked up glasses filled with sparkling cider. The fire blazed. The music buzzed behind conversations while Mr. Cannady wandered about, brightly talking about this and that, business and pleasure. Elliot smiled and waved to Mark, and the lights went out.

Except for the fire it was pitch black. Sparks hissed and spat in the dark as the guests stammered nervously. A great crash of pots reverberated from the kitchen and ten children suddenly raced down the stairs, weaving in between the shadowy bodies of the party-goers.

Fiona ran up to Mark, a slight glow emanating from her whiteness, her body almost translucent. At that moment, he was grateful it was dark so that his guests couldn't see the children clearly.

"Mark, we're scared! Have you looked out the windows?" she asked.

"Why?"

"Everything is coated in ice! That's why the power is out," Rollo exclaimed, pulling on Mark's sleeve. "The cold has come for us!"

"No, it hasn't. Now calm down."

Sam flung himself into Ashley's arms and knocked her over into Elliot who had worked his way through the crowd. They fell like bowling pins, people falling into other people who fell into furniture, which slid ever so slightly, taking the next person by surprise, piling them into one another like some cosmic comedy.

Mirabella laughed with a little animal sound, her eyes glowing yellow in the darkness. "Oooo," she giggled, "everyone is falling down like London Bridge."

"Anyone hurt?" Mark whispered to her.

"No, no one, but there is a lady worrying over her new dress being ruined, and another who is mad at her husband for bringing her. There is a man who ripped his pants when he fell because they were too tight, and Mr. Cannady has something wet running down his undershirt."

"Okay, enough." Across the room, Mark saw Ashley's bright smile by the firelight where she still lay tangled in a heap with Sam.

"Try the phone," Mark said to Traxon, who didn't seem to be having any trouble moving about.

"I did already. It's out, too."

"I told you she was coming," Ailithe rasped eerily.

Castor tugged on Mark's arm and whispered. "I would be happy to act as a small, temporary generator."

Mark turned slowly and stared at the boy. "No, absolutely not. You'd electrocute yourself."

"Not so, but I would reduce my life span. However, it is my duty to serve people."

"You are people, Castor," Mark said. "You'd electrocute yourself." He cleared his throat and announced, "Ladies and gentlemen, I would like to extend the hospitality of my home to all of you for as long as necessary."

"I'm going home," someone said.

"Not me! You couldn't pay me be drive in this weather," a man said.

"Carl, I want to go home, right now."

"No," Carl said, "and don't whine about it either, Frances."

The caterers didn't follow Carl's example. They packed up and went home, leaving the food in serving dishes, slowly cooling.

Twenty minutes later the crowd had thinned by half. Each person who left went with a blast of cold wind. Each time Mark returned to the great room from seeing someone out, he was halfway to permafrost. The fire crackled and hissed as he re-warmed his hands after the fifteenth farewell. The conversation came to an awkward halt as the wind whipped and howled at the windows.

"I know!" Paul said, jumping up in the darkened room and running off. Back he came with marshmallows and graham crackers.

"Add some chocolate, and you have S'mores," Mrs. Cannady said.

Soon they were supping on S'more appetizers and then a dinner of slightly cold gourmet food. The S'mores were the better part. As everyone calmed down, the evening took on a pleasant atmosphere. Several people browsed the bookshelves and settled in to read by candlelight. Others chatted. Ashley snuggled against Mark as he read softly from his father's copy of the *Wizard of Lost Land*. Rollo sat rigidly intent, his mouth slightly open. "It seems so familiar," he said.

Castor and Sam brought wood from the woodpile, dumping huge armfuls on the porch and returning shivering and wet.

Mary Blount, a new empoyee was staring at Castor with her mouth open as he came in. "Uh, aren't these kids a little strange?"

"Huh?" Mark was taken off guard.

"Oh," Elliot called to her. "They love to play dress up."

"Whose are they?" Carl asked from where he sat.

"Mark is foster parenting them," Elliot said.

"He would," Carl said with disgust in his voice.

"How bad is it outside, anyway?" Mary asked. "Do you think I could still get home?"

Castor surprised Mark when he anwered, "Oh, I doubt it, but if you want to go out and look, it's a lovely otherworld out there."

"Lovely? We're trapped, prisoners!" Mary whined.

"But it's still lovely," Fiona insisted, defending Castor. "Just take a look."

"Lovely? What is wrong with all you children?" Mary asked.

Fiona laughed at her, a soft, eerie kind of laugh, and Mark saw the woman instinctively draw back.

"My, my," Mrs. Cannady said, "wherever do you get such catalogs and why do you keep them on your bookshelves?" She held an open magazine before her.

"They come to the house every day. I guess when we straightened up for the party, the kids must have put them there," Mark said, hoping Mrs. Cannady wouldn't pursue the topic. She nodded thoughtfully. Mark felt a moment of relief and then Mr. Cannady turned and joined the conversation.

"They come to your house everyday, Mark? Why don't you put a stop on their delivery," Mr. Cannady suggested.

"Easier said than done," Pete said.

"Then just throw them away," Mr. Cannady said impatiently.

Mark opened his mouth to answer, but Ashley stepped in quickly, and said diplomatically, "They're actually quite amusing, and they're also quite a mystery."

"What do you mean, my dear?" Mr. Cannady asked.

"Well, you see, they come every day, ten to fifteen of them every morning like clockwork, except on Sundays," she said.

"A neighbor claims they have been coming to this house, rain or shine, whether it was occupied or empty, every day, for fifty-two years," Pete added.

"Hogwash! Someone has been pulling your leg."

"It's a pretty weird joke, doncha think?" Pete said, urging the game along.

What was Pete thinking? This was too dangerous. Mark opened his mouth to divert the conversation, but Mr. Cannady, who had taken a catalog and was flipping through it, spoke first.

"What a lot of junk. Who would order this stuff? Probably some sort of scam to get money."

Mark was about to agree just to close down the conversation when Ashley asked, "But why send the catalogs for so long?"

"It's a prank, my dear, a prank," Mr. Cannady said firmly.

"Why don't you order something from it," Fiona said to Mr. Cannady, "just to see what happens."

"Yes, yes," Elflet said, bouncing up to Mr. Cannady who had by now sat down on the sofa, catalog still in hand. "But not from that one. Here," Elflet said, pulling one from under the cushions, already marked with little slips of white paper. "Try this one."

Mr. Cannady smiled condescendingly.

"Why not?" Randal Potter said. "Just to put it to rest."

"Hurrumph, well then, what shall I order?" He flipped the pages to the markings and scanned the possibilities.

"Let's vote," Elflet suggested.

"I don't think this is a good idea," Mark said. "Let's let the whole matter drop."

"Oh, look here," a young woman who clung to Randal Potter's arm cooed. "How about this darling thing?"

She held up a page, pointing to a picture of a fluffy mutant from the planet Orb. The caption read: *Noted for their strength, this child's ancestors were developed to terra-form other worlds. She has seven clawed, opposable toes for digging, and sports a prehensile tail which she uses for superior climbing abilities.*

"No, I don't think so," Mark said and glared at Traxon, whom he was sure had marked that page.

"How about this sweet one? Little Miss Muffett," Mrs. Cannady suggested. "We could always have it sent to Suzanna, our granddaughter. She's so fond of cuddly things. Look what it says: *Sweet, soft little girl, with pillow, and a particular aversion to spiders.*"

"Maybe, maybe." Mr. Cannady muttered, then threw the catalog down, and said, "This is ridiculous! I tell you, nothing will come of it."

"Ask Mark," Jack said quickly.

"What? Have you actually ordered from these things?"

"Well, you must admit, if they came to your home they would make you curious," Mark said, giving Jack a very angry glare.

"Well, did you get what you ordered?" Mr. Cannady asked.

"No, not what I ordered," Mark said.

"You see? You wasted your money."

Mark didn't answer and for once the children were quiet, until Castor said, "Not really wasted. Not exactly, sir."

"So you got something? But not what you ordered?"

"Right," Mark said. "So you see, you were right, sir, don't order from them." He picked up all the catalogs and placed them back on the shelf.

"But," Mrs. Cannady said, "that doesn't explain why the catalogs have come for so long. Surely no one would order from them twice if they were cheated, so why keep sending them?"

"Obviously, the perpetrators are desperate to unload their bogus goods," Mr. Cannady said.

Bogus goods was exactly right. Bogus in more than one way, but the question remained. Why had they persisted all these years?

Why it's obvious, Mark heard Mirabella say in his mind. *They want to get us out of the cold.*

He hoped she was right. He hoped their purpose was to get the kids out of cold storage and into the world. But why had they been put there to begin with? What was the point? It was a conundrum. Mark chewed on his thumb absently, momentarily forgetting the party and the people around him until he heard Mirabella ask, "Did anyone ever come up with a way to grow children artificially?" She must have been eavesdropping on his or Pete's thoughts.

"What an extraordinarily odd question for a child to ask," Elliot's wife said.

"Well, did they?" Mirabella asked again.

"For heavens sake, child, that technology was abandoned long ago. Never did pull it off," Mr. Cannady said.

"What? You mean someone tried it? That's an abomination," Ashley declared without hesitation.

"My father invested in that project," Elliot said. "He thought it was going to be the biggest economic boom ever. It failed miserably."

"I should hope so," Ashley said unsympathetically.

Mr. Cannady cleared his throat. "Lots of people lost their shirts investing in that, but if they could have pulled it off, think of the money they would have made."

Elliot bit his lip and said, "It certainly ruined my father."

"I'm sorry, Elliot," Ashley said sheepishly.

"Yes, me, too, but it's just as well it failed."

Mark thought at Mirabella, *Don't pursue this. It's not a good idea.*

But, she thought back, *it's what you were thinking about.*

He gave her a dirty look and asked Elliot, "What did your father do after that?"

"I don't know. He never told us. When I was fifteen, he left my mother and I never saw him again. He was a lot older than my mother and he died a few years later."

"Sorry, I didn't mean to pry."

"It's okay. I got over it long ago. They sent us all of his belongings squeezed into one tattered suitcase a few months after he died, but none of us ever even went through them." Elliot added beneath his breath, "But I wish I had taken the time."

No one but Mark seemed to have heard him. It made him think about the box his own father had left for him. It felt wrong for it to have been ignored for so long. *I'll look at it as soon as everyone leaves*, he promised himself.

"Maybe we should sample the cheesecake the caterers brought. It'll help keep our minds off the weather. Traxon and Jack and Rollo will get some more wood with me, while you all start. Please, enjoy!" he said out loud to his guests.

The boys and he bundled into coats and slipped out the door as quickly as possible to keep the heat in and the cold out. Mark huffed puffs of white breath into his gloves and stepped carefully across the slippery porch. Broad trees were enshrouded in ice. Golden seed pods in glassy jackets dangled rigidly from the dry remnants of summer plantings. Nothing moved even though the wind stung their cheeks. The boys hurriedly filled their arms with wood and were at the door when a thunderous cracking filled the air. An ancient tree limb crashed to the ground, splintering ice as it fell and sending little crystal spears sliding across the frozen yard. Startled, the boys stood immobilized by the sound.

"Come on, hurry now, boys," Mark called.

They scurried back into the great room, dumping their loads by the hearth. The fire spit more loudly as bits of ice fell into it from their coats. The guests were eating cheesecake rather quietly, sipping at tepid coffee that had ceased to heat when the electricity had died.

Ashley's head swiveled back and forth as she glanced around the room. "Mark, I think we need to entertain them a little. I've got an idea," she said. "Hey, everybody, let's play a game, okay? How about, *Just Suppose*. It was what we played whenever the lights went out when I was little."

"Sure," Jack said. "How do you play?"

"It's simple. First you think of something absurd. For example, uh, let me see. Okay, I'm ready. Just suppose we could grow children artificially. Now, Mr. Cannady, what do you think would happen if we could do that? You say, and then ask someone else, and we'll go around the room. At the end, we'll vote on who made the original Just Suppose most plausible."

"This is stupid," Mary Blount complained.

"Have you got a better suggestion on how to pass the time?" Ashley asked her.

"No, but…"

Lucy Cannady stopped Mary in mid-sentence. "Let's play. I think it'll be fun."

"What do we win?" Sam asked.

"That I can answer," Mr. Cannady said. "I will offer the prize, but I get to decide who wins. None of this voting." He paused, and hearing no objections or grumbling, said, "Whoever wins can pick anything he or she wants out of one of the catalogs!"

Everyone laughed loudly except for Mark and Pete and Ashley.

Smiling, Mr. Cannady said, "I'll go first. Just suppose, if they could grow children artificially — hmmm." He put his finger in the air as he came up with an idea. "They would start selling them at a great profit. They would advertise them with phrases like, pick your kid, no sass back, no worries, choose their interests and their eye color. Okay, Carl, you and Frances are next."

"Me? Okay, okay. I think they would find ways to market the kids they created with other special products like clothes, games, accessories," Carl said blandly, obviously disinterested.

"Like invisibility screens," Traxon said gleefully.

"It is not your turn, young man." Frances pouted possessively. "It's mine and I think they would promise high achievers. Everybody wants smart children."

"You," Carl said, appointing Pete. "You're next."

"I don't even hafta think about it. They'd grow people who could change their DNA at will so they could do what they wanted without getting caught," Pete said without even a moment's hesitation.

"We can't do that," Sam said.

"Of course not, little boy," Frances said. "No one can. Besides, who would want to be able to do that?"

"Crooks? People who wanna a way to make a lot of money quick and easy. Think of the ads. Grow a gang of untraceable henchmen! I know some guys who'd pay big bucks for that," Pete declared.

"That seems very improbable," Randal Potter said.

"That is an absolutely disgusting idea," Mary Blount said.

"More disgusting than engineering children to some artificial standard so they're all alike and then marketing them? Not to me. Least ways, my idea would put some challenge back in a cop's job," Pete said almost longingly.

"What outlandish ideas!" Carl said. "Nobody wants to increase opportunities for criminals to escape. Besides, there isn't any crime anymore."

"Not that anybody admits to, anyways," Pete mumbled. "Your turn, Fiona," he said, passing the next turn to his granddaughter.

"They would make people who have been lost," she volunteered immediately.

"Lost? Why bother? Somebody might still find them," Jack said.

"Maybe, unless they're dead," Fiona murmured.

"Then they'd be making ghosts," Jack pointed out.

"Ghosts do not exist," Elliot said stolidly.

"Are you sure?" Fiona asked, her voice slightly shaky.

"Absolutely."

"All right, then it's your turn, Elliot," Fiona said, passing the task along quickly.

"I suppose they might try to make perfect people."

"What does that mean?" Mark asked. "What's a perfect person?"

Elliot laughed. "I have absolutely no idea. I guess I wasted my turn. To you, Mark."

Mark took in a deep breath and said, "I think they'd recreate people or characters who no longer exist, but whom the world still needs."

"How quaint," Carl commented condescendingly.

"Like who? That might actually have some commercial potential," Mr. Cannady asked seriously.

"Servants that would be reliable?" Frances suggested. "My servants can't be trusted to do anything correctly."

Ashley laughed at the woman. "That would be an awfully expensive solution, don't you think?"

"Any other suggestions?" Mr. Cannady asked. "I like Mark's idea."

"Perhaps a hero for the times, an inventor of imagination, or some-one like that?" Elliot said whimsically. "We could use more of those."

"Like me?" Rollo said in an awed voice.

"Like you?" Mr. Cannady said. "You're just a rather chubby boy."

"I'm an inventor and I have a great imagination."

"Oh, I see," Mr. Cannady said patronizingly.

"Maybe like you, Rollo," Mark agreed.

"Come now, no one would bother with any of these ideas," Mary Blount said. "This is ridiculous!"

"I pass to Mirabella," Mark said, ignoring the woman.

"What about making people who could bring magic back to the world? Isn't that what you think we've lost, Mark? Magic?"

Everyone's head turned towards Mark, almost in unison, and stared at him.

"Magic?" Mr. Cannady finally said, incredulously. "You can't believe in magic!"

"No, not magic, but something magical and unexpected. Something barely this side of impossible," Mark said, hoping the longing wasn't obvious in his voice.

"Like the ice storm," Ailithe whispered.

Before anyone could protest, Lucy Cannady spoke brightly as she turned away from the window. "The child is absolutely right! Just look out there with the moonlight on the ice. It is absolutely, without a doubt, magical."

"Lucy, enough," Mr. Cannady commanded. "This game is over. I'm giving the prize to Carl. Pick which toy you want from the catalogs, Carl."

"Oh, goody," Frances giggled.

Quiet descended on the room. The storm raged and the cold seeped through the house except around the hearth. People huddled together, spellbound by the crackle and fire-fly sparks of embers and soft-floating soot. Slowly, as the night dragged on, they drifted into sleep, except for Mark. He spent the night watching Ashley sleep on the pillow next to him, thinking about how lucky he was.

At the first dim sign of light, Mark shook Ashley awake and pulled her into the kitchen. "Let's go outside and watch the sunrise together."

She poked him gently with one finger. "I think you're a romantic under there, Mark Perralt."

"Come," he said awkwardly, "or the sun will come up without us."

That sounded so trite he wanted to hide. The best he could do was swathe his face in a scarf. They bundled into their coats and gloves and tiptoed out the kitchen door into a still, dark morning. Not a sound, not a squeak, not a buzz broke the pre-dawn moments. Then the sun rose, and the first rays bounced off the sleeves of ice that bound the world.

"Beautiful," Ashley whispered and squeezed his hand. "Magical," she added in an awe-struck voice.

They were held there, entranced and hypnotized, until from somewhere down the street, the crash of another mighty limb brought them back to reality. She took her hand from his and breathed into her cupped fingers.

Frowning a little, she asked, "Mark, do you really think they grew the children in tanks?"

"I don't know," he said. "I hope not."

"Mr. Cannady said the scientists never learned how."

"What if they did, except no one ever found out about it?"

"That was a long time ago. Who'd be making them now?"

"I'd guess some of the scientists who had worked on it, lost their licenses and went into hiding."

"Wouldn't they be awfully old by now?"

"Maybe. Maybe they trained younger people to carry on."

"And these scientists, who once engaged in serious research, who were at the forefront of cutting edge technology, decided to make storybook children? And then marketed them as toys for fifty years? What a joke! Give me a break, Mark."

"Ashley, they're marketing them as toys because no one would purchase them otherwise. And maybe they chose story characters because no one would care about the results."

She backed away. "I care, you care! I don't believe anyone would do that! No one could be that cruel!"

She pushed past him and back into the house, shattering the magic, but he didn't blame her. It did sound cruel, but he couldn't shake the idea. He didn't want it to be the truth, but it was all he could come up with.

Pete came out and said, "Need any help?"

He hung his head. "More than I can say. I wish I knew the truth."

Pete patted Mark on the back gently. "It'll work out, bud."

They went back inside. Everyone was looking at catalogs.

"They're bored," Ailithe said. "They complain a lot, so we offered them catalogs to look at."

"Oh, great!" Mark frantically clapped his hands to divert their attention, and called out, "How about some breakfast?"

Everyone instantly shed the catalogs onto the chairs and sofa. Mark offered cold cereal and bread and some fruit. No one complained. They were finishing when the house shuddered and the furnace began to purr.

"Electricity!" everyone cried. "We'll be able to go home soon."

"Now, I hope," Mark whispered happily to Pete.

Mark gathered the coats, gloves, hats, that had been piled all night on his bed. People claimed them in a rush to get ready to leave.

"In some pitifully small way, this has been entertaining," Carl said with a smirk. "By the way, have you seen my wife's boots?"

"Boots? No, I haven't."

"How about mine?" Mrs. Cannady asked.

"Yours?" Mark said uncomfortably. "Uh, excuse me for a minute. I'll ask the children."

He found Elflet in the kitchen.

"Come here, Elflet." Mark held his hands out to the child. "Boots!" he demanded.

"I can't, I mean they're a bit, uh . . . "

"Disassembled," Castor volunteered. "Here are the pieces. I put them in neat piles for you."

"Good grief! Elflet, the guests want their boots. How many pairs did you take apart?"

The child held up four fingers.

"But if they go home," Rollo said, "their furnaces won't be on. Just ours. So it doesn't matter anyway."

"You? You made it come on? But everyone thinks . . ."

"I know, I'm sorry, Mark. I just wanted everyone to be warm. I thought you would notice the lights were still out. I didn't count on the sun being so bright you wouldn't need to turn on the lights."

"She deceives the eye with the brightness of her ice," Ailithe pronounced like an augur.

Elflet, who had his nose up against the window, said, "Everything is all shiny like a million mirrors.

How was he going to explain this? Everyone thought they could go home, that their heat would be on, except it wouldn't be.

"Markham, come in here please," Elliot said. "Laura's boots have vanished and the clocks don't seem to be working. We tried the phone to check in with the babysitter and the lines are still dead. What's going on?"

"Rollo seems to have brought the furnace back on by. . . " He thought as quickly as he could. "By hooking it up to an old generator I had picked up for parts. So we have heat."

"Do you think the electricity is down all across the city?"

"I've no idea," Mark said.

"Who would have dreamed we could be cut off from the world and reduced to shivering fools?" Elliot moaned.

He's quite worried about his little girl, Mirabella thought to Mark.

"Do you think Lisa's okay?" Elliot asked as if he had heard her.

Mark patted Elliot's back gently.

"I have an idea. Sam?" He called to the little boy and took the child into the kitchen. "How would you like to perform a superhero act? Your first!"

"Really?" the child asked, his face lighting up with happiness. "Yes, yes. What do you want me to do?"

"Fly to Elliot's house and check on his daughter. Also, perhaps you could see how widespread the damage is?"

"Aw, that's too easy. Don't you have anything harder for me to do?"

"Like what?"

"Stopping a great evil or something?"

"Where did you get such an idea, Sam?" Mirabella asked as she joined them.

"From a comic book in the box Traxon took. It had this guy named Sam Mann, The Strongman who is really strong and can fly and kick bad guys real hard with steel-toed black boots and never looses a fight."

"Sam, I don't want you to try kicking bad guys. You're only a little boy and we have no idea what you can really do," Mark said as firmly as he could.

"But, I'm just like him. I can fly and I'm strong and he even has a great dog, just like me!"

"Sam," Mirabella said, "we all seem to be like someone in a book, usually a children's book, but none of us is quite right. There is always something a bit wrong. Don't try anything in a book. We have to figure out what we can and can't do, just like any other children would."

"Okay, okay. I'll just do what Mark wants. But I hope I'm like the guy in the comic book. He was a real hero."

Mark wasn't sure about the 'real' part of that statement. None of the kids seemed like they were quite real, but Mirabella was right. Just like all children, these kids had to find out who they were as they grew up. Or maybe, he thought, find out who they were not. He wrote down directions for Sam to Elliot's house and gave him a street map in case he got lost.

"And take Speedy with you," Mark added at the last minute, thinking surely the dog would always be able to find its way home.

"Okay, but first I have to get dressed in my costume. It's black and I cut a hole in the shirt so I could write *SAM* on my chest with a marker. And Pete let me get black rubber boots, too."

Mark suppressed a laugh as Sam ran upstairs to change. He returned to his guests. "Listen, everyone, I'm sure Elliot told you already that our heat is the result of an old generator I had picked up and not a return of the power. So, I guess you will not be able to go home yet."

Mr. Cannady was standing by the window. "You were right, Lucy. It's actually beautiful outside. Who would think such beauty could wreak such havoc?" He continued to stare out the window, when suddenly he jerked his head up. "What, what the devil is that?" he asked, pointing up.

"What?" Elliot asked, peering out.

"It's gone! I swear it looked like — no never mind, not possible." Mr. Cannady continued to chew on his knuckle and kept looking back up at the sky.

"Oh, look!" Ailithe cried, joining him at the window "A red bird, there on that branch!"

The red blazed out amid the translucent ice.

"I'm going out for some more logs," Mark said.

"I'd like to come," Mr. Cannady said.

They bundled up, pulled on gloves and slipped out the front door.

"Mark, uh, listen, I'm a bit worried. I, uh, swear I saw one of the children fly off. I mean fly off into the sky!"

Mark didn't answer. He wondered if Mr. Cannady could accept the truth.

"Perhaps all the silence has given rise to a hallucination?" Mr. Cannady suggested almost hopefully.

"Could be, sir," Mark agreed quickly. "Don't worry, I am sure this won't last much longer. "

Mr. Cannady took an armload of wood and left Mark looking out into the icy beauty. The redbird had flown and only the ice was left, clear, thin, delicate yet so strong it had becalmed the whole world. He reached for one more log when he heard the sound. It was so close that he felt as if he was drowning in its reverberations. He didn't even have time to look up as the tree that grew through the porch crashed down on him.

HEROES AND HEROINES

A.
B.
C.

A. Teen King Arthur: 6th century, British, king
of chivalry, founder of the Round table - 75
(Knights of Round table also available on p.55)
B. Jeanne d'Arc: 15th c. brave girl warrior,
immortalized in songs, plays, art and film.- 75
C. Tarzan: raised by great apes, boy in touch
with natural world, great sense of justice. From
book by Edgar Rice Burroughs. 75
(Mechanical gorilla, elephant and chimpanzee
available on page 88.)

ark! Mirabella was shouting into his mind. *It's so dark where you are! Please come back to the light!*

He tried, really he did, but he couldn't see her. He couldn't see anything but a murky darkness. He tried to hear, but the only sounds he could hear were Mirabella's thoughts and a loud buzzing in his ears. He tried to answer her.

You're alive. I knew it. They think you may be dead, under the porch roof and the tree. I'll tell them.

Dim, rather vague light crept under his eyelids. He could hear, but what he knew must be words had a tinny, distant quality that prevented him from understanding them. He focused as best he could and his hearing began to filter noise into words.

"What are we going to do?" Elliot was saying. "We can't just leave him there!"

"Well, we aren't going to be able to move that tree by ourselves."

"We gotta try," Pete said.

"Move," a small voice said. Mark heard a clunk and then another. The rhythm seemed like it should mean something. It was Paul and his ax! The rhythm got faster, and faster, and faster.

"Do you believe that?" someone said. "How can that be?"

"Cause he's Paul Bunyan, you big dopes," Jack's voice said, indignantly admonishing them.

"Who?" Carl asked.

"Paul Bunyan. Don't you guys know nothing? He's the big woodsman with the giant blue ox named Babe."

"You need to curb your imagination, young man. And anyway, that ax is not big enough to do the job."

"Wanna bet?" Jack asked.

"I could fit through that opening and see how badly hurt he is," Fiona soon said.

"My dear child, that is barely a crack. No one could get through that," Lucy Cannady protested.

"Please, Grandpa Pete, please let me try. What if he's bleeding or something?"

He didn't hear an answer, only the thump of the ax, but a few moments later he felt Fiona close by.

"Mark, how do you feel?"

He opened his mouth, but couldn't get any sound out of it.

"Mirabella, interpret for me," Fiona called out.

He's cold and his chest hurts. He's having trouble getting enough air. Pete says to give him your coat and get out of there.

Mark saw the child melt out of her coat and then stretch and pull her body like a contortionist until she was flexible enough to slide between the chunks of debris and tree that had buried him.

"Did you see that?" Mrs. Cannady asked.

"I did not see a thing." Carl was in denial, but his voice was on the edge of hysteria.

"Quiet!" Pete said. "I wish Sam was here. He could lift these logs right off."

"That little child?" Mr. Cannady protested.

"I could help," Castor said. "I'm quite strong, really."

"Sure, kid," someone said.

"Castor, be careful," Mirabella warned.

Mark felt a lowering blackness and fell past consciousness.

"How is he?" someone was asking.

"I think his leg is broken," another voice said.

"I think his ribs are broken." The first voice spoke again.

"Get outta the way, everybody," Pete instructed. He stuffed something under Mark's nose. Ammonia. Marks eyes snapped open. "Okay, back off. Howya feeling, Mark?"

He wanted to answer, but couldn't yet. His throat was raw from the cold.

"Move over," Ashley said to Pete and held warm tea to Mark's lips. "Sip, just a little at first. You were out there two hours before Paul chopped you out and we got you in here."

"I want to talk to him as soon as I can," Mr. Cannady said.

"About what?" Ashley said, turning on the man, hands on hips like a ferocious watch dog.

"About, well, about these kids."

"It can wait, unless you think they are going to magically vanish in a poof of smoke?"

"Uh, no, of course not, but . . ."

"Then back off," she said firmly.

"Ashley," Mark whispered hoarsely. "Where's Sam?"

"He hasn't come back yet, but don't worry, okay. How are you?" she said gently. He was lying near the fire on a heavy blanket.

"I think I need a doctor."

She nodded in agreement.

"Let's take a look and see how bad it really is," Pete said.

"The ice, she has done this," Ailithe declared as tears trickled down her face.

"All you kids, go in the kitchen, now!" Pete said. "And for that matter, everybody but Elliot and Ashley can go in there. This might hurt, Mark, but we gotta take a look. Try and think about something else."

Mirabella, tell me what everyone is thinking, he called to her mentally to distract himself.

Mr. Cannady is mad that you hid all our talents from him. He thinks we're marketable at least as advertising. Elliot's wife keeps thinking about Lisa. She doesn't care about much else, really. This guy Carl, he thinks there's something fishy going on. He's ready to check and see if any of us have papers. His wife, she's just scared. There's a woman who works with you who is denying everything. It's Mr. Cannady's wife who is interesting. Oh, and I keep vaguely hearing your sister Kate, somewhere. She's desperately trying to find out if we're all okay. She is really upset. She loves you, you know.

Mark lost her voice to pain as Ashley and Elliot took off his jacket. They cut part of it away so they wouldn't have to pull on his arms. Pete did the same to one of his pants' legs.

"His left knee sure is puffed up. Hope it's not broken. I got some experience with emergency medicine. but I can't tell for sure," Pete said, and scratched his head. "It's easy to see he's got a lot of bruises all over, probably a broken rib or two from the discoloration there, and I'd guess he's got a concussion from the look of the knot on his head and the way his eyes are dilated. Not as bad as it coulda been."

"Good," Mark mumbled groggily, "but it still hurts."

"Gotta wrap those ribs. Can you sit up?"

"I'll try."

It made him dizzy. Ashley held him and Elliot helped Pete tear strips of cloth to tie around his chest.

"It's okay, Mark," Ashley said as he gasped. "I'm here. I'm not going anywhere."

"You mean, you'll be," he gasped, "my girl?"

"I'll think about it," she said softly. "Now shut up."

FAIRY DUSTINGS

SPECIAL OFFER..75.00
TINKERBELL, TEENY FAIRY FROM THE FAMOUS
BOOK BY J.M. BARRIE ---PETER AND WENDY.

ALSO AVAILABLE: DOLL HOUSE WITH SPECIAL
FAIRY FURNITURE, KITCHEN EQUIPPED WITH BAGS
OF FAIRY DUST. 125.00

He sipped at a little tea warmed over the fire in a kettle Pete had found in the basement. His stomach was empty and he still felt like throwing up. Pete said it was from the concussion and, since they couldn't contact a doctor, it was the best guess anyone had. He tried hard not to think about the drumming in his head or the ringing in his ears. He was just dozing off when he heard Frances Ellerby exclaim.

"This is it! This is the toy we want!"

"What is it?" Ashley asked, irritation clearly showing in her voice.

"Here, take a look."

Mark called to her hoarsely, his throat still raw, "Well, what is it?"

"*Jack the Giant Killer. Takes on tasks bigger than he, especially bullies and other bad guys,*" Ashley read out loud.

"Why this one?" Mr. Cannady asked.

"Well, our son is six, and there is a boy who is picking on him. It just seems like the perfect toy to give him confidence right now."

Ashley, Mark and Pete exchanged glances.

"Couldn't do too much harm, I suppose," Mr. Cannady said.

I hope not, Mark thought to himself.

"I wonder where the catalog got such a wonderful idea?" Frances sang sweetly.

"From stories, of course," Jack snorted. "Where'd you think?"

"Oh, now, now, boy, don't get all excited."

"You know, I've got a name, and it isn't boy. My name is Jack — like Jack the Giant Killer!"

"Oh, good grief. There are no giants, and no giant killers. We're ordering a toy!" Carl said angrily.

"How do you know there are no giants?" Jack asked them. "You think you know everything! I was going to be the giant killer some day!" He ran out of the room, jumping over the balustrade of the staircase in an impossibly high Jack-Be-Nimble jump and ran upstairs, presumably to his room. Mark heard the door slam.

"He's right, you know, nobody knows everything," Pete said. "Who knows, maybe you'll need a giant killer someday, just like Mark needed Paul Bunyan."

"That little boy is not this Paul Bunyan person," Carl insisted.

"He is very good with an ax," Ailithe said. Her mouth turned into a thin-lined smile as she asked, "Do you suppose that I can fly, Mr. Ellerby?"

"No, you cannot," Mark said pointedly. "Please, Ailithe, go make sure Jack is okay. And walk up the stairs, do not fly up them too quickly."

"Right! fly! Why would any child think she could fly?"

"I thought I could fly when I was little," Mrs. Cannady said.

"What are you talking about, my dear?" Mr. Cannady asked.

"I was three, and they had a showing of an old movie — *Peter Pan*. Peter sprinkled fairy dust over these three children, Wendy, Michael and John, and they could fly. So, I thought I might be able to fly, too. I stood at the top of the steps, sprinkled a little salt on my head, and then yelled out, 'Daddy, I'm going to fly' and jumped. My daddy caught me halfway down the stairs, but I thought I could really fly. I really did believe it for quite a long time!"

"See, that's exactly why all these silly fairy tales and stories are dangerous!" Frances exclaimed. "You could have been killed."

"But it was the most wonderful feeling while I believed it," Mrs. Cannady whispered to Mark where he was lying. "So magical."

"There's a Peter Pan in the catalogs," Traxon said. "Want me to show him to you?"

"Oh, would you, Traxon? Thank you."

He went to the shelves and straight to a thick catalog. "If you order Peter, he comes with the book by J.M. Barrie, *Peter and Wendy*," he explained.

"And look, I could order the three children, too," Lucy Cannady cried out, clearly delighted.

"Yes, but I'd advise against the Captain Hook," Fiona said, sidling up to join their conversation.

"Oh, darling," Mrs. Cannady said to Mr. Cannady, "do you mind if I order these? I know it's silly, but it reminds me of a lovely time in my life."

"Whatever you want, my dear, whatever, although I hardly think jumping off a staircase is something to be memorialized."

"As soon as the power returns!" she said. The smile that covered her face made her pretty.

At that moment there was a light tapping at the door. Pete opened it and Speedy scooted inside, jumped on him and lapped his cheek with his tongue. Behind the dog stood Sam, holding a small girl by the hand.

"Lisa!" Elliot exclaimed, scooping the child up into his arms. "How on earth did you get here?"

"Sam brought me," she said.

"How?"

"We flew," she said. "Whee, it was fun!"

"Now Lisa, people can't fly."

"Uh huh!" she insisted. "And dogs, too."

Elliot hugged his little girl, choosing not to ask anymore.

Sam looked at Mark and said, "What happened?"

"The tree fell, but it's okay. Paul chopped me out," Mark said. He felt oddly calm. "Castor lifted the wood off of me. I'll be fine." He reached out and patted Sam's arm.

"Good." Sam lowered his voice. "Mark, the whole city is down. And it looks like it's clouding up for another storm."

"The sky is clear," Ashley pointed out.

"Not from up really high. I checked. I could see storm clouds."

Ailithe came up to them. "It's a warmer wind than the ice lady. She brings snow. Thick, deep white, whirling about, covering the ice."

"That could make more trees come down. Mark, what are we going to do?" Ashley asked. "How long can you feed all these people?"

"Ailithe, how much time do we have?"

"Not today," was all the child said.

"Then maybe we have time to get everyone out of here and back home before the next storm hits." Ashley said. "But how?"

They looked at each other, but none of them had an idea until Castor cleared his throat and said timidly, "Perhaps I could lay my hands on the cars."

"How's that gonna help?" Jack asked.

"I have the ability to super-heat or super-chill my extremities," Castor explained.

"Really? Wow!" Rollo said admiringly. "Wish I could do that."

"The function is designed to help me regulate my body temperature, but I believe I can use it to melt the ice. Once I get down to the

238

metal of the car itself, I should be able to heat it so that the ice will liquefy easily."

"This isn't going to damage you, is it?" Mark asked.

"It's perfectly natural for me. I'll be fine."

"In that case, unless someone else has a better idea, go for it, Castor," Mark said.

"But what about the roads?" Sam asked. "They're really thick with ice. Castor can't melt all that."

"Are they salted yet?"

"Why would they salt roads?" Elflet asked.

"To melt the ice."

"Wouldn't it take a long, long time to sprinkle all that salt onto the streets?" Elflet said, scratching behind one of his pointy ears.

"They do it with big trucks," Ashley explained.

"Big white trucks? I saw some of those rumbling around out there," Sam said.

"You did?" Mr. Cannady said, walking over to their group. "So if we can get to the main roads we might be able to get home."

The discussion spread around the room as people perked up at the thought of going home.

"But the cars are iced in," Carl said, "and I don't think we could chop them out with a pick ax."

"I think Castor can take care of it," Mark said.

"Oh really? How's that? Is he a superhero or something?"

"Oh no, sir. I'm a cyborg," the boy corrected Carl.

Carl snickered, rolled his eyes and twirled a finger around pointing at his own head. "Crazy, crazy!" he said.

"Why's he doing that?" Elflet squeaked between giggles as he watched Carl.

"I don't know," Sam said.

Carl was laughing openly now. "Melt the ice!" He smirked between laughs, then laughed again and again.

"Once the ice on the cars is melted, I can pull them out to the main roads with my truck. It'll be slow, one at a time, but I should be able to do it," Pete suggested. "I only wish we had more than one old truck, so we could get everyone out of here faster, especially him," Pete said, pointing at Carl.

"What you need is a replicator," Traxon said, "so we could make more trucks."

"What's a replicator?" Castor asked.

"A machine that can copy exactly whatever you want it to."

"Now that would be a hot item!" Mr. Cannady observed.

"Mr. Cannady, you don't believe such a thing could exist, do you? It's ridiculous!" Carl said derisively.

"I've seen a lot of things since this party began that I never would have believed."

"Old people!" accidentally slipped out of Carl's mouth.

"Pardon me?" Mr. Cannady said threateningly.

"It's only — I mean — well . . ."

"Yes, Carl, what do you mean?"

"We all know that, um, older people aren't always, uh, you know, with it."

"What?" Mark asked.

"They get weird ideas, sometimes." Carl stuttered, saw Mr. Cannady glaring at him and tried again. "I mean, they, uh, read a lot when they were young, so they acquired some, uh, odd, old-fashioned ideas."

"You can't mean Mr. Cannady, can you?" Ashley asked, exaggerating an expression of amazement.

Carl stammered inarticulately without finding a response.

Mr. Cannady looked from Carl to Ashley and back again. His brow creased. "I have never pretended to like imaginative stories. Always left that to Lucy. But there is a difference between stories and direct observation. If it happens, then that makes it fact. If you deny facts, why then, Carl, I think you are the one imagining things. I saw a toddler chop through a whole tree. I saw another young boy pick up logs that ten men would have struggled with. Was that just my imagination? Was it just a story? I saw it!"

"Yes, dear, but it would sound like a very crazy tale if it got out on the Net news," Lucy Cannady said to her husband. "Perhaps it would be better not to mention all this, don't you think?"

"Perhaps," her husband growled, "but in this room, is anyone willing to deny what has happened?"

No one said a word.

"Does this make us conspirators?" Ashley asked slyly.

"Conspirators!" Carl exclaimed. "Oh no, I'm not going to be drawn into that!"

"Fine, then," Mark said. "Go report the story."

Carl spluttered and then clamped his lips together.

"I'm going to get started," Castor said.

"Come on, you guys," Pete called to the kids. "Get bundled up and we'll scrape at the ice as soon as it starts melting.

Mark noticed Fiona and Rollo were missing. He was about to ask where they were when Lucy Cannady said, "Mark, do you have some paper so I can write down the ordering information for Peter and his friends? Perhaps I should order Tinkerbell as well. Our grandchildren would have such fun with them."

"Lucy, those children have too many toys at their houses already," Mr. Cannady said. "You keep whatever you order for them to play with at our house."

She nodded and looked a little sheepish as she tried to suppress her smile. "Of course, you're quite right, my dear. They'll stay with us." Then she whispered to Mark again. "He's always a bit grumpy when something unexpected happens to him. Except for the tree, I think this has all been quite delightful, myself."

Rollo came out of the kitchen. "We can listen to the news."

"What? How?" Mr. Cannady asked.

"I got Mark's short-wave radio to work, but the batteries aren't going to last long. Be careful not to jiggle it or move it."

Rollo put on his coat, wrapped his face in a muffler and went outside to help as all the guests rushed past him, shoving to get through the kitchen door. Only Ashley, Mrs. Cannady and Elliot remained with Mark.

"My, my, they're all in such a rush to get back home. I rather like it here, with all of you children," Mrs. Cannady said, gesturing to include Ashley and Mark. "May I come back to visit?"

"Of course," Mark said. "Any time."

"I'll let you know when my order from the catalog arrives," she said and winked. "You won't mind if I bring my new toys over for your children to play with, will you?" She smiled very sweetly and took Ashley's hand. "Come, my dear, let us go get a piece of that cheesecake." They followed the crowd into the kitchen, leaving Elliot alone in the room with Mark.

Rollo stuck his head inside and yelled, "Whose car do you want us to do first?"

"Elliot's," Mark called back.

"Thanks, Mark," Elliot said very quietly. "And not just about the car. All of my life I have walked the straight and narrow until I met you. I have no idea what's going on and I don't really want to know, but thank you for bringing Lisa to us, however you did it." He turned to leave and stopped. "And thanks for making life more fun."

"It has been my pleasure, Elliot." Mark smiled. "Go home now and play with Lisa."

"I will," Elliot said. "See you soon, and feel better."

He gathered Lisa and Laura. They bundled into their coats. Speedy barked, and Lisa giggled and waved her little hand at the dog as they left.

COMIX

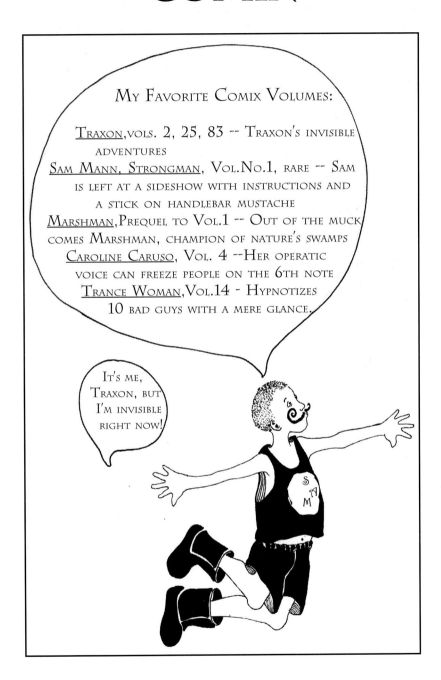

My Favorite Comix Volumes:

Traxon, vols. 2, 25, 83 -- Traxon's invisible adventures

Sam Mann, Strongman, Vol. No. 1, rare -- Sam is left at a sideshow with instructions and a stick on handlebar mustache

Marshman, Prequel to Vol. 1 -- Out of the muck comes Marshman, champion of nature's swamps

Caroline Caruso, Vol. 4 -- Her operatic voice can freeze people on the 6th note

Trance Woman, Vol. 14 - Hypnotizes 10 bad guys with a mere glance.

It's me, Traxon, but I'm invisible right now!

he guests' fancy cars were pulled out one by one to the main road behind Pete's rattle-trap old truck. It took several hours and by the time they were all finally gone, the phone had come back on. Mark had Ashley call Kate and tell her they were fine.

"Kate's nice," Ashley said. "I like her."

"Good," Mark said. "I hoped you two would like each other."

"Do you think Mrs. Cannady knew?" Pete asked, as he rejoined them by the fire, holding cold-reddened hands up to the warmth. "Sure sounded like it. How'd she figure it out?"

"Uh, Peter and Wendy, John and Michael, and Tinkerbell were in the same catalog as Rollo," Fiona said, handing Mark the magazine.

"Good grief!" Ashley exclaimed.

"Well, well," Pete said.

"I bet Mr. Cannady is grumpy for a while after those kids arrive."

"Could be, but I bet Lucy Cannady can handle it," Mark said softly. "Listen, could you all help pick up now that our guests have gone home?"

The children scattered like little mice, picking up the scraps and debris left from the party.

"I'm hungry," Paul said.

"You're always hungry," Jack noted.

Mark listened to them as they chattered and squeaked at each other just like all siblings. They really did seem like any other kids as they played. He closed his eyes and let his mind drift. Somewhere he started to see images, not dreams, but thoughts connected by thin threads that began to knot themselves together more tightly, but before he could tie it all up he dozed off.

"Mark," Ashley said, stroking his head. "How are you feeling?"

"Sore. How long was I asleep?"

"Long enough for it to start snowing again. Sam and Ailithe bundled up and flew off to get some food and other things we'll need. Rollo got the short-wave running again and we've been listening to newscasts. The whole city is reeling from what Jack calls the one-two knock-out of the storms. It's really beautiful outside, but I wish we could have a doctor check you out."

"It's okay. I'm feeling better, really. I think I'll try and do some work on my plans for the game. I almost had the whole thing before I fell asleep. It's all there if I can just hold onto it."

"Right now you should concentrate on getting well. Can you sit up? I'll help you."

He slowly, painfully raised himself. "You know, Ashley, this is the first time in my life that I've felt like I belonged anywhere. I never really had anything in common with anyone before. But the kids, well, they have made me feel real!" He laughed. "Ironic, huh?"

Ashley nodded and helped lift him into a wing chair and eased his legs onto a foot stool. "Want to read a book while I toast you a little bread over the fire?"

"Sure. I'll take something light. Maybe a comic book?"

She handed him one. It was decorated in bright blues, greens and yellows outlined in black. The main character was a teenage alien, raised as a feral child in the hills of a distant planet. Mark turned the page and did a double take. The character had the ability to become invisible.

Ashley offered him the buttered toast with a glass of water.

"How'd you get the water so cold?"

"Mark, the whole world is covered in ice. I just borrowed a little."

He grinned crookedly. "Look at this comic. Do you see anything familiar?"

"I do! Do you think that's how Traxon will look when he's older?"

"I don't know, but if so, forget about trying to be inconspicuous. Look at the size of that guy. He's huge! Uh oh! That's what the tag said. It said Traxon would grow-up to be seven feet tall!"

She patted his shoulder gently. "Maybe it won't matter. Did you notice how nobody at the party thought the kids were particularly strange? Instead, they thought Mr. Cannady was weird when he realized the kids weren't normal children. Only Mrs. Cannady seemed to have figured it all out."

"It was as if everyone else was blind."

"I know the feeling," Ashley remarked.

She went back in the kitchen. Mark stared out the window. The snow was falling thickly, turning the night sky light grey. It was heavy, wet snow, and as it piled on the tree limbs they began snapping again.

He watched the icy night and listened to the falling limbs, muffled this time by the billowy snow cover.

"You hungry?" Pete asked. "Rollo and I fixed up an old Bunsen burner you'd picked up somewhere. I guess it came in useful, you being a junk-rat. You got any other stashes we can raid?"

"Boxes of it in the attic, but I don't know if there's anything useful in them."

"Maybe I'll check in a little while. Meantime, here's some soup."

Mark sipped at the soup and watched the snowflakes. He was feeling warm and cozy when the door burst open and Sam and Ailithe floated in, shaking snow from themselves so that it spiraled from where they flew down to the floor in small flurries.

"Supplies," Ailithe said, shaking white flakes off a grocery bag.

"Uh, we left some money. No one is in the stores. We added it up and left the right amount, we think."

"When did you learn to add?" Mark asked. "Never mind, go to bed. Both of you."

They flew up the stairs soundlessly, their feet never touching a step, but he heard doors open and shut.

Mark closed his eyes, trying to keep the headache that had receded at bay. The strings of thought started to intertwine again. It was the game. He concentrated, and suddenly saw the leap that made it work. His eyes snapped open.

"Pete. I need some paper and something to write with."

"Now?" he called.

"Yes, now, quickly."

Mark pulled a catalog off a shelf near him and used it to support his papers as he wrote. His handwriting was shaky, but he didn't care. He scribbled until he fell asleep in the chair. When morning came, someone had laid him on the sofa, neatly laid his papers together and covered him with a quilt.

"Elflet and I found you sitting there, sound asleep," Fiona said. "We got Castor and Sam to help us put you on the sofa."

"Thanks. What time is it?"

"Early. The snow just stopped," Fiona said. "If I went out into it, I would fade right away from view, just like a true ghost!"

"Do you mind being ghostly, Fiona?" Mark asked.

"Not since I came here. I feel as if I have come home. The house, the catalogs, even you. Mark, why did they make us and leave us in the cold for so long?"

"I don't know, Fiona."

"I bet it was because nobody wanted a bunch of legends and fairy tales and storybook people wandering around on the streets or going to school with their kids. You saw what the lady at the book store did. You heard your guests. Nobody likes stories."

"Mrs. Cannady does. Pete does. I do. There are others who do, too."

"But would they want stories to be real? Would you have ordered the kids if you had known what you were getting?"

"Probably not."

"My parents wished they could have sent me back. I heard them say that once. You would have sent everyone back, too, if you could have."

"Maybe at first," Mark admitted. "But, not now. I've told them all, I'll never let them go!"

"Will you order some more of us?"

"I can't. Where would I put them?"

Fiona looked sad. "It makes me want to cry. Why did they make us? Why?" she asked brokenly.

She wandered off quietly, leaving her sadness hanging in the air. He wished he had an answer for her, for himself. Was it really possible that all those dolls and action figures and figurines in the catalogs were really children? Where were they stored? How could whoever did this stay hidden all this time? Why, *why* would anyone do it, and how many times had he asked these questions without getting any closer to a real answer?

Pete came in. "I overheard your conversation with Fiona. What kind of sickos would play with kids' lives like this?"

"I'd like to think it is somebody who didn't want all our magical and moonlit childhoods to vanish forever. Maybe they thought they could preserve them by bringing book characters to life?"

"This ain't a fantasy! More likely someone just thought like your Mr. Cannady, just thought they had a hot product, only it didn't sell."

"Pete, I hope you're wrong. And I hope some scientists didn't make the kids just to prove they could do it, either, but I suppose that's another possibility."

"It'd be an awful expensive trick to pull off. They'd have needed investors, and to have promised their backers big, big bucks!"

"Maybe they had scientific funding, but lost it," Mark said, thinking again of the fragile clipping under a magnet on his refrigerator. "Maybe they were disgraced, maybe prosecuted, maybe banished? If this was a movie, the ones who escaped would decide to take revenge." He stopped speaking. His line of thought had dead-ended.

"The old mad-scientists-in-hiding plot, huh? That's pretty far-fetched," Pete said. "I'm still betting on a plot to make big bucks that went awry and left them with lots of defective products. Their investors got mad and the perpetrators slithered away into hiding."

"Well, either way, I doubt they made big bucks," Mark said.

"Maybe not." Pete paused and then snarled, "Or maybe that's why they made so many kids, 'cause they're reaping in a bundle of loot. How do we know how many kids they've sold? Nobody's gonna stand up and announce, 'Hey world, I bought a child today!' You didn't, my daughter didn't."

"True, but I can't believe scientists would be that opportunistic," Mark said.

"You're an idealist and a dreamer, Mark!" Pete said, shaking his head. "Wish I had your power to think the good in people."

"So be it then. I'm a dreamer," Mark admitted, at last accepting the old, once detested label.

"None of us may ever know the truth," Ashley interrupted them from the doorway to the kitchen, "but no matter what the reason, it is a tragedy if all those toys in the catalogs are children lying in the cold, waiting for someone to order them."

"Unless the alternative is something even worse," Mark said.

"What could be worse?" Ashley asked.

He could barely vocalize it. He had to clear his throat twice before he got it out. "Destroying them."

The words hung there in the silence, until Pete finally said, "So the question is, what are we going to do?"

"There probably isn't much we can do," Ashley said with a catch in her voice. "There must be thousands of kids in those catalogs, waiting for someone to adopt them." A crystal teardrop slid down to the corner of her mouth. She stopped it with the tip of her finger and said, "You should be resting, Mark."

"Yeah, she's right," Pete said. "You want me to help you into your own bed?"

Mark nodded. He leaned on Pete shakily and limped painfully into his room. Long after the other two had gone to bed, he lay in the dark listening to his thoughts fight with each other. He kept imagining little cold minds crying into the liquid where they were suspended. He kept seeing the pictures in the catalogs. He felt positive they were out there. His skin crawled at the thought and tears formed at the corners of his own eyes. Maybe in the morning, things wouldn't look so bleak. At least the Cannadys were going to be proud new parents. He smiled as he remembered Lucy Cannady's wink as she left. Then he imagined Carl's expression as he opened his delivery. Mark wouldn't be surprised if one morning he found Jack-the Giant-Killer dropped off on the Perralt front porch.

GAME PIECES

Three days later the snow finally stopped and the sun came out, turning the sky hard blue and burning the whiteness into a blaze of light. The snow dropped from the trees and the bushes and the roofs and the street signs in heavy, wet clumps. Inside of a few hours, everything was dripping water, and rivulets ran down the curbs and flooded the sidewalks and roads. At night the water froze over, but finally after a week, there was nothing left to melt except islands of snow with grass peeking through their crusts.

By the time it was over and Net service was returned, Mark was almost steady on his feet. As the swelling around his knee went down, Pete decided it wasn't broken and taped it up tightly. They carted him to the doctor who x-rayed it to be sure, put it into a brace and re-taped his ribs, leaving him with instructions to get lots of rest, no physical exertion for a month and then physical therapy for his knee. As they came home from the doctor's they passed the Book Stop. It was gone, its doors boarded up, its sign and bookcases discarded in heaps on the sidewalk.

"The last book store in town," Mark said.

Ashley patted his arm.

"I need to send something to Mr. Cannady. It's the computer game. It's finished."

"Really? Finished? How does it work?"

He began hesitantly. "It plays better than it sounds."

"Go ahead. We ain't got nothing better to do," Pete said.

"Here goes then. Okay, Pete, pick a character to be."

"What're my choices?"

"Let me see. Gulliver? Wild Bill Hickock? The Pied Piper? Queen Esther? Orville or Wilbur Wright? Robinson Crusoe? Helen of Troy?"

Pete shook his head *no* after each suggestion.

"All right, Pete, just pick someone. It can be anyone you want."

"How 'bout one of your old favorites? Tarzan of the Apes, I'd like to be him," he said and pounded on his chest.

"Okay, sure! So now that you're Tarzan, the game gives you an on-screen summary of the story from which Tarzan originates. Once you've read it, your player comes up on screen."

251

"Yeah? What's he look like?"

"Just like Tarzan. Tall, muscled, dark hair, wears a loin cloth, just like the real character."

"Yep, that's me, all right!" Pete smiled broadly and rubbed his bald spot.

"And because he's Tarzan, he'll have certain strengths and skills like expert vine-swinging, knife throwing, extra strength and special communication with animals."

"That's me, too," Pete said and put up one finger as if he was keeping track of something. "Go on. What's next?"

"Tarzan goes into a warehouse and picks five types of building materials he wants to carry with him as he tries to beat the game. Because he's Tarzan, the computer offers him a choice of building supplies he might come on in the jungle."

"So far, so good," Pete said. "And then?"

"Your hero sticks his choices into a napsack and steps onto a path that leads into the jungle undergrowth."

"Could he have gone to Great Britain instead?" Pete asked.

"I suppose, but for today, it's Africa," Mark said.

"So, there he is in the lush jungle with a buncha materials and a few skills," Pete said expectantly. "What's he doing there?"

"There's a maze made of pieces sort of like an old-fashioned board game, except you can't see the edges of the board. Tarzan lopes along the path, stopping on question pieces as they pop up. He can leap over one if he wants to, but to accumulate points, he has to answer them. And if he misses one, he loses a quarter of a strength. The questions are all based on the original story the character is extracted from, so if Tarzan, also known as Pete, can't answer one, Pete can pause the game and save it until he reads the orginial book that would be sent as a courtesy by the manufacturer, which of course is Canady & Company."

"Do you think anybody's gonna read the books?" Pete asked.

"If they want to win the game, they will," Mark answered quickly.

"Neat little trick. I like it," Pete said and popped up a second finger.

"I liked it, too." Mark grinned and continued with the explanation. "When Tarzan does answer a question, he can choose to add to his strengths or he can save points up for later use. There are booby-traps like alligator infested swamps and quicksand and army ants and rogue gorillas, and if he can't avoid them, he loses some of his strengths."

Finger three and four joined one and two on Pete's hand.

"What are you doing, Pete?" Ashley asked.

"Keeping track of the rules," he answered.

"Why?" Ashley asked.

"Cause I'm the player and I wanna know the best way to win."

"Oh," she said.

Mark cleared his throat as he went on. "When Tarzan gets to an intersection in the maze, he has to pick which way to go. If he goes down, he will have lower levels to his maze. If he goes up, he'll add upper stories. If he goes forward or sideways, the maze expands in that direction. There are clues he can buy with his points to help him determine his direction, but all the clues are based on the original story, too. If he gets to a dead end, he loses a point. If he comes to the edge of the maze, he marks it with the materials he's carrying."

"So, does he want to find the edges?" Ashley asked.

"Actually he does," Mark said.

"What's Tarzan supposed to be doing, constructing a building?" Pete asked.

"Exactly. Contructing a building. If he gets through the whole maze, he will have defined a cathedral or a castle or a geodesic dome or a needle building or more likely, in Tarzan's case, a tree house. But, no matter how many people chose Tarzan as their character, no one will ever build the exact building that has been built before."

Pete's thumb popped up to join finger one, two, three and four, and he said, "Bingo!"

"Where'd you get such an idea?" Ashley asked.

"Wait, wait, there's more," Mark said, feeling excited now. "The further along he goes, the faster the dangers pop up. That's when the points and strengths he's earned really count because he needs them to get through the maze so he can finish his building. But, he also can't use up all his points or strength, not yet anyway."

"Mark, what does Tarzan's building look like?" Ashley asked.

"I don't know for sure. It depends on lots of things: the building supplies, the directions he takes, even which questions he answers. If he chooses glass to take along, it could have a glass roof etched with elephants and great apes. If he chooses bamboo and palm leaves, it might be a house hanging from the jungle trees."

"Can a player get a printout of the final building?" she asked.

"That's a great idea, Ashley! I'll add it to the game," Mark said.

"All right, I got it so far, but how do you win this thing?" Pete asked. "Do you just finish the building? Is that it?"

"Nope," Mark said.

A finger on Pete's other hand joined the first five, straight up. "I'm really glad to hear that."

"If Tarzan can complete his building, he gets to move to the final level of play and re-enter the structure he just created. Inside there's a shorter maze and to win the game, Tarzan has to get to the treasure at the heart of the small maze. There aren't anymore questions and he doesn't build anything. He wins on pure reflexes, combined with the points and strengths he has left to get him past a collection of booby-traps and dangers he encounters as he tries to get to the exact middle of the building. If his points get too low, he can get more by taking a quiz on the computer about his story."

"Uh, huh. Another way to get the kid to read the story?" Pete asked.

Mark smiled.

"You devised a computer program to do all that?" Ashley asked.

"Sure he did," Pete answered. "He can do anything when it comes to computers."

"It was easy as long as I thought of it as making something three-dimensional and real, and not as designing a computer program in some netherworld cyber-place. Do you really like it?" he asked.

"It's great!" Ashley said. "I can't wait to play it!"

"Pretty good, bud, but I've got a question. Whatcha get if you win?" Pete asked.

"Your treasure," Mark said.

"Yeah? A virtual treasure, huh? I guess kids will like that, but me, I'd rather get the dime store toy from the box of candy-coated pop-corn," Pete said.

"Definitely a generation gap there," Ashley noted.

That night Mark finally looked at his Web posting. He had eighty-three responses from people who claimed to receive toy catalogs through snail-mail. Sixty-five of them mentioned that they had ordered from them. It was nice to know that he and Pete weren't alone. Mark sent them all a message, and went to bed.

In the middle of the night, he sat straight up. He smiled and, for the first time in a long while, felt better.

Traxon appeared at breakfast with a backpack on.

"Where did you get that?" Mark asked suspiciously.

"From a catalog." Traxon looked sheepish, then brightened and announced, "I'm ready to go to school."

Ashley looked sadly at Mark.

"Not today, Traxon," Mark said, "but soon!"

"Soon? Really?" Traxon asked, fixing his gaze on Mark.

"Yes, really."

"Good," the boy said, and went off to get ready to go outside with the other kids.

"How could you promise that?" Ashley asked.

"Because it's true."

"Mark, these kids will never go to regular school. You know it, I know it, Pete knows it. How could you mislead Traxon like that?"

"If our kids were the only ones who were different, you might be right. But, just suppose that there were others?"

"Oh, come on, Mark! You are so exasperating. There aren't any others like these kids. They would have been noticed. The government would be swarming over this place, or at a minimum, my father's company would be."

"Uh huh? Just suppose you met a ghost. You would know it, right?" he asked.

"Ghosts do not exist, so it isn't even an issue," she said firmly.

He smiled broadly. "But, you have met Fiona?"

"What?" she exclaimed, her face caught in dawning awareness punctuated by amazement.

"Ashley, people don't see the impossible because they are sure it can't happen. If it does, they deny it. Besides, the more weirdness there is, the less it would seem weird."

"Fiona? A ghost?" she said dazedly.

"I've got one thing left to do, then we can talk some more."

He pushed her gently towards the great room where the sun was warming the sofa, and left her chewing on her thumb.

He went to his computer and added to the game proposal. The treasure you won at the heart of each building would be the opportunity to choose from an online catalog, a unique one-of-a-kind child character to be featured in a movie brought to you by the newly established *Lady A Perralt Production Company*. Game winners would have the opportunity to invite their movie characters to visit their homes and schools. The circle would be complete. The movie tie-ins to the game would support the children, and certainly some families would want to adopt famous kids. Nobody would question their eccentricities, assuming it was some kind of stunt. People always mistook movie stars for the characters they played. It wouldn't be long before weirdness became acceptable, maybe even desirable.

He smiled to himself again. It also gave him something to invest all his money in, and he could legitimately invent gadgets and toy tie-ins to the movies for fun. Kate would approve, so would Larry, without suspecting what he was really doing until it was too late. And they wouldn't need as many special effects for the movies because of the natural abilities of the children who starred in them. Mark printed the proposal and folded it into an envelope.

He pulled at his hair and found it had grown out. He messed it up and hobbled into the bathroom to have a look in the mirror. He didn't look like the old Mark Perralt and he didn't look like Cannady & Company's Markham Perralt either. He laughed out loud. He looked like himself.

He went to his desk and began to type another letter to arrange to include online versions of the catalogs with every game. He assured the anonymous suppliers that this would be an effective way to market their products. He promised that the catalogs would have an unbreakable code and be absolutely untraceable. In addition, if they sent him DNA samples, Cannady's would provide official ID's for all the orders they filled. He had made sure it wasn't illegal, just an unnoticed loophole in the law. He put the letter into another envelope and put one of the stickers from the catalogs on it. He was confident he would hear back within forty-eight hours. He would wait to send the package to Mr. Cannady until then.

He went back to the great room, but Ashley was asleep. She looked so peaceful. He covered her with an afghan. She didn't stir. He watched her for a few minutes and then limped stiffly down the steps to the basement, none too quickly, nursing his knee as he pulled out the box from his father. He lifted out books and snapshots, medals and picture books, and carefully sorted them into stacks. At the bottom was a journal entitled *My Part in the Great Experiment*. Mark opened it eagerly, but all the pages had been ripped out. He reached into the very bottom of the box, and pulled out an old, fox-eared pale yellow tag. Typed in worn letters the tag said, "One true genius of far ranging talents. No name assigned. No book connection. A random selection of genes. Likely to be an imaginative maverick who loves to make things." Printed in red letters in what he knew as his father's handwriting were the words: "My Son."

My Son. The two words rattled in his stunned brain and bounced off an eidetic memory. He saw his two-year-old self, so bundled into winter clothes he looked like a fat snowman except for the skinny little face that peeked from beneath the hood.

Come on, son! Let's go out and play in the snow with Katie and Mommy. It'll be fun.

Little Mark stood staunchly unmoving, backed up against a wall in terror.

Markie, you have on: two pairs of socks, rubber boots up to your knees, a pair of gloves under a pair of mittens, and a big scarf; long underwear, pants, a shirt, a sweater, a hat, ear-muffs, all under a down snow suit. If we put one more piece of clothing on you, you will be paralyzed by all the paraphernalia.

Tears dripped down Mark's small face. *It's cold, Daddy. The cold will take me back!*

It won't, Mark! I promise, son.

His father reached out, but Mark cringed back against the wall.

That's it! You have to get over this. His father reached for him, picked him up and slung him over his shoulder. Mark was too encased in clothes to be able to kick, but he screamed.

His father stepped to the door and sang out loudly over the screams, *Throw him over your shoulder...*

"What's that?" Elflet asked from the corner, startling Mark.

For a moment, he wasn't sure who Elflet was. "What?"

"Whatcha got in your hand, Mark?"

He looked down at what he was clutching. "Oh! An old tag. What are you doing down here?"

"Making shoes," Elflet said proudly and held up a beautiful pair of leather boots. "I started with new leather. I can't fix them, but I can make them. These are for Fiona." His ears wiggled as his face broke out in a smile. "Whose tag is that?"

Mark stuffed the tag into his pocket. "It doesn't really matter," he said. "Let's go upstairs and ask Lady A if she'll make us into a real family."

"That's a good idea, Mark. How are we gonna do that?"

"I'll show you."

He held the child's hand in one of his, and pulled himself up the stairs with the other. At the top of the steps he reached into his pocket, pulled out the old tag, and as they passed the trash basket in the hall, he threw it in.

"Don't you want it?" Elflet asked.

"Why would I?" Mark smiled down at the little boy as they went to wake Lady A.